Dating Can Be Deadly

50

WENDY ROBERTS

was born and raised in Winnipeg, Canada, where she alternated between fending off frostbite in winter and mosquito bites in summer. Her earliest childhood memories are the musky, dusty scent of the local library bookmobile and losing herself in the adventures of Nancy Drew.

At the tender age of eight, Wendy's writing career sprouted when she penned the poignant tale of a cup of flour's journey to become a birthday cake. After a writing hiatus that lasted a few decades, she rediscovered her muse, her sanity and a sated harmony in putting pen to paper once again.

Wendy now resides on the west coast of Canada with her five biggest fans—her husband and their four beautiful children. This is her debut novel.

Dating Can Be Deadly

Wendy Roberts

RED DRESS **INK**

First edition February 2005

DATING CAN BE DEADLY

A Red Dress Ink novel

ISBN 0-373-89512-7

Grateful acknowledgment is made for the permission of A P Watt Ltd on behalf of Michael B. Yeats to reprint an excerpt from the poem "Lines Written in Dejection" by W. B. Yeats.

www.RedDressInk.com

Printed in U.S.A.

Deepest thanks to my mom and dad
for showing me laughter through all things.

For my husband, Brent, for saying I could,
and for my children, Sarah, Daniel, Donovan
and Devin, for making it all worthwhile.

chapter one

I charged through Seattle's Memorial Cemetery with my arms pumping and heart pounding. My mouth wheezed in great mouthfuls of dreary afternoon drizzle while I ruined a perfectly good pair of black leather sling-backs. To top that off, the purse snatcher, who was at least double my twenty-six years and probably a heroin addict as well, had easily outrun me.

I had a choice, I could either A) continue to run with the hope that I'd eventually wear the thief down with my persistence or B) give up on ever seeing my shoulder bag, a suede Prada knockoff, ever again.

Exhaustion won. I gave up and staggered to a stop. I apologized to Samuel Harvey, 1910-1973, whose tombstone I leaned against while recovering from the impromptu workout.

"He got away?" Stumbling in my direction, with high

heels sinking in the sodden grass and with ample bosom rising and falling in deep gasps, was my good friend Jenny. She propped herself up at the opposite corner of Samuel Harvey's resting place. "Damn! I thought you had him."

"This is what happens when you can no longer afford to go to the gym." I panted. "A senior citizen junky makes off with your bag and leaves you whimpering in a graveyard."

"This is what happens when your car dies and you're forced to stand around on Baldwin Street," corrected Jenny. She tucked a strand of hair behind her ear, the red hair color, Claret Classic, was courtesy of this week's sale at Neuman Drugs. Next, Jenny dug in her purse and pulled out a cigarette. She lit up then nodded her head in the direction the thief had taken. "Let's go after him."

"I'd rather—" stick a pen in my eye, have a pap test, visit my mother… "—not."

"Well, we should check. Maybe he ditched your bag somewhere?"

"What's the point?" I asked, sulkily digging up sod with the toe of one of my wrecked shoes.

"Maybe he just snatched the cash and dumped the rest." Jenny took a deep drag on the cigarette and blew the smoke out in a long stream. "Of course I'd be able to catch him myself, if I wasn't retaining all this water."

I knew Jenny was retaining twenty-five years of fried food, not water, but she was my best friend so I supported her delusions of water retention, just like she supported my fantasy that being able to type seventy words a minute meant I was physically fit.

"Replacing your ID and credit card is going to be a real pain," Jenny added.

I hit my forehead with the heel of my hand. "Damn! My Visa!"

My credit card was the only thing preventing me from having to beg dinners off my mother until next payday. I had a sudden and nauseating vision of endless meals sitting across from Mom explaining why I haven't married and have no prospects, why I haven't a better job and no prospects and why I haven't cut my hair, lowered my hemlines, taken a class....

I hurled myself down the stone pathway.

"Wait up, Tab! I'll come with ya!" Jenny flicked her smoke into a nearby puddle and followed in my wake up a narrow walkway.

The path led us between tombstones and grave markers. When we began to climb a slight incline nearing a clump of tall blue spruce, I suddenly stopped walking and Jenny slammed right into me.

"What is it? Do you see your bag?" Jenny flicked her gaze left and right then sidestepped around me to look at me full in the face. Her eyes widened. "Oh, no."

"What?"

"You're doing that thing."

"What thing?"

"That thing you do with your eyes when you blink a lot."

"I do *not* blink a lot."

"Uh-huh." Jenny planted thick fingers on wide hips. "Yeah, well, tell your eyelids that 'cause right now they're doing the mambo."

I pinched the bridge of my nose with my fingers and squeezed my eyes shut.

"What is it?" she demanded impatiently.

"Nothing." I nibbled my lower lip and glanced nervously at a nearby tree. "Let's go." I whirled on my heel to beat a fast retreat.

"Whoa!" Jenny clamped her fingers on my elbow. "You had one of those premonitions, right?"

I sighed, "I don't have *premonitions.* It's more like a deep feeling of foreboding." With the occasional bleary snapshot thrown in for good measure.

Jenny nodded vigorously. "Yeah, like the time you knew something was wrong at home and you found out your dad had just had a heart attack, or that time you knew Martha was preggers even before she did."

I pulled my elbow from her grasp and crossed my arms over my chest. "Actually, it's more like that feeling I got when you fixed me up with your cousin Ted and his leg-humping dog, or the time you told me the shrimp in your fridge were fresh."

"Well, maybe this time your bad feeling is telling you that your purse is over there behind that tree and the bad part is that only the cash is missing."

The feeling in my gut wasn't exactly saying *purse,* it was saying something darker. Evil. I shuddered and wished I hadn't quit smoking last month.

Then again, I reasoned, I'd had the same feeling when I was sixteen and Mom found me out behind the garden shed with Todd Verbicki's hands down my pants. I relented and Jenny and I made our way across the mossy grass to the spruce that had garnered my attention. We walked around it.

"Huh. Nothing," I said, then Jenny was suddenly doing deep breathing exercises behind me.

"Aw, man," she whispered hoarsely. "I think I'm gonna puke."

I reluctantly turned and scanned the source of her nausea. My gaze landed on a grisly scene. At the foot of the next tree, a cat—or whatever was left of one—had been brutally eviscerated. Its corpse lay in the center of a blood-soaked pentagram that had been dug into the dirt.

"Let's bolt," I choked out.

"And it was just totally and completely gross!" Jenny announced, concluding her description of our escapade. The three of us—me, Jenny and her roommate—were huddled in their small apartment at the kitchen table over a plate of brownies.

"You really predicted it, Tabitha?" Lara asked, eyes wide from behind thick black-rimmed glasses.

"No." I sighed, because now I'd have to correct all of Jenny's exaggerations. "To start with, my car was not carjacked, it merely died over on Baldwin Street. Jen and I were waiting for a bus when the purse snatcher grabbed my bag. He was at least fifty and most likely a druggy, not a green beret set on revenge." I rolled my eyes at Jen, who was biting into her fourth brownie. "But, yes, there was a cat that was cut up and it was humongously gross. I only had a bad feeling about what was behind the tree, I didn't drop into a trancelike state and predict the second coming."

Jenny harrumphed. "Nothing wrong with adding a bit of color to a story."

Why would you need to make a horrible event sound even worse?

"Did you call the cops?" Lara asked.

Jenny and I looked at each other then back at Lara and shrugged.

"You should call someone, shouldn't you?" She pushed. "The ASPCA? The groundskeeper for the cemetery?"

We shook our heads.

"What for?" Jenny asked. "They never catch purse snatchers and the cat's dead—nothing will change that."

"And it's not like the Seattle PD is going to launch a door-to-door search for either my forty dollars or for some sicko who likes to hurt animals," I put in.

"Yeah, but the pentagram." Lara shook her head slowly from side to side. "That says bad shit, like satanic stuff or something."

"Actually I think pentagrams are usually linked more to Wicca and witches, right?" Jenny asked.

Both turned and stared expectantly at me.

"What?" I demanded. "I don't follow that stuff anymore, you know that! Anyway, mutilated animals…" I shuddered. "That sounds satanic to me."

"If it's the devil, then we'll say a prayer," Jenny commented sarcastically. "That doesn't mean we need to get in his face."

There was a pause while we each considered our own thoughts on the matter.

"So, where's your car?" Lara asked, brushing brownie crumbs from her sweater.

"We towed it to Doug's garage," I replied.

"Your cousin, Doug?" Lara asked Jenny. "The one with no neck?"

"Yeah, that's the one," Jenny agreed.

Then, as if thinking of my 1995 Ford Escort summoned it to respond, my cell phone rang. It was the mechanic. The conversation was short and afterward I laid my head down on the table and moaned.

"Is she having another one of her visions?" Lara asked Jenny.

"Nah." Jenny chewed another brownie. "Just an emotional meltdown."

"My car," I murmured against the cool pine table. "It's going to cost almost eight hundred bucks to fix it."

"Wow," Jenny sympathized. "You could probably just buy another Escort for that price, right?"

I lifted my head to glare at her.

"Okay, maybe not one as nice as yours," she conceded. "Guess you'll be taking the bus for a while."

"I hate the bus," I whined. "Where am I going to get that kind of cash?"

Half an hour later we concluded that I could save up enough to pay for the repair if I gave up a few necessities like Starbucks, *Vogue* magazine and food for the next six months.

"Or you could just get another job," Lara suggested, placing a soup-bowl size mug of thick black coffee in front of me. "They're looking for another person to help behind the concession counter at the Movie Megaplex."

Lara was the queen of part-time. She held four part-time jobs and kept her schedules straight on a large white wipe-off board in her bedroom.

"No way! I'm already putting in my forty hours a week at McAuley and Malcolm." And it felt more like fifty.

"Well, technically you don't work a full forty hours," Jenny pointed out. "You're usually at least a half hour late, you take long lunches and you leave early. My guess is you really only work about thirty hours a week. Of course, it's better than when you were smoking and taking all those puff breaks."

Jenny and I worked together at the law firm of McAuley and Malcolm. Jenny had the prestigious title of legal secretary while I was only the lowly receptionist. Jenny also covered my ass whenever I was away from my desk so she knew all about my lack of attendance.

"Still, what about my social life?" I drank from the hot coffee and felt my armor crumpling. This *was* my social life.

"I'll loan you fifty bucks until payday, Tab," Jen offered generously.

"Come with me tonight and I'll get Harold to hire you," Lara announced, as if it were all settled. "A few nights a week and you'll quickly have your car repairs paid for."

After a little more coffee and lots more cajoling, Lara convinced me. I called in to report my stolen Visa and then we headed out to the movie theatre where I was introduced to Harold Wembly. He was a beanpole young man with acne-scarred skin and the manager of the Movie Megaplex.

"So you want a career as a Megaplex counter assistant?" his eyes gleamed with power.

"Um, well sure, I guess." I turned and raised my eyebrows at Lara.

"You're in luck." He clapped his hands. "You can start tonight. Joan called in sick and Lara here can show you the ropes. After tonight you'll work from Wednesday to Saturday, six-thirty 'til midnight."

"F-four nights a week?" I stuttered. "I was thinking maybe two."

"Bus," Lara hissed in my ear. "Do it his way and you'll get your car back before the November downpours start."

I sighed. "That'll be fine."

Harold tossed me a yellow button-down Henley shirt that had Megaplex embroidered in green over the pocket and popcorn-butter stains on the cuffs.

It was still half an hour before the theater would open so Lara took me to the staff room and introduced me to the two other girls who'd be dishing up popcorn with us. Then she brought me down to the huge counter and familiarized me with movie munchie etiquette.

"There are three basic sizes—jumbo, enormous and colossal." She pointed to the three-dimensional poster on the wall.

"You mean small, medium and large."

Lara covered my mouth with her hand and slid her gaze to the left and right. "Don't ever let Harold hear you refer to the sizes that way, or you'll be fired on the spot."

Oh, boy.

"The drinks are the same sizes and you need to fill the cups half with ice before pouring in the pop." She opened a refrigerator beneath the counter. "Bottled water is kept here."

"What if they want regular water, from a tap?"

Lara shook her head. "Strictly forbidden. There's a firing squad outside waiting to shoot the first person who offers free water."

I *almost* thought she was kidding.

A few minutes later, after I solemnly swore to never ever touch the popcorn maker, Lara pronounced me ready to serve.

"This isn't so bad," I said. "Other than the fact that I'm a fashion nightmare." Looking down at the running shoes Lara had loaned me, I adjusted the black skirt I'd worn to the office that day and tugged a strand of my wispy brown hair out of my eyes.

Obviously I'd spoken too soon because less than two hours later I was run off my feet and had a river of perspiration flowing between my breasts.

"Great. You survived the first half," Lara said, smiling and wiping at drink spills on the counter. "Other than the time you nearly dumped a tray of drinks on that asshole who grabbed your boob."

I groaned and pressed a hand to my lower back. "How much longer?"

"Those were the early moviegoers," Lara stated, pushing her glasses back on her nose and blowing her black hair out of her eyes. "Thursdays can get pretty busy. The next wave will start in about twenty minutes."

"The next wave?" I replied weakly.

"We can take a break now, if you'd like."

The second wave wasn't a wave; it was a tidal storm.

Huge lineups formed in front of each of the four cashiers but my lineup was continuously longer than all the rest. Not only was I slower at serving than the others, but I was also working the register nearest the ticket counter. I was tired. Exhausted. My mind was in a complete daze and my contact lenses were beginning to fuse permanently to my corneas. But suddenly, things came back into focus, or rather, someone. Oh, no!

I whirled to fill an order and met up with Lara at the popcorn. "You gotta switch lines with me!" I hissed.

"No way. The new girl *always* gets the first register."

"But Clay Sanderson's in my line! He's one of the part-ners at the law firm. I don't want him to see me!"

Lara glanced over her shoulder. "Which one is he?"

I continued to scoop popcorn into an already overflow-ing jumbo-size container. "Golden hair, body like a Greek god, has on a brown leather jacket and there's a blonde, a model-type, hanging off his arm," I whispered.

Lara looked again. "He's gorgeous! Sure, I'll wait on him." She undid the top button on her shirt. "But after he's gone, we switch back."

Lara hustled up to my line that was easily double the length of hers and I scrambled over to the next cash regis-ter trying to keep my gaze away from Clay Sanderson in case he spotted me. No chance of that, though; he only had eyes for the blonde in the stiletto heels.

A few minutes later I glanced over and couldn't see Clay in Lara's lineup. I figured he'd already gone, so I was prepar-ing to switch back when I noticed Lara had a weird look on her face and was nodding sideways in my direction.

"I'll have two medium Cokes and a large popcorn," a deep baritone voice sounded in front of me.

I turned my head and looked straight into Clay Sander-son's azure eyes. I guess being a partner in a law firm meant you had enough brains to switch to the snack lineup that had less of a crowd.

I swallowed thickly. "You mean two enormous drinks and a colossal popcorn?" I asked, offering up a tentative smile.

The corners of his mouth twitched into a lopsided grin. "Sure."

I quickly headed to the drink dispenser. Maybe he didn't

recognize me? Sure we saw each other every day, when he walked into the office, but I *did* have a forgettable face. Not like his blond girlfriend.

Returning to the counter with his order, I rang up the total. I offered two dollars in change to him and he reached across and held my hand while he took the bills and stated, "Your secret is safe with me."

When I looked at my hand I expected melted flesh where he'd touched me. Then he leaned in, and for a split second I actually thought he was going to kiss me, when instead, he whispered, "By the way, you have some popcorn, uh—" His gaze moved down to my chest then back up to my face. I could feel my cheeks becoming red.

I noticed there were a few popcorn kernels balanced precariously in my cleavage. When I looked up again he was gone.

The rest of the shift was quieter, but I was relieved when it finally ended just before midnight. Lara linked her arm in mine as we stepped out of the theatre and into the chilly night air.

"He said he'd keep it a secret, right? So what are you so worried about?"

"I dunno," I replied glumly, as we cut across the parking lot.

"Oh. I get it." Lara nudged me with her elbow. "This is the suit you've been drooling over for years, huh? Mr. Sexy Lawyer at your firm."

I began to protest, then relented. "I was surprised he even recognized me."

"Why wouldn't he? You've been working at that firm for what? Two years?"

"Yeah, but did you get a load of his girlfriend?"

"Yeah, I see your point."

We continued our walk. My apartment was less than a block from the movie theatre but I was accompanying Lara across the street to her bus stop.

"You don't have to wait with me," Lara said. "The bus will be here in less than five minutes. Go on home. You look beat."

"I am beat. It's just that…" My eyes were drawn to the old building behind us. It looked like it had been a store at one point, but now it was boarded up with posted signs indicating it was zoned for demolition. My heart was jackhammering painfully inside my chest.

"Oh, my God! You're doing that thing with your eyes!" Lara grabbed me by the shoulders and shook me roughly. "What is it?" She looked around wildly.

"I've got a real bad feeling about that place." I looked up the road and nodded with my chin. "There's another bus stop a block up. I'll walk you over there."

She shook her head. "No way." She pointed to the building behind us. "Besides, there's nobody in there, it's pitch-dark."

"Yeah, but still…" My palms were beginning to sweat and I had more than a bad feeling now—I had an image of a woman flash in my mind. A very dead woman. "Oh jeez." I rubbed at my eyes. "Come on!" I yanked Lara by the elbow and tried pulling her up the road.

She tugged her arm free and studied my face. "You're really scared. Is this another cat thing? I don't spook easily but you are making me so curious." She headed for the main entrance to the vacant building.

My stomach was churning as I followed her. There wasn't much to see. It was a dilapidated gray stucco building with Keep Out signs hammered to the front door and a cement lot that circled the structure. Lara walked determinedly around the perimeter of the building. At the back, where a board had fallen away, she paused before peering inside the abandoned structure.

"Nothing!" She let out a disgusted breath. "I'm telling you, Tabitha, after everything Jenny's told me about this psychic thing you've got going on, I'm kinda disappointed."

"Yeah, well, Jenny does tend to exaggerate." I glanced around and sighed with relief that no bogeymen were lurking in the parking lot behind us either. "Guess my feeling was off." I didn't want to think about the image that had flashed through my mind. "Let's go."

"Hey, what's that?" Lara asked before we'd taken a step.

"What?"

"Painted on that Dumpster." She nodded to the corner of the parking lot with her chin. "Could that be…" She began walking toward it. "Oh, my God, it is! It's a pentagram! You said there was one at the cemetery, too, right?!"

My feet froze to the pavement. A streetlight in the corner of the lot angled a dim yellow sheen bathing the Dumpster in an eerie glow. Spray-painted over the words, *Pacific Refuse Inc.,* was a black pentagram. That real bad feeling I'd had earlier returned. Lara walked closer to the bin and was now only a couple of feet away.

"Don't," I said weakly.

"It's just a Dumpster." She looked over her shoulder at

me and made clucking noises. "Unless you're thinking there's something in here besides trash, like maybe another mutilated cat or something."

"It's the *or something* that bothers me and I'm not hanging around to find out." I stomped away hoping that Lara would follow, but after a dozen steps I looked over my shoulder and saw that she was not behind me. She'd done the exact opposite—she'd shimmied up the side of the Dumpster.

"You know what?" Her voice echoed loudly inside the container. She shoved herself off, landed on her feet and wiped her hands on her jacket with a look of revulsion.

"What?"

"The Dumpster's empty but there's a puddle of something inside there. It looks like it could be blood. Of course, it's hard to tell in the dark."

My throat tightened. "I'm guessing there's a lot more blood than would come from a cat, right?"

"Yep. A lot more."

I wanted to run. Run far. Run fast. Lara, on the other hand, did the exact opposite, again. She called the cops.

Twenty minutes later I was sitting curbside with a good view of one of Seattle's finest shining his flashlight into the Dumpster. He pushed himself off it in much the same manner as Lara had and then his partner climbed up and did a similar look-see inside with *his* flashlight. Lara was pacing nonstop in front of me, her face bright with excitement.

After a few minutes, the cops strode over. One was a fiftyish Hispanic guy with a thick mustache. The other was a younger cop who was built like a refrigerator with stringy blond hair.

Refrigerator Cop spoke first, addressing Lara. "You're right that it looks like blood but, obviously, we can't tell just by looking at it that it's from a human. Probably somebody just dumped some meat."

I let out a snort from my place at the curb and Refrigerator Cop turned and narrowed his eyes at me. "Tell me again what brought you around the building to look in the Dumpster."

"Hey, I didn't look in there," I protested. "I was just following *her*." I indicated Lara with my chin.

"Yeah, and she wanted to check because you had a psychic vision or something," Mustache Cop said sarcastically and he and his partner shared identical smirks.

I got to my feet and clapped my hands together. "Well, looks like you guys have everything under control, so I'm going to go home to bed."

"We've got the crime lab guys on their way and they'll check out the Dumpster to be sure," said Mustache Cop. "And we've got your information, so we'll be in touch if anything further comes up."

The look on his face said that he didn't believe anything further would come up. He believed the pentagram on the side of the Dumpster was teenage graffiti and that the gooey stuff in the Dumpster was not human blood. I slid my gaze to the Dumpster and fear made my nerves ping.

Lara caught her bus and I ran the rest of the way to my apartment. I spent the better part of the night not able to sleep because of an unending slide show of morbid snapshots that flashed behind my eyelids. It began with the poor mutilated kitty in the graveyard, then that picture faded and the image of a woman's bloody torso took its place. In the final slide, I saw the inside of a dimly lit building where someone was lighting a large black candle. I could almost smell the wax at this point. That's when I would wake up in a cold sweat. Needless to say, fighting the dreams meant that sleep eluded me until I finally helped it along at three-thirty in the morning with tequila—kept for medicinal use only.

Since my car was sick I'd set my alarm for 6:00 a.m. It was an hour earlier than usual, but it would give me plenty of time to catch a bus and get to the office promptly. However, tequila-induced sleep does what it's supposed to do. I slammed my fist on the snooze button no less than a dozen times. When I finally did roll out of bed—groggily at that—it was after eight.

"Holy shit!" I yelped and stumbled into the shower.

My apartment was described in the ad as a cozy, metro-politan unit with a parklike view. Actually, it was a dumpy basement studio with narrow, dirty windows, one of which looked out onto the parking lot and some sparse shrubs. The pipes grumbled before spewing hot water for my five-minute shower, then I wrestled my eyelids to remain open long enough for me to impale them with contact lenses. I was hopping into pumps and running out the door a couple minutes later.

As usual, my neighbor, Mrs. Sumner, opened her door a crack and peered at me. Also, as usual, Mrs. Sumner, a stale fiftyish woman, had her hair in curlers, a cigarette dangling from the corner of her mouth and sported a ratty pink housecoat. The only time I ever saw poor Mr. Sumner, a meek whipped form of a man, was when he was sneaking out the door and tiptoeing down the hall.

"Mornin', Mrs. Sumner." I nodded as I passed.

"If you're gonna be comin' in late and leavin' early don't always be slammin' your door!" she shouted after me.

"Bye, Mrs. Sumner," I shouted back and ran as fast as I could.

The prestigious law firm of McAuley and Malcolm practiced family and criminal law at its location on the twelfth floor of the Bay Tower. It blended with similar glass office buildings downtown that hugged the shores of Elliott Bay. The good news was that there was a bus stop directly in front of the gleaming office tower. The bad news was that I fell asleep on the bus and woke up six blocks past my stop and had to jog back.

In the elevator I attempted to compose myself. I smoothed down my frazzled hair, straightened my skirt and took deep calming breaths. At the twelfth floor, the elevator doors whooshed open onto the reception area. A large mahogany desk, in the shape of a horseshoe, stood front and center. It was my duty to sit behind it and answer telephones. Since I was now an hour late, Jenny was there instead. She looked up at me, her eyebrows raised in amusement.

"You look like shit," she said, getting to her feet so that I could slip behind the desk.

"I also *feel* like shit."

"First morning taking the bus didn't go well?"

"I've discovered a fascinating fact about morning transit commuters," I announced, depositing my purse into the bottom desk drawer. "Most people who take the bus do not bathe and those that do, choose to do so in loathsome perfumes."

A call came in and I put on my office voice and sang, "Good morning, McAuley and Malcolm. How may I direct your call?" I managed to transfer the call without cutting the person off.

"I thought maybe you looked like shit because of the whole pentagram and bloody Dumpster thing," Jenny put in.

"Oh, that. I guess Lara told you."

Jenny grinned. "She woke me out of a dead sleep to tell me every detail." She leaned in. "Do you really think somebody was killed and tossed in that Dumpster?"

Before I could reply, the elevator doors opened and Clay Sanderson stepped out along with senior partner Ted McAuley. They appeared to be engrossed in a serious discussion as they passed through the reception area with barely a nod in my direction, but suddenly Clay stopped.

"Do you smell that?" he asked.

Old Ted McAuley sniffed loudly. "Huh? What? I don't smell anything."

Clay shrugged. "Odd. For a second I was sure I smelled popcorn." He glanced over at me, behind Ted's back, and winked before they continued on their way.

"Oh, my God," Jenny breathed. "He actually winked at you!"

"Yeah. Every time he points his baby blues in my direction I almost have an orgasm."

Jenny laughed. "Lara told me he saw you working the theater last night but he agreed to keep it a secret."

"I guess I'm pretty lucky. If word got around the firm that I was dishing up popcorn at night I'd be a laughing-stock and I'd never be considered worthy of anything above receptionist."

The day trudged on as it usually did. I answered calls, transferred most, lost some and muscled the word processor into producing a couple of interoffice memos. Jenny and I went to the deli next door for lunch where she interrogated me further on Lara's Dumpster diving and I filled her in on the details of my nightmares.

The day picked up speed after lunch and the staff made their usual dash for the elevator at five.

Jenny paused while she slipped her arms inside her coat. "How come you didn't sneak out with the FedEx guy?"

I shook my head. "Can't today. I don't have enough time to go home before I need to be at the Megaplex. I might as well hang around here for a half hour. Maybe I'll get caught up on my typing."

Jenny blinked at me and frowned. "Are you sure you're feeling okay?"

I assured her I was, even though bobbing aimlessly inside my head were bleary images of a bloodstained Dumpster and a woman's mutilated remains. If I had my way those images would be forcibly tucked away into the furthest reaches of my gray matter.

"Okay," she said, eyeing me skeptically. "But if you need to talk just call me on my cell. I'm having dinner with Jed."

"Jed? Is he the guy from last week, the one from the meat packing plant?"

"No that was Ed. Jed's the guy from that doughnut shop in North Queen Anne."

"I thought that was Fred."

She shook her head. "Fred was the guy I faked orgasms with. The one who was into scented candles."

"Oh." Between the butcher, the baker and the candle-sex-faker it was getting harder and harder to distinguish Jenny's dates from one another.

After Jenny left, the partners began filing out of their offices. Clay Sanderson was the last to appear. He pushed the call button for the elevator then sauntered casually back to my desk and stood smiling rakishly.

Feeling as though I should say something, I blurted, "Thanks for last night." I nibbled my lower lip. "I mean, thanks for not saying anything about seeing me last night, working at the Megaplex."

His eyes sparked and he leaned a hip against my desk then reached over and playfully tugged at a strand of my hair. "Lucky for you I have a weakness for a woman who smells of melted butter."

Oh, boy.

Clay picked up his briefcase and strode back toward the elevator, which was taking an eternity to arrive. Suddenly, the doors did open and out stepped a stocky middle-aged man with skin the color of espresso. He wore a rumpled overcoat, a worn tweed suit and a dour expression.

The sight of him triggered another premonition, and fear tripped up my spine like a lover's knowing touch.

chapter two

"Tabitha Emery?" the man asked, his feet eating up the floor between the elevator and my desk.

"Yes?" I gulped.

Reaching into a pocket he pulled out his identification. "Detective Jackson." He tilted his head. "Is there something wrong with your eyes?"

"No." I tried to control the flutter of my eyelids that came with a premonition, stress or after eating bad clams. My fluttering eyes noted that Clay Sanderson's hand was holding the elevator door open, but he had yet to step inside.

"I'd like to talk to you about last night," Detective Jackson announced.

"Yeah, well, I'm kinda busy right now."

He frowned at his Timex. "You only work until five and it's presently five-o-three. I think you can spare me a few minutes."

Clay gave up on the elevator and let it leave without him. He walked directly toward me.

"Is there something that I can help you with, officer?"

Detective Jackson flicked a gaze in Clay's direction. "And you are...?"

"Miss Emery's attorney, if she needs one."

My eyelids popped wide open. Aw geez! I did *not* need Clay Sanderson wading right into the cesspool section of my life.

"It's okay!" I announced to Clay with a smile before turning to the detective. "I'll answer your questions, but I don't have lots of time because I have to get to my other job."

Clay put his briefcase down and his eyes leveled with mine. "Tabitha, if you're having a discussion with the police, don't you think it would be helpful to have an attorney present?"

"I don't need a lawyer. This is nothing."

The detective merely shrugged. "I wouldn't exactly call murder *nothing*."

"Murder?" Clay and I chorused.

Clay's voice was hard and clipped. "My office. Now."

Clay Sanderson's office had a large rectangular desk in golden oak and I'd often visualized him tossing files to the floor and taking me next to his inbox. There was also a large window that had a stunning view of Elliot Bay. A row of pigeons sat glaring at me from the ledge like feathered jurors. In the corner of the office there was a small round glass table circled by four chairs where Clay headed and parked his rather fine ass. The detective, who definitely did *not* have a fine ass, followed and sat across from Clay, and I took the chair between the two.

"What's this about? From the beginning," Clay barked.

"Well, after we finished work at the movie theater," I began.

"I want to hear it from him," Clay snapped.

I rolled my eyes.

"And don't roll your eyes," he added.

Sheesh!

"Well, sir—" Detective Jackson leaned back in his chair and pulled a small notebook from his pocket "—shortly after midnight Miss Emery called in a situation and—"

"I did not call it in, Lara did," I corrected and received an icy glare from Clay.

"Fine. I just won't say anything," I sulked.

"That would be best," Clay said, sounding too professional for my liking. It was getting so that I was having a hard time maintaining visuals of sex in his office.

"What situation was called in?" Clay asked.

"There's an old boarded-up building at the corner of 156th Avenue and Eighth Street," Jackson began.

"Across from the Movie Megaplex," Clay added.

"That's right. Last night Miss Emery and—" he glanced down at his notes then up again "—her friend, Lara Caruth, had a sudden desire to go Dumpster diving and—"

"We did *not* Dumpster dive!" I shouted.

The detective smothered a chuckle and cleared his throat. "Apparently the ladies felt a sudden *calling*—" he sneered "—to investigate the Dumpster behind the building. Then they called in the fact that there appeared to be blood inside said Dumpster."

"Blood?" Clay questioned. "I thought you said this was about murder. Was there a body found?"

"No, sir, there was not. That is what brings me here to discuss the matter with Miss Emery." The detective swiveled his chair to focus granite black eyes on mine. "Somebody spray-painted a pentagram on the Dumpster and the crime lab confirmed today that it was human blood found. There was enough blood to suggest that whoever lost it, did not walk away."

"That poor woman," I murmured.

Detective Jackson quickly stated, "I never mentioned that the blood was from a woman."

It was Clay's turn for an eye roll. "I'd say she had a fifty-fifty chance of getting that one right."

Jackson lowered his voice. "All right then, perhaps you'd like to clarify what you and your friend were doing in the rear parking lot of an abandoned building after midnight, peering into a Dumpster?"

"You don't have to answer that," Clay stated firmly.

"It's no big deal." I shrugged. "Lara's bus stops right in front of the building."

"That still doesn't explain what you were doing *behind* the building."

I offered the detective a pissed-off glare. "I didn't *want* to go behind the building. I had a real bad feeling about it, but Lara insisted because…" Again I shrugged. "Well, just because she was curious and thought it might be like the mutilated cat and—"

"Cat?" both men chimed in unison. Uh-oh.

"Um." I pinched the bridge of my nose with my fingers. "Yesterday after work I had my purse snatched and the guy ran through a cemetery. I had a bad feeling at the cemetery."

"Most people have bad feelings in a cemetery." Jackson snorted.

"This bad feeling led me to a mutilated cat lying inside a pentagram."

Clay sucked in air through his perfect white teeth.

Detective Jackson's gaze narrowed. "And it didn't occur to you to mention this little tidbit of information to the officers on the scene last night?" He flipped open his notebook and demanded details. I offered him what few there were.

"I've been twenty years on the force, Miss Emery, and I've learned not to believe in coincidences." Jackson snapped his notebook shut and buried it inside his coat. "Now would be a good time for you to tell me anything else you may be withholding."

Clay stood abruptly. "This interview is over. Miss Emery has been more than cooperative."

Detective Jackson left but not before uttering, "I'll be back," like an Arnold Schwartzenegger wanna-be.

After the detective left I realized I'd better hit the road, too, if I was going to make it to the Movie Megaplex by six.

"I appreciate that you stayed on my account, Mr. Sanderson but—" I began.

"Call me Clay and tell me about this *bad feeling* stuff you were mentioning."

"There's not much to tell. I'm not some weirdo psychic carrying a crystal ball. I just get a feeling for things sometimes, that's all." I shuddered and didn't mention that this time bad dreams and foggy apparitions of a woman in a pool of blood were also included.

"Do you want to tell me about this so-called premonition?"

I shook my head. "Nothing really to tell, it was just a bad feeling I had."

He smiled. "My grandmother used to claim to have second sight."

"Did she make predictions?"

Chuckling, he said, "Well, her second sight was usually assisted by her love for vodka."

Clay held the door to his office open and I walked through. When he followed behind me I couldn't help but clench my butt muscles, just in case he happened to be watching that part of my anatomy. It was a habit.

At the reception area I pressed the call button for the elevator.

"I'm sorry you had to waste your time like this."

"I never consider spending time with a beautiful woman—or a new client—to be a waste of time."

"Um, I'm an employee, not a client. Just because I answered some questions from Detective Jackson doesn't mean I'll be needing to lawyer up." As for the beautiful part, well I'd just savor that while I cuddled with my pillow tonight.

"Look, Tabitha, I don't want you to take this lightly. This is a murder investigation and so far it sounds as though the only leads they've had were provided by you."

I didn't reply and we rode the elevator in silence except for the Muzak version of an Olivia Newton John song playing overhead.

I survived another shift at the Movie Megaplex even though Friday was even busier than Thursday. Afterward

I discovered that my bra had increased a full cup size thanks to the amount of popcorn that had found its way down my shirt.

"You coming to Jimbo's?" Lara asked while slipping from her yellow Movie Megaplex shirt into a sheer black blouse. Jimbo's was our usual watering hole on Friday nights. I was usually there sitting with Jenny and a few others trashing old boyfriends and halfway drunk by the time Lara showed up after her shift at the theater.

"I don't think so. I'm trounced," I said, inwardly admitting to a new respect for Lara who'd never missed our Friday skunking even with a brassiere filled with popcorn.

I told Lara about my visit from Detective Jackson and Clay Sanderson's unexpected rising to my defense.

"The man of your wet dreams finally spoke to you for longer than it takes to ask for his phone messages? All the more reason for you to come out and celebrate," Lara argued.

"No."

"You'll change your mind," Lara remarked pushing her glasses up her nose. "Jenny told me that Cathy is bringing her roommate."

"Oh, my God, not that insufferable nerd, Jeff! He's a disgrace to gay men everywhere, as dull as my aunt Ruth and less hairy." I straightened the drab black skirt and white blouse that I'd worn nine to five at McAuley and Malcolm. "Why on earth did you think I'd change my mind knowing that Jeff would be there?"

"Because, you dolt," Lara breathed while peering into the small mirror in the employee lounge and layering new mascara over old, "Jeff still works at that New Age shop, the Crying Room."

"The *Scrying* Room," I corrected and let out a bubble of laughter. "Don't you know the difference between *scrying* and *crying*?"

"No, I don't. But *you* do." Lara turned and raised her eyebrows at me. "That's why I'm sure you'll come tonight. After Jeff's had a couple martinis you can pump him for information."

"Oh, really? What kind of information would I be pumping from Jeff? How to bore Seattle's entire homosexual population into becoming straight?"

"No."

By the hand, Lara tugged me out the rear entrance of the theater and into an icy West Coast shower. "Everything you've always wanted to know about pentagrams but were afraid to ask."

Lara and I split a fifteen-dollar cab ride to Jimbo's. Even though the clock was halfway to 1:00 a.m. when we entered, I felt rejuvenated by the dim lighting, noxious aroma of stale smoke and beer and the vibration of heavy base from the sound system. Our comrades, Jenny, Cathy and Jeff were engrossed in a conversation of earth-shattering magnitude, namely, whether or not tongue piercing really could provide an advantage during oral sex.

Lara and I tugged two more chairs over to the scarred pine table that was the one preferred by our group due to its equal proximity to the self-serve bar and the toilets. I noticed that Jenny had swept up her red hair and wore jeans and a V-neck black sweater. The sweater hid her tummy roll while the low cut of her top enhanced what she considered to be her two best features. Cathy, at the other end of the table, waved bloodred fingernails and mouthed *hello*. She wore black as well but had no fat to hide and her hair had been the same blond, spiked Rod Stewart style since we were in high school. Jeff, who sat on my right, wore brown corduroy pants, a brown cable sweater and nearly succeeded in camouflaging himself into the brown chair he was sitting in. His hair, what little he had, was fine and pale against an equally pallid complexion. He offered us a nearly imperceptible nod as a greeting.

"What's tonight's poison?" Lara asked, pushing glasses up her nose and bottom into the chair on my left.

We were informed that tonight they were debating the merits of butterscotch schnapps. It was our group's mission to set a booze theme to coincide with our weekly imbibing.

"I'm drinking a Buttery Nipple," Jenny announced holding up a nearly empty shot glass. "It's made with butterscotch schnapps and Baileys."

"And Cathy is consuming a Poopy Puppy," Jeff said, failing to even crack a grin at the ridiculous drink name. "Ingredients are a blend of amaretto, Kahlúa, Baileys and the butterscotch schnapps with a splash of Coke."

Cathy licked her red lipsticked mouth. "It's really quite yummy in a sickening sweet kinda way."

"I see you're being your usual stick-in-the-mud self and just drinking a martini," I commented to Jeff.

He peered at me with a serious expression. "If one has to consume alcohol, this is the purest choice." He downed what was left in his glass.

Lara was already on her feet, anxious to make her way to the self-serve bar. I handed her a five and told her to surprise me. The one thing our bunch had in common was the fact that we could hold our liquor. There wasn't a puker amongst us, save the time last summer when we tried to combine crème de menthe night with tequila night.

When Lara returned she had a Poopy Puppy for herself and a Buttery Nipple for me. I downed the Nipple in one smooth move while Lara brought the gathering up to speed on my horrific twenty-four hours ending with my office visit from Detective Jackson. Jenny congratulated me on attracting the attention of Clay, but reprimanded me for not taking advantage of our shared elevator ride and trying to seduce Clay using a thank-you kiss as an excuse.

"Discussing murder does not exactly put me in a romantic mood," I replied dryly.

"Who's talking romance?" Jenny laughed. "I was talking hot jungle sex in an elevator."

"Speaking of jungle sex, how was your date?" I asked.

Jenny shrugged. "A dud." But didn't elaborate and for the millionth time I admired her for her tenacity in pursuing the opposite sex.

"Anyway," Lara piped up, "I was figuring Jeff could probably help Tabitha out."

Everyone turned their attention to Jeff who squirmed in his seat.

"Wh-wh-what can I do?" In addition to Jeff's many charms, he tended to stutter when he was uncomfortable.

"You're the one who has the spiritual or Wiccan connection. For starters, you can fill us in on this pentagram stuff."

"Sure, Jeff," Cathy encouraged. "You looove that junk, it's right up your alley."

Jeff blinked and cleared his throat before beginning his dissertation. "Well, Medieval Christians attributed the pentagram to the five wounds of Christ. To the Gnostics, the pentagram was the Blazing Star and it wasn't until the 1960s that it became a Wiccan symbol."

We all stared at him openmouthed.

"W-w-well, it's kinda my job," he said, embarrassed. When he recovered he twisted toward me. "You should come down to the shop and I can show you around. You can look at some books on the subject or I can show you our variety of pentagrams. I'm working tomorrow, if you're interested."

"No, thanks, I'm busy. I still have to work at the movie theater."

Jeff cleared his throat and headed for the self-serve bar.

"That's not until six-thirty," Lara pointed out. "It might be fun to check out the Scrying Room. I've always been kind of curious about that place."

"Thanks, but I have other plans for my day." Like sleeping until noon and scrounging through all of my pockets for quarters to see if I had enough cash to do laundry.

"I'll go with you," Jenny offered.

"I have no need to expand my knowledge of penta-grams. Just because I've seen two lately does not exactly mean I have to become an expert on the subject."

"Well, if I were you, I'd certainly be curious," Cathy piped up. "I'd even offer to join you but I promised to baby-sit my sister's brats."

When I didn't give in, Jenny added, "If you don't go

with me," she taunted in a singsong voice, "I won't tell you some really juicy office gossip."

I felt myself waver. "I want to hear the tittle-tattle first before I promise to go to the Scrying Room."

"No way."

"What if I've already heard it?"

"You haven't and, trust me, it's good."

I caved. "Fine. I'll go with you to the Scrying Room. Now spill."

"Well, you know Martha's pregnant."

Cathy burst out, "Of course Tab knows! She knew it before Martha knew. She had one of her spells and—"

"I do *not* have spells!"

"Whatever," Cathy countered.

"Don't leave us hanging here!" Lara exclaimed.

Jenny put up her hands to stop us. "This isn't about Martha being pregnant. This is about her maternity leave and who is going to be filling her space during that time."

"Who?"

Jenny leaned back. "I don't know for certain, of course, but I *do* know that Muriel's husband is being transferred to San Francisco and it sounds like they'll be packing up. So that means Muriel won't be available to fill in for Martha's maternity leave."

"Omigod!" I was getting excited. Ever since I was hired on permanently after a brief temp job, I'd been hoping to be promoted from receptionist but Muriel was next in line. Although only a mere filing clerk, Muriel was still a smidgen above my position in the McAuley and Malcolm food chain. "Is this a sure thing?"

Jenny nodded. "I heard her tell The Bitch today."

The Bitch, aka Sonya Suderman, was office manager and in charge of all the nonlawyer staff.

I could almost taste victory. Last year I'd taken some extra computer classes and a course on legal terminology to bring me up to speed. It wasn't like it was *a dream come true* to be a legal secretary, but it was a *nightmare come alive* to remain a receptionist. I'd actually had my eye on Marie Laraby's secretarial position since she was old as dirt and there was a pool going as to whether or not she would retire or simply slip into a doughnut coma behind her desk. Marie worked for George Ferguson who was equally ancient, had trouble with intestinal gas and was head of the wrongful dismissal department.

"And you know the best part," Jenny said, grinning like a Cheshire cat. "You wouldn't have to work for Flatulent Ferguson."

I suddenly felt melancholy. "If my dad hadn't died I would've gotten my degree by now. I'd certainly have more than a secretarial position to look forward to."

"Tabitha, I hate to break it to you, but going for a degree in Women's Studies was not going to help you. You should've been studying men all along." She laughed.

"Aw, man." I hung my head with a sudden realization. "Martha works for Clay. If I get the job I'll be Clay Sanderson's secretary."

"That's great!" Lara exclaimed. "Isn't it?"

"Of course it's great," Cathy reasoned. "Tab's been soppy and doe-eyed over that suit for years."

"How could I possibly work for him?" I moaned. "I can't work with a man who ties me up in knots."

"I know exactly how you feel," Jeff commented, returning with his martini in time to hear my last comment.

Soppy and doe-eyed was exactly the way Jeff was staring at the Scrying Room's owner, Lucien Roskell, when Jen and I arrived just after ten the next morning. Only problem was, the way Lucien scraped his gaze hotly across my breasts when I walked in, told me that Jeff's boss didn't have an ounce of gay in him.

When a few possible customers came into the store Jeff and Lucien left Jen and I to look around or, as Lucien put it, "meander their metaphysical retail establishment." I was quite content to meander since I had no idea what the hell I was doing there in the first place. Jenny, on the other hand, was having a hard time taking her eyes off the proprietor.

"Did you get a load of that guy?" she whispered in my ear.

"Yeah, I did. He's good-looking." I picked up a crystal dangling from a long silver chain and held it up for examination. "Do you wear this thing or hang it as a decoration?"

"Good-looking?" Jenny slapped my back so hard I stumbled forward and nearly dropped the crystal. "The guy isn't good-looking he's friggin' gorgeous!" Jenny insisted. "Under that black turtleneck you can see washboard abs!"

"Well, sure, but he's got a bum-chin."

Jenny rolled her eyes, "You mean a *cleft* chin? If I could stick my tongue in that cleft I'd die a happy woman."

I glanced across the shop to where Lucien was showing a collection of tarot cards to a balding middle-aged man. Lucien looked up and his carbon eyes gripped mine and held. I felt my toes curl.

I tore my gaze away. "I don't know, there's something weird or strange about the guy."

"It's probably the fact that he's six feet tall with broad shoulders, a smooth olive complexion, thick dark hair and those bottomless eyes," Jenny sighed. "We've heard of male perfection, we're just not used to seeing it away from a GQ cover."

"Sorry to leave you," Jeff offered when he returned. "Our pentagram stuff is over here."

Jeff brought us to another section of the L-shaped store that was floor-to-ceiling glass shelves.

"This is our Wicca section." He glanced over his shoulder. "Look, I gotta go fill an order in the back room so take a look around. There are a number of good books in our witches library that you might find interesting and, if you want, I'll give you my twenty-percent employee discount." He turned and scuttled in the opposite direction.

Jenny and I stared at the massive quantity of items surrounding us.

"Wow," Jenny said. *Wow* just about covered it.

"No eye of toad or hair of newt," I observed, but there certainly were shelves containing everything else you would expect your modern witch to have. There were spell candles, witch balls, incense sticks, intricately carved wands and, of course, crystal balls in your choice of green, blue and black. One shelf held a weighty selection of scrying mirrors that gave me the heebie-jeebies.

"Well, I'm definitely getting *this*," Jenny announced holding up a book titled *Red Hot Love Spells*. "Maybe I can find a spell to put on Tim tonight."

"Is Tim the one who's Lara's cousin?"

"No, that was Todd."

"So he's your neighbor's nephew?"

"No, that's Terry. Tim is my cousin's neighbor's stepson."
I just shook my head clear and changed the subject.

"To own this kind of a store this Roskell guy is either
very strange—" I fingered a brass chalice and gasped at the
price tag "—or very smart."

"I see you're interested in The Craft," a deep voice
sounded behind us. "'All the wild witches, the most noble
ladies, for all their broomsticks and their tears, their angry
tears, are gone.'"

We turned to look into Lucien's smiling face.

"I don't know what that means—" Jenny giggled "—but it sure sounds nice. Was that Shakespeare?"

"Yeats," Lucien replied. He flashed a wide smile at Jenny
then focused his obsidian eyes on mine. "Jeff tells me
you're interested in pentagrams."

I didn't answer. It felt as if his cavernous gaze was
extracting my ability to speak. I controlled my urge to
fidget and my other urge to run.

Jenny stepped closer so that she was shoulder to shoulder with me. "Yes, Tabitha has had a rather interesting few
days, pentagram speaking."

"Really?" His eyebrows rose in amusement, his gaze still
securely locked on mine. "It sounds like an interesting
story, perhaps one that should be told over dinner?
Tonight?"

"Um, sorry. Actually, I'm working tonight."

"Oh? Jeff told me you work in a law office, is there an
emergency legal matter to attend to?" The corners of his
mouth twitched.

"I have a second job at a movie theater."

"But she's not busy now," Jenny piped in and I would've pinched her if she hadn't sidestepped out of pinching distance. "You could always go for coffee."

"Splendid idea." Lucien grinned. "I'll just let Jeff know that he'll be running the store."

He turned on his heel and then I *did* pinch Jenny.

"Ow!"

"What the hell did you do that for?" I snapped. "I don't want to go out with him!"

"You're the one who is always saying that coffee with a man is the perfect predate test," Jenny reasoned thumbing through the pages of her love spell book. "What's so awful? So you spend a few minutes together. Big deal. You can determine whether or not there's a spark and whether or not he's capable of stringing a few words together, then if he passes the predate test you're safe to attempt dinner."

I hated having my own lecture tossed back in my face.

"Well, you're coming with us."

"No way! The man doesn't even look at me when I'm standing right next to you."

"I don't care. I need a buffer because he's just so—" I groped for the word "—intense."

Jen rolled her eyes. "I'm sure you can handle him on your own for a few minutes. I'll be right across the street at that discount shoe place. When you're done having coffee with Mr. Intense you can meet me there."

Before I could protest further Mr. Intense was at my side and shrugging into a black leather jacket and within minutes we were at a coffee shop next door cozily sipping steaming lattes.

"So tell me about your pentagram escapades," Lucien urged.

"Jenny likes to be a little dramatic," I replied, and after taking a deep drink of my coffee I relayed to him all about the purse snatcher, the following cat yukiness and then the incident at the Dumpster. I omitted Detective Jackson's subsequent visit.

Lucien leaned in, listened patiently and made tsk-tsking sounds at all the appropriate places. Once I'd completed my story he leaned back and considered me with his scrutinizing gaze.

"Having the sight must be both a blessing and a curse for you."

I jumped enough to slosh a little coffee on my fingers. "I do *not* have 'the sight.'" I drew quotes in the air with my fingers then wiped the coffee from them with a napkin. "I assure you that I cannot foretell the future or read minds." I took a long pull from my coffee cup. "Occasionally I *do* have intuition," I begrudgingly admitted, then I laughed nervously. "Women's intuition. Ha ha. We all have it."

But he wasn't buying it. "But you did know something was wrong even before you saw the dead cat or the Dumpster. I'm willing to bet that you've also had premonitions about what actually did happen at that Dumpster."

"You'd lose that bet."

He shrugged. "But you do believe a woman was killed and put in the Dumpster and you also believe the pentagram in the cemetery and the one on the Dumpster were made by the same person."

"I never said that."

"You don't need to say it."

"Oh, so now you're the clairvoyant?"

He sipped his coffee and grinned. "I think some people have a sixth sense but most ignore it."

I considered that to be true as well and told him so.

We sat in silence for a moment then suddenly he reached inside his turtleneck and pulled out a long silver chain. Dangling from the chain was a silver disc, an amulet, with a pentagram carved into its center. Intricate letters and figures I couldn't quite make out were engraved around and inside of it.

"That's a different kind of pentagram," I commented. "Do all those symbols on it have a meaning?"

He nodded. "It's called the Pentagram of Solomon. It protects from danger." Grinning he said, "You know, many people get a kick out of playing around with witchcraft or the occult. A few satanic or Wicca doodads around the house can make great conversation pieces." He rolled the amulet between his fingers and it glinted in the florescent lighting of the coffee shop, then he tucked it back inside his shirt. "I'd say the majority of my customers are just curious and some may even dabble occasionally but that doesn't make them satanic cultists or evil murderers."

"Of course not, just like going to church doesn't make you a Christian any more than standing in a garage makes you a car."

He tossed back his head and laughed throatily. "Exactly."

"Still—" I downed the rest of my coffee "—you must get some so-called true believers in your store."

"Sure, in Washington state alone there are over a dozen Wicca covens practicing on a regular basis." As if he were tossing them away with a wave of his hand he continued, "They're harmless. It's those who don't belong to the groups, those who follow their own path, who are probably more likely to be dangerous."

Suddenly, he leaned on our small table until his face was scant inches away from mine. "Have you tried to focus your visions? I have a terrific assortment of scrying mirrors."

I leaned back. "I don't believe in them."

He frowned and drew his brows together. "I'm sure it doesn't work for all but many seers trust in scrying. How can you not believe in scrying when your own ability should be enough to convince you of its possibilities? Perhaps you should learn more about the subject before saying you don't believe."

I sighed. "Scrying is the art of clairvoyance achieved by concentrating on an object," I recited. "The word *scrying* comes from the English word *descry,* which means 'to make out dimly' or 'to reveal.'"

He clapped his hands politely. "Obviously you've already done your homework on the subject. Yet you still claim not to be a believer. Why is that?"

"A couple years ago I got curious. I spent some time at the library and with a psychic. The so-called psychic cured me and proved to me that most of what's out there is a lot of horse hockey."

I didn't reveal to him the fact that my sudden interest was triggered by a premonition of my father's demise followed by his actual death in precisely the manner I envisioned.

"Most—but not all—of the stuff is bunk, I'll give you that, but how do you explain the fact that some people have very accurate visions while scrying?"

"It's simple, if you've ever sat staring at a blank wall until you began to see images, or if you've ever lain in bed staring up at the ceiling until you saw blurry patterns in the stucco, then you're doing the exact same thing as staring into a scrying mirror until a so-called vision manifests itself."

He didn't respond except to finish his coffee. When he spoke again he abruptly changed the subject. We spent the remaining few minutes discussing the weather and then whether or not the Seahawks had a hope in hell of beating the Chicago Bears tomorrow.

When we parted company in front of the coffee shop I had to admit I was a tiny bit disappointed that he didn't ask me out. Not that I was sure I'd even accept, still, it was always nice to have a gorgeous guy ask.

Jenny had used our few minutes apart to add to her shoe collection. She lived valiantly by the credo that if the shoe fits buy it in every color. She picked up a prized pair of red stilettos for her date that night. Jenny was a full-figured gal and with stiletto heels she looked like a pear on stilts. Then again I was probably just jealous because, unlike me, Jenny rarely was desperate and dateless on a Saturday night. True, the guys she dated were usually blind dates that never asked for seconds—hell some even went to the bathroom halfway through the evening and didn't return. Still, Jenny was an optimist and figured Seattle had a lot of men and she was determined to date all the single ungay ones or die trying. You have to admire someone with that kind of tenacity.

Jenny and I grabbed a burger for lunch then parted company. I did laundry at home and then shuffled off to work. That night at the Movie Megaplex I was friendless 'cause Lara had scored a night off. The first wave wasn't too bad—there were lots of groups of singles. Then the second wave hit and there were lots of couples all smoochy and cuddly after a romantic dinner. I tried to dish out the popcorn, drinks and candy without making eye contact. If I saw that glazed lust-on-its-way-to-love look on one more face I'd start slamming my head into the counter. Then, just when it couldn't get any worse, a warm male voice forced me to look up.

"A diet cola, bottled water and a jumbo popcorn." Clay Sanderson beamed down at me. He had that same challenging spark in his eyes and the same glittery blonde hanging off his arm.

I swallowed and dared to meet his gaze. "Uh, if you order the enormous popcorn you'll get a free box of Rosebuds."

"You're the boss," he joked.

Why me? If he insisted on taking his date to the movies so often why did he have to come to *this* theatre and *my* lineup? I filled his order then returned and took his cash, trying to be as quick as possible.

Clay offered me a wink before traipsing in the direction of the theaters. I noticed his girlfriend was wearing high heels similar to the ones Jenny had bought. Only Clay's girlfriend did *not* look like a pear on stilts—she had the legs of a dancer. All of a sudden I was depressed.

I took a ten-minute break and ate my way through a supersize Oh Henry! and a box of Junior Mints then returned to do clean up. After the second wave of shows started things got pretty slow behind the concession stand so we began to close the station down. The two pimple-faced teenagers working with me talked excitedly about their plans to attend a party later. It was downright embarrassing that I had nothing to do. I decided that my chocolate binge would need the assistance of a few beers to make me feel better. Yeah, a few beers and maybe a pack of Virginia Slims. When I quit smoking last month I'd not counted on being pummeled by all these new obstacles in my life. Bad dreams. Detective interrogations. A chance I may get a promotion and work with Clay. I needed nicotine to calm my frazzled nerves.

The second wave of moviegoers were spilling into the parking lot as I returned to the staff room to change out of my yellow uniform shirt. I slipped into my Seahawks jersey and shrugged into my Gore-Tex jacket. It was raining when I stepped outside, which matched my mood perfectly. Actually, it wasn't official rain. Seattleites had many names for the various forms of wet drops that fell and this was a mizzle—a mist increasing to a drizzle. Regardless, it was wet, it was cold and I had to walk home in it.

Most of the second-wavers were darting to their cars and I envied them. I wanted my car. I *needed* my car. When you had a car you had freedom. I cut diagonally between the parked vehicles but paused midway across as I found myself looking at the abandoned building where Lara and I had discovered the bloody Dumpster. I stopped and stared at it. I was *not* going near there. Nope. I wasn't. Really.

"You're not going over there," Clay's voice commanded from behind me.

I turned sharply with surprise. "Of course I'm not!" I said defensively.

He opened the passenger door to a sporty yellow Miata soft-top and the modelesque blonde slipped into the passenger seat, eyeing me dismissively.

"Because you sure looked like you were *thinking* of going over there and if that is what you're thinking, I have to advise you against it."

I felt a dribble of rain dangling from the tip of my nose and swiped it away with my hand. "I was *not* thinking of going there. I was just wondering if the cops had checked inside the building."

Clay narrowed his eyes and folded his arms across his chest. When he narrowed his eyes they crinkled in the corners, making him look a little older than his midthirties. I wasn't used to having his undivided attention. I didn't sigh, even though I wanted to.

"I'm sure that the police have thoroughly checked the entire area and I am just as sure they would not want you checking to see if they checked."

"Clay, I'm cooold," whined Modelesque Girl.

"I'll be just a second, Candy," Clay replied, and pushed her door shut.

Her name was Candy. Perfect. How could I ever compete with a combination of thinness, blondness and someone whose name was a sweet confection?

"So you're going straight home then, right?" he asked.

Suddenly I was annoyed. Just because I moonlighted at a movie theater did *not* mean I didn't have a life! Okay, well it *did* mean that but *he* didn't need to know it!

"It so happens that I have a date," I lied.

The corners of his lips twitched. "It's almost midnight. You should've had your date pick you up."

I jammed my hands into my pockets. "Todd's meeting me at my place. I live only a couple blocks away and I *like* to walk."

Todd was the name of my first boyfriend. I don't know why his name sprung to my lips but I figured having a name for my fake boyfriend lent some credibility to my lie.

Candy tapped her window impatiently with a long manicured nail.

"Cool it," Clay said to the window.

Yeah, cool it, Candy, Clay and I are having a conversation here, I thought.

"Okay." He chucked a finger under my chin. "Just be careful, huh?"

The underneath part of my chin tingled where he touched it. I turned and strode purposely across the parking lot. After a few steps I could hear his car roar to life and that's when I let out the breath I'd been holding. The chuck under my chin was not exactly the lip-crushing kiss of my fantasies but it had definitely thrown me off guard.

When I reached the edge of the lot I hesitated. I should turn right onto 156th Avenue and continue my walk. I could stop at the corner store and pick up that pack of Virginia Slims. The ciggies combined with the six-pack of Rainier beer that was waiting in my fridge would take me well on my way to having my own little pity party inside of half an hour. Or I could do all of those things *after* I checked out the building across the street.

It's not like I have a death wish. I'm just a curious kind of person and my inquisitiveness was now centered on that dilapidated building. All I wanted was a peek inside. I wasn't going to go near the Dumpster. No way. I just wanted to know if the inside of this building was what I'd seen in my dream.

I crossed the street. Instead of that eerie feeling I'd felt the other day about the building, there was only a general uneasiness, but it wasn't thundering inside me. It was just sort of…there, hovering in the background…like when you eat hot wings and you know the heartburn'll follow, but I could handle that. I mean if the place was *really* dangerous I'd have that deep sense of foreboding snaking through my veins, right?

Trusting my instincts in this weird kind of way, I scurried toward the building and dipped into the shadows. The front door was padlocked and boarded; the windows along the front and side were also secured with plywood. I inched around to the back, to where one of the boards had fallen away. Standing on tiptoe, I pressed my face close to the window. It was black as ink inside. Damn.

Just then, the clouds opened and it started raining hard. There was a slight overhang covering the back entrance and I scooted out of the wet. Of course the door was also criss-crossed in canary-yellow crime-scene tape, but all I wanted was to wait until the rain tapered back to a sprinkle then I'd head home. It was a shame I hadn't gotten a better look. Too bad I didn't have a flashlight. Wait a second! I didn't have a flashlight but I still carried a Bic lighter. I rummaged through my purse. Lucky for me I hadn't changed purses since I'd quit smoking. I dug around the bottom of my bag until my fingers clamped onto the smooth familiar feel of the Bic. I lifted it out triumphantly and stumbled backward hitting the door with my shoulder. The tape tore away and the door sprang wide open. Holy shit!

I recovered from my stumble and stared into the dark cavernous building. Swallowing my fear, I fumbled with the lighter until I was able to flick it ablaze. I stuck my arm straight out and the tall flame illuminated the way as I walked inside.

The flame flickered as I walked farther and farther. The back door opened into a hall and after a few steps to my left it turned into one big room. It had the appearance of an old convenience store. On the far wall, shelves were still mounted from floor to almost the ceiling. The lighter was heating up so I let it go out. Using the wall to guide me, I inched along. Suddenly, my foot plunged into a hole. I flicked my Bic and saw that my foot was lodged into a heating vent with a missing cover grate. I had to tug my foot out, leaving my shoe behind, balance on one foot and then do some wriggling to get my shoe free from the crevice. After that, my eyes adjusted quickly to the dim light coming through the opened back door.

The room smelled of dampness, rotting wood and something else. The something else was candle wax. I felt my heart rate pick up when the scent rushed a flash from my dreams. I remembered a room like this and a hand reaching to light a thick black candle.

I switched on the lighter again and something caught my eye. On the wall to my right was a drawing in black marker. Not the large scrawling curse words or tagging of graffiti, but two symbols each about a foot high. The first was a crude drawing that looked kind of like an angel but instead of a halo it had a horizontal crescent shape on top of its head. The second was a circle with a cross inside of it. My fingers reached out to touch the drawings.

"What the hell are you doing?" A voice boomed from the doorway.

I let out a squeak, dropped my lighter and nearly passed out.

chapter three

"What the hell are *you* doing sneaking up on me?" I demanded in turn.

Clay Sanderson fisted his hands on his hips. "I distinctly recall telling you *not* to come in here!"

"You may be my boss at McAuley and Malcolm but I'm on my own time now and if I want to go snooping then—"

He strode dangerously toward me and stopped scant inches away. "You broke into a crime scene!"

"Whoa." I held up a hand. "I did *not* break in. The tape came down when I fell against the door, and then it just flew open."

He grabbed me by the elbow and dragged me away, all but shoving me into the door frame. The door itself was still wide open and I could see, not to mention hear, his Miata purring in the lot.

"Look!" he commanded, stabbing a finger at splintered wood around the doorjamb. "This definitely looks like a break-in."

I stared at it. "Yes. You're right, but that does not mean *I* was the one who broke in. Maybe the cops broke the door when they investigated this place or maybe whoever drew on the walls did it or maybe—"

A car horn sounded loud and we both turned to see Candy inside Clay's car. She had a most pissed-off look on her face.

"Your date's getting impatient," I said.

"Fuck her," he growled.

"I'll leave that to you. She's not my type."

He chuckled wearily, then his gaze clashed with mine. "Yeah, and what *is* your type, huh? Todd? Is he your type?"

I was hypnotized by Clay's baby blues. "Who?"

"Aha!" he shouted. "I knew you didn't have a date and I suppose if I just leave you here you're going to go right back to snooping, aren't you?" he barked.

Actually, I was planning on just going home but I didn't like his tone. He was beginning to sound like my mother. "So what if I am?"

He looked to the heavens for assistance but when none came he lowered his gaze to mine and glared. "I am going to drive you home and make sure that you stay there."

"Oh, yeah, and how do you propose to manage that? Are you gonna strap me to the roof of your car 'cause last time I checked you only had two seats."

He reached into his pocket and flipped open his cell phone. Seconds later he was giving directions to a taxi dispatcher.

"Look, I don't need a cab," I said. "I'll just walk home." Not to mention the fact that I didn't even have enough cash in my purse for the one-block cab fare. How embarrassing is that?

Clay walked over to his car, opened the driver's side door and spoke at length to Candy. Something soft nudged my ankle and I glanced down to see the largest rat I'd ever laid eyes on. I yelped and jumped at the same time. The black fur ball looked up at me and mewed softly. It was a cat, or more accurately, a skinny, black, soaking-wet kitten.

"Aww," I bent down and scooped up the pathetic creature and held it to my chest. It was all ribs and felt as if it hadn't had a good meal in its entire life. I held the black furry face up to mine and it tentatively licked my chin. I immediately fell in love.

Meanwhile, Clay slammed his car door shut and returned to me.

He stopped short and stared. "What is that?"

"It's a cat."

"I can see that it's a cat. What are you doing with it?"

"I'm holding it. For a lawyer you don't have much of a grasp of the obvious."

I took a step away and he yanked me back by the collar of my jacket.

"Where are you going?"

"Home."

"You're waiting right here until the taxi comes."

I turned to look at Clay. His jaw was set angrily and his eyes were sparked with fury. He looked like he could plow a fist through concrete. I'd never been more attracted to him. If I continued to stay in his close proximity I was going to have serious orgasmic trouble. Luckily, Candy motioned him back to the car.

I closed my eyes and thought of a plan. Okay, so I'd let him stick me in a cab and once we were around the corner I'd get the cabbie to drop me off and I'd walk the rest of the way. I petted the wet furry mass in my arms and it snuggled deeper against me.

The taxi pulled up only seconds later. Clay walked around his Miata and opened the passenger door. Candy unfolded her shapely legs and got to her feet. She shot me a lethal glare then strode angrily to the cab, got in the back and it squealed out of the lot.

Huh.

So Candy's the one taking the cab.

"Get in," Clay commanded, holding the passenger door of his Miata open.

"I thought the cab was for me," I said sheepishly. "I didn't mean to ruin your date."

"Get in," he repeated.

I sighed and slipped into the vehicle.

"You're not taking that *thing* with you, are you?"

I looked up at him incredulously. "This kitten? Of course! What do you want me to do, just leave it out here in the rain?"

He growled, slammed the car door shut and walked around to the driver's side. I gave him directions to my place and we drove in silence. The car smelled intoxicatingly of his cologne and worn leather. If I could bottle that scent and sprinkle it on my pillow I'd never leave my bed.

He curbed his car in front of my building and got out.

What a gentleman, he was even going to open my door for me. I wasn't used to this kind of treatment.

"Thanks," I said and tucked kitty under my arm as I climbed out of the car. "Look, I'm sorry again about your date."

"I'll walk you up," he offered.

"No, that's okay,"

"I'll walk you up," he said more firmly.

I shrugged and headed for my place, stuffing kitty inside my jacket along the way.

"You'll have to walk me *down*," I said and jabbed my key into the front door of the building. "I live in the basement."

I wasn't too thrilled about the prospect of Clay Sanderson seeing my drab studio apartment but I quieted my concerns with the fact that he had already seen me working concession at the Megaplex so, technically, I'd already exceeded my embarrassment limit.

As we walked along the hallway Mrs. Sumner poked her head around. Curlers in hair. Cigarette in mouth. Ratty housecoat.

"Don't be slammin' your door!" she snapped, eyed Clay critically and then retreated.

When I opened the door of my suite Clay followed without waiting for an invitation and he nudged the door closed with his hip. I put kitty down on the floor. He—I discretely checked gender on the way over—scampered up onto my sofa bed that was glaringly still in the bed position and snuggled into my blankets. Luckily there were two pine chairs to sit in and Clay already had lowered himself into one.

"So what's the plan? Are you going to keep the cat?" he asked.

I made a face. "I'm not sure. We're not allowed pets here."

As if on cue there was a sharp rap at my door and a voice boomed, "Tabitha, I got a package for you!"

"Ah, shit!" I scooped up kitty and handed him to Clay. "Hide! It's my landlord!"

"Do you always get deliveries at one in the morning?" Clay whispered. "And where exactly am I supposed to hide?"

I pushed him into the bathroom then answered the knock just as Mel the Mole Man was raising his fist to bang again. The tenants lovingly referred to Mel as the Mole Man because no one had ever seen him in the light of day and he tended to shrink against bright light.

I smiled sweetly through the crack of the door at my landlord's rotund form and his small squinty eyes that were behind huge thick lenses.

"Hi, Mel."

"Here." He pushed the door open farther and thrust a box into my hands. "Somebody dropped this off a few hours ago. I heard you come in so I figured I might as well give it to you now."

"Thanks," I started to shut the door but he stopped it with a beefy hand.

"Since we're both up, maybe you'd like to come over, I got popcorn made and I was just about to watch a Star Trek marathon."

"Um, as appealing as that sounds—" I flicked him a brief smile "—I gotta say no. Thanks for the package."

I slammed the door and locked it.

Clay appeared immediately with kitty still in his arms. He opened his mouth to speak but I held a finger to my lips to shush him. A couple seconds later I heard a door across the hall open and then shut.

"Sorry about that, my landlord would've had a fit if he saw the cat."

I tossed the package to the counter, opened a cupboard and pulled down a tin of tuna. After opening the can I dumped the contents into a bowl and put it on the floor. Kitty skidded over so quickly he almost knocked the whole bowl over. I burst out laughing and then looked over at Clay who was staring at me but was not sharing in my mirth.

"Aren't you going to open it?" He indicated the package I'd left on the counter.

"Oh." I picked it up and traced the brown paper wrapping where my name had been scrawled in an unfamiliar hand. I tore away the wrapping then unfolded the flaps of the box. A small gift card was nestled on top of layers of white tissue.

The card read, "'There are more things in heaven and earth, Tabitha, than are dreamt of in your philosophy.' Let's continue our discussion sometime...." It was signed, "Lucien."

I dropped the card carelessly to the counter where Clay eyed it with a wry expression, "Your boyfriend's fond of quoting Shakespeare's *Hamlet,* hmm? I thought you said his name was Todd."

I pushed the tissue aside and stared down into the box. All blood drained from my face.

Clay asked, "What is it?"

"Nothing." I hastily tried to recover the gift beneath the tissue.

"If it's nothing why are you looking like death warmed over and why are your hands shaking?" I caught his swift frown as Clay elbowed his way in front of me, dug into the box to reveal the gift. "What is this thing?"

"It's a scrying mirror." I dragged my fingers uneasily through my hair.

"A mirror." He turned the object over in his hands.

It was beautiful really—circular, about ten inches in diameter with an expensive pewter beaded frame. Just touching it had sparked a deep feeling of revulsion similar to inhaling the aroma of blue cheese.

"What kind of a mirror is black?" Clay asked.

I ignored his question.

"Sorry, I'm being rude, I should at least offer you a drink." I opened the refrigerator and peered inside. "Beer? Wine?"

I looked over my shoulder and he was eyeing me curiously. "A beer will be fine."

I tossed him a can and popped the tab on one for myself. The situation was beginning to feel strange. I hadn't expected Clay to come into my apartment and now that he had, I had no idea what to do with him. Of course, I knew what I'd like to do to him.

"Who is Lucien?" he asked, interrupting an emerging fantasy involving Clay and me on my linoleum.

"Um, a friend of a friend. He runs a New Age store called the Scrying Room—" I nodded toward the box "—hence the gift of a scrying mirror."

I crossed the floor and fiddled with my small stereo until I found a station playing soft jazz. I returned to my seat and drank deeply from my beer.

"You don't seem pleased by the gift."

I shrugged. "It's the thought that counts."

"Hmm—" his eyes challenged mine "—and I'm betting his thoughts are beyond friendship."

Before I could reply he asked, "So what does this scrying mirror thing do?"

"Nothing. It does nothing."

"It's just an ornament, then?"

"No. Um, scrying mirrors are used to help induce visions."

He paused with his beer halfway to his lips and smiled. "Visions? And this Lucien," he said the name mockingly, "he believes that crap?"

I rankled at his tone. "You know, many people have their minds open to the metaphysical."

"If you're *too* open-minded, your brains will fall out."

I laughed.

"And since you just said yourself that it does nothing—" he gulped some beer "—perhaps neither one of us has an open mind on the subject."

"Okay, so I'm not as open to the whole scrying thing as some people."

"Like Lucien."

"Exactly, but I do believe in a sixth sense that's more developed in some people than in others."

"Like you."

I didn't reply. Kitty snaked between my ankles purring his thanks for the tuna and marking me with his scent. I bent down and stroked his fur that was quickly drying to black fluff.

"So are you going to try that thing, then?" He nodded toward the package.

"No, of course not." I wondered if my voice sounded as unsure about that answer as I felt. I went to drink more of my beer and discovered it disappointingly empty and his looked the same.

"Can I get you another?"

He got to his feet.

"No, that's all right, I should go anyway. I only came inside because…" He seemed to grasp to finish his sentence as if he wasn't sure himself what he was doing here. Well, I certainly couldn't help him because I was still trying to figure that out myself.

"I guess I just wanted to make sure you weren't planning on returning to that vacant building. It's not a good idea to be stomping all over a crime scene."

I walked him the four baby steps from my living room-bedroom over to my apartment door.

"Thanks for seeing me home and I apologize for spoiling your date. Let Candy know that I'm sorry that she had to take a cab just because you felt obligated to take me home."

"I don't think I'll be telling Candy that I was in your apartment."

"Why not? It's perfectly innocent and—"

"Perfectly innocent except for this."

He bent his head and his lips brushed mine tentatively. I was in a bewildered daze as he nibbled my lower lip. Before it occurred to me to respond, he ended the kiss and wordlessly slipped out of my apartment.

I remained leaning against the wall in a state of complete shock for at least a few minutes, afraid I'd collapse. He kissed me. Huh.

I awoke Sunday morning bleary-eyed from dreams that ranged from a woman bathed in blood to Clay bathed with my tongue. The latter actually caused me to call an emergency brunch meeting. We ducked out of the tapering drizzle and gathered inside Michael's Diner at ten-thirty in the a.m. Michael's is a quaint narrow restaurant with a terrific long counter where you can spin on stools while you eat. It wasn't exactly dinner theater but it was reasonably priced.

First things first, we ordered food and coffee and dug into the serious conversation once both had been received.

"Was there tongue, or no tongue?" Jenny inquired from the stool on my right.

"No tongue," I replied drinking deeply from my coffee cup.

"What about breast?" Lara asked from the stool on my left. "Did he go for a grope?"

"Nope, no grope."

We were silent while my friends absorbed the news that the lawyer I'd craved and pined for over the last two years had surprised me with a late-night, passionate kiss.

"So the guy kissed you? He kissed you in your apartment?" Jenny shook her head slowly. "I don't get it, why didn't you just drag him into bed?"

"Because she's not a slut, that's why," Lara reasoned dipping a corner of her toast into egg yolk.

"Well, maybe I would've tried harder to at least return the kiss if I'd known it was coming," I explained. "I was frozen in shock. I just stood there like an idiot."

"Did you put your arms around him, or anything?" Jenny asked slathering cream cheese on a bagel.

"No. Nothing. I was a statue. He'll probably take that as a rejection, right? He'll think I'm either not attracted to him or that I'm frigid as a Popsicle."

Jenny and Lara leaned forward across the counter to look at each other; then they looked back at me and shrugged in unison.

"Nobody knows how the male mind works," Lara breathed. "It's a mystery."

"So, are you keeping the cat?" Jen asked.

"I don't know, if Mole Man finds out he'll have a fit but Inky is such a cute little furball."

"Inky, huh? You're keeping him," Lara pointed out.

"Yep," Jenny added. "If you've named him, you're definitely keeping him."

I decided they were right. I did want to keep Inky. I guess that meant a trip to the store for a litter box and cat toys.

"I wish we could have a cat." Lara sighed. "But I'm allergic."

"What about Lucien?" Jenny prompted. "Are you going to call him?"

"What for?"

"You need to at least thank him for the gift."

"Oh. Yeah, I guess I should." I downed the rest of my coffee.

"And he'll probably ask you out again," Jenny added. She leaned forward to talk to Lara. "You should see this guy, tall, dark and yummy from head to toe."

"You must be giving off some kind of sex vibrations," Lara said to me, obviously impressed. "Two interested men in one weekend. That must be some kind of record."

"Hell, two in one year would be a record," I agreed.

"By the way," Jenny began around a mouthful of bagel. "I talked to Doug last night and convinced him to let you have your car if you can come up with half the cash."

"That's great news!" I beamed. "Payday's tomorrow, right? I could pay him half as soon as I cash my check!"

"Yeah, but you gotta promise to pay him the other half by mid-November. He won't carry you longer than a month."

"With the extra cash I'm making at the Megaplex it won't be a problem."

"Just make sure you don't quit without giving proper notice once you earn your car repair cash," Lara warned. "Harold'll kill me if you're a no-show one night."

"I wouldn't just up and quit," I said defensively.

"Sure you would," Jen corrected. "You've done it at every other job you've had, well, except the ones where you got fired first."

Lara looked at her watch. "Speaking of being fired, I better fly or I'll get canned." She worked at a mom-and-pop grocery on Sundays. "I'll see you tonight, right?"

"Nope, not me," I sighed with relief. "Harold said I only had to work Wednesday to Saturday remember? I'm gloriously free all day."

"Oh, right." Lara smiled. "Guess I'll talk to ya tomorrow then. I'm dying to hear how things go between you and Mr. Lawyer at the office."

I definitely did *not* want to think about that.

Jenny and I parted company because she was doing the Sunday brunch thing with her folks in Renton. I should have been doing a Sunday visit with my mom but I talked to her in the morning when she called and explained that I was working a second job to pay for car repairs. I figured that information ought to buy me at least a few Sundays without parental guilt. Although I felt a twinge of it anyway since she'd sounded pretty disappointed. I knew mom was trying to mend fences between us. I also knew it was going to take an awful lot of lumber to repair the gaping hole she made when she chose to screw the neighbor while my dad lay dying.

With a few hours to myself I did the grocery-shopping thing and the pet-shopping thing and then returned to my apartment to do the laundry thing. Inky attacked my ankles when I walked in the door and used the litter box the second it was ready without any prompting. I decided that in addition to being gorgeous he was an absolute genius.

The box that Lucien had sent over was still sitting on my counter and it glowered at me to pick up the telephone and call in a thank-you. I figured the shop was only open until six on Sundays so I'd wait until six-thirty and hope he had an answering machine. Yes, I was chicken.

At precisely six-thirty, after tossing a load of whites into the washer and a load of colors into the dryer, I returned to my apartment, after apologizing to Mrs. Sumner for more nonexistent door slamming, then looked up the Scrying Room's number. As I hoped, the answering machine picked up. There was some eerie organ music that played first and then Lucien's low smooth voice came over the line.

"You've reached the Scrying Room and we are now closed. Samhain is fast approaching and to help you celebrate this wondrous event, our ritual candles are twenty-five percent off. If you wish to leave a message you may do so now."

I waited for the beep then blurted out in a mad rush, "Hello Lucien, it's Tabitha, thank you for the gift, for the scrying mirror you sent, it was very thoughtful of you. Bye." I slammed my cordless phone onto the counter with a sigh of relief. About ten seconds later the phone rang.

My eyelids began to twitch and I tentatively answered, "Hello?"

"I would've picked up your call but you didn't stay on the line very long." Lucien's voice rolled silkily into my ear.

The hairs on my arm stood up. I cleared my throat nervously. "Yes, well, I didn't think you were there."

Silence.

"So anyway, thanks again for the scrying mirror. It's a real nice one. Pewter and all."

"But…?" I could hear him grinning.

"But nothing. It was a nice gesture and I appreciate it."

He chuckled, "But you haven't used it yet, have you?"

"What's Samhain?" I asked changing the subject. "You mentioned the holiday on your machine."

"It's the festival of remembrance for the dead. Followers of The Craft tend to use a lot of candles during that time."

"Oh." *How morbid was that?* "And it's coming up soon?"

He laughed softly. "Yes. The eve of November first."

"Oh, Halloween!" *Jeez, why didn't the guy just say that?*

"So, have you?"

"Have I what?"

"Have you used your scrying mirror yet?"

"No, to tell you the truth it's not really my cup of tea. I thought I'd mentioned that the other day over coffee."

Silence.

"Not that I'm not grateful for your gift, or anything, it's just that..." I grasped for some explanation.

"You're scared," he offered. "I understand perfectly."

"I am *not* scared."

"Okay."

"I'm *not*."

"Hmmm. Do you know what I love, Tabitha?"

I swallowed. "Um, no, what do you love?"

"I love to challenge my fears. To face them head-on. It's soooo—" he exhaled "—so invigorating. 'To conquer fear is the beginning of wisdom.'"

"Shakespeare, right?"

"No."

"Oh. Well I've really got to go, I just wanted to thank you again for the gift,"

"You're welcome... And Tabitha?"

"Yes?"

"Call me after you've used it."

He clicked off and I stared at the phone. It rang again before I could put the receiver down. I let it ring three times while I debated whether or not to pick up and finally I stabbed the talk button impatiently.

"Hello?"

"You sound out of breath," Jenny commented.

"Not out of breath, just out of patience. I just hung up after talking to Lucien."

"So you thanked him for the thingy?"

"Yeah."

"And Mr. Intense asked you out?"

"Well, no." Hey, the guy didn't even ask me out!

"So you're disappointed he didn't ask you out?"

"No. Well maybe a little, I guess, but I don't think he's right for me."

"Why? Because he's successful and good-looking?"

"He's intense, kinda strange and mysterious."

"In a good way though, right?"

"I don't know…I guess he's got this real sexy aura thing."

"Aura? Have you been spending more time in his shop?" She giggled.

I replayed our conversation to her.

"Well, he's right about one thing," Jenny stated. "You're definitely afraid to use that mirror."

"I'm *not* afraid. I just don't see the point."

"Uh-huh. Sure. Have you had any more creepy dreams about the dead woman?"

I shivered. "Yeah."

"Did you ever think that maybe this dead woman is trying to tell you something?"

"Now it sounds like you're the one spending too much time at the Scrying Room."

"Hey, if Lucien looked at me the way he looks at you I'd be hanging out there night and day. Seriously though, what if you could use your visions to help solve her murder?"

I made *Twilight Zone* noises and then said, "Jen, you've

been watching too much TV. Dead people don't call up law office receptionists to help them solve their murders."

But the words sounded hollow and unconvincing, even to me.

chapter four

Through the haze, there was the barely audible hum. Low. Murmured. Hypnotic.

A single figure stood clad in a dark shroud, concealing his face from view. The chanting stopped and a single hand reached out, struck a match and set flame to a tall black pillar candle. On the third finger of the hand glistened a large silver skull ring. The moment seized in still frame for a split second. I could hear his breathing, shallow and quick with excitement. Then, suddenly, the skull ring began to writhe and pulse with blood oozing from silver eye sockets.

"No!" I jolted upright in my bed, drenched in perspiration with my hand pressed to my chest to keep my heart from pounding right out of it. Terrified by my reaction, Inky leaped from the edge of my bed, somersaulted to the floor and skidded across the room with a loud hiss of protest.

★ ★ ★

"Maybe you need to see a therapist or something," Jenny suggested as we jaywalked across the street to the deli for our lunch.

"I don't need therapy! I'm having nightmares," I stated with exasperation. "I don't need to be told I hate my mother, I already *know* that!"

Jenny held up her hands in surrender. "Okay, okay. I'm just saying these dreams sound like they're out of hand. How much sleep can you afford to lose? You were two hours late this morning! At this rate you don't need to worry about impressing The Bitch in order to get Martha's job, you're just gonna have to worry about *keeping* the job you've already got."

She was right. The Bitch had formally warned me this morning that *this kind of tardiness would not be tolerated*. The only bright spot was that Clay was scheduled to be in court all day so he wasn't around to see me in my state of disheveled sleep deprivation.

"I've got an idea," Jenny said. "How about if you stay with me and Lara tonight? You can couch it and then you can drive us both to work in the morning."

I didn't want to sleep on Jenny's couch, but I also didn't want to be fired so I reluctantly agreed.

The deli was jammed and we had barely enough time to eat our usual—tuna for me and pastrami for her—before we had to return to the firm. For the rest of our lunch Jenny restrained herself from mentioning my problem and, instead, worked on distracting me by discussing whether or not we should try the new cucumber facial in *O* magazine.

After lunch we jaywalked back across the street with me walking downwind of Jenny so that I could inhale the secondhand smoke from her postlunch ciggie. I told myself that it wasn't really cheating on my quit-smoking thing since the nicotine I was sucking into my lungs was tainted by car exhaust fumes.

Remembering that I could cash my check and pick up my car after five o'clock was the beacon of light at the end of my day. After work, Jenny and I tripped over to the ATM to cash our checks and then, in celebration of our newfound wealth, we sprung for a cab to the Grease Pit Garage in Renton.

When we arrived at the garage, Doug met us out front.

"I've fixed her up good as new," he announced proudly and wiped his greasy fingers on his gray coveralls. He had a square head that sported a squarish black brush cut, a square, short body and the lack of any discernable neck that made him appear even more cubelike. The rotten teeth in his mouth forced him promptly onto the ten-most-ugly list I kept in my head. The only reason he wasn't at the top of the list was because he was letting me have my car back.

"You said she could pay half now, right?" Jenny asked her cousin.

Doug reluctantly nodded, a difficulty when you have no neck. "Yeah, but you gotta pay off the rest by November 15. I won't let it go any longer."

"No problem," I stated and counted four hundred of my hard-earned dollars into his chunky hands.

"If it does turn out to be a problem I'm gonna have to charge you interest," Doug said with black ratlike eyes trained on my boobs. "And I'm not talking cash, either."

He tossed the keys to my Escort in the air and I caught them.

"No offence, Jen, but your cousin definitely makes my top ten." I jammed the key into the door of my car.

Jenny walked around to the passenger side and sighed. "He's definitely at the shallow end of our gene pool but he's a good mechanic and gives a family discount, so we tend to overlook that he's really a caveman."

Inside the car we buckled up and I turned my key in the ignition. When it puttered to life I had to blink back the tears. No more gagging on the pungent aroma of body odor on the bus.

We spun my wheels over to my place first and I gathered a few things in a bag for overnight at Jenny's and played toss the rubber mouse with Inky while we waited for delivery of a pepperoni pizza. When the pizza guy showed I paid him while Jenny squeezed passed me and scooped up the Mole Man's newspaper that lay outside his door.

"Don't do that!"

"I've already done it," Jenny stated and strolled back into my apartment with Mole Man's paper.

I hastily closed the door behind her.

"Why'd you steal his paper? I don't need to be on the outs with my landlord. If he starts snooping around, he's gonna discover I've got Inky."

Inky appeared and twitched his whiskers at me as if answering to his own name, or he could've been reacting to the aroma of melted cheese. It was hard to tell.

"I always read the news after work, you know that," Jenny pointed out. "Besides, it's not stealing, I'll put it back when we leave." She scooped up Inky and nuzzled into his neck. "Aren't you the cutest little fuzzball?" she cooed.

I opened the pizza box and fetched us each a beer. Jenny made herself comfortable with Inky on her lap, licking mozzarella off her fingers while she flipped through the pages of the paper.

I chomped into a slice of pizza and noticed my answering machine light was winking so I stabbed the message button.

"Miss Emery, this is Detective Jackson. Call me when you get this message." His gravelly voice left a number where he could be reached.

My gaze met Jen's and we shared identical curious looks, except mine was combined with a pinch of unease.

"Wonder what he wants now?" I drank uneasily from my beer to quiet my apprehension.

"Maybe it has something to do with this." Jenny stabbed a finger at the newspaper and I came around to read over her shoulder.

It was a two-inch article at the bottom of page five that was headed Mutilated Felines Point To Satanic Cultists. The blurb stated that a smattering of maimed cats had been discovered throughout the greater Seattle area and that the police had no leads. The writer went on to state that similar mutilations in other cities had been linked to a cult called the Scarab Sentry.

We hmm'd over that while we ate the rest of our pizza. Inky volleyed between my lap and Jenny's begging bits of cheese and purring happily.

"Maybe you should just call this detective and get it over

with," Jenny suggested. "You know you won't be able to get it out of your head until you find out what he wants."

"I'm sure whatever he wants won't be good."

"Do you want him just showing up at work again tomorrow?"

She had a point. I reluctantly punched Jackson's number into the cordless phone and a couple minutes later I hung up with Jenny anxiously at my elbow wanting to know what he said.

"He only said he didn't want to talk over the phone but would like me to come down to the station to talk to him and his lieutenant."

"When does he want you to come?"

"Now."

"Wow! This is exciting!" Jenny gushed and snatched up her purse raring to go.

"Whoa, I never said I was going to do it."

"Why not?"

"Maybe I just don't *feel* like meeting with Jackson and his boss for a little chat. Did you think of that? Maybe I'd rather—" do cardio aerobics, get a huge zit on my nose, take my appendix out with a spoon… "—not."

"Aren't you curious? Maybe you've forgotten some clue that will lead them right to the murderer, or maybe they want you to do something undercover and wear a wire."

"You've been watching too many cop shows."

"Come on, don't you have any Nancy Drew in you?"

"Not even a drop. I was busy reading Archie comic books instead, Betty and Veronica crack me up. Besides, haven't you heard?" I covered Inky's ears with my hands and whispered, "Curiosity killed the cat."

Jenny wore me down with her persistent pouting and begging. Finally I relented, and once the pizza was gone we left my apartment.

After walking a couple steps down the hallway, Jenny piped up, "We didn't slam the door, Mrs. Sumner."

Abruptly Mrs. Sumner's door closed without her saying anything.

Thirty minutes later, Jenny half dragged me into the precinct station.

"We're here to see Detective Jackson," Jenny told the bored-looking desk sergeant.

"Name?"

"Tell him Tabitha Emery is here," she said winking at me.

Oh, brother, she was so excited she was nearly leaping like a cheerleader. My excitement was more contained. If I'd suddenly discovered a pack of Virginia Slims in my purse I may have been convinced to do a cartwheel or two.

Detective Jackson appeared wearing the same tweed suit and pissed-off expression he'd had when he'd shown up at my office. He offered me a quick nod, then glanced questioningly at Jenny.

"Who's this?"

"My friend, Jenny Arton."

He shook his head. "She's gonna have to wait here. The lieutenant asked to meet with you, not your friend."

"Hey." Jenny jumped in his face. "She needs me! I'm kinda her representative."

Jackson looked at me. "I thought that lawyer guy was your representative?"

"I don't need a representative."

"But I was with her when she found that first penta-gram where that cat was all cut up! I have a right to come into the meeting."

Jackson just glared. "You never mentioned there was someone else with you."

I shrugged. "You never asked."

His jaw tightened. "Fine. You both come in."

We followed Jackson out of the reception area into a large open space painted dull gray. The room bustled with the ring of phones and cops and complainants sat at desks both looking equally despondent.

Detective Jackson opened a door at the far end of the room and Jenny and I stepped inside.

"This is Lieutenant McGillvray," Jackson stated, then turned to his boss. "This is Tabitha Emery and her friend, Jenny Arton. The friend is here on account of she was with Miss Emery in the cemetery."

Lieutenant McGillvray had a round face, thinning sil-ver hair and a wide thin-lipped smile. He reached across his obsessively neat desk and stuck his hand out at me. I shook the pale, cool, manicured fingers.

"It's nice of you to come in at such short notice, Miss Emery." He flicked his wide mouth at Jenny. "You, too, Miss Arton. Please have a seat."

We sat down in the two hard wooden chairs opposite his desk and Jackson stood beside his boss, hands clasped behind his back, looking unmoved.

"Is this about the murdered woman?" Jenny asked, lean-ing forward excitedly. "Do you want us to operate a sting, or something? Because I'm a very good actress and— Ow! Why'd you kick me?"

"Why don't we let the lieutenant do the talking?" I said through my gritted teeth.

For a second, Lieutenant McGillvray's grin grew wider, if that was possible, and his lips totally disappeared. Then his smile was gone and his voice grew serious. "Detective Jackson has been keeping me informed and, of course, we are quite concerned that a murder may have been committed. Yet we have no body or knowledge of the victim."

I thought I could probably A) gather all the facts and make an informed decision, B) just keep my mouth shut or C) hop right on the train to denial.

"Maybe there isn't a body. Maybe someone just got hurt or something?"

"There was enough evidence in the Dumpster to suggest that, er, how can I put this delicately?" McGillvray glanced to Jackson for help but the detective offered none. "Let's just say the evidence suggests that the remains were in much the same condition as the cat."

Jenny's eyes grew wide. "Holy smokes! You mean she was disemboweled? How can you tell? Was there like intestinal goop all over the Dumpster, too?"

So much for trying to put things delicately. Lieutenant McGillvray paled considerably then bright patches of red appeared on his cheeks as if somebody had slapped him.

"Is there any chance that the body could be discovered at the garbage dump?" I asked.

"Miss Emery," Detective Jackson began, "the city of Seattle carts fifty railcars carrying one hundred containers of trash to the Columbia Ridge Landfill in Oregon five evenings a week. That's a couple dozen *tons* of garbage a week that gets spread over about six hundred and forty acres."

I tilted my head and stared at him. "We ship our trash to Oregon?"

"Yes."

"Oh." I'd lived all of my life in the city of Seattle and never known that. I don't know why, but I felt strangely smug by the thought that I could throw something away in Seattle and it would leave the state.

Lieutenant McGillvray cleared his throat. "Perhaps I should make it clearer as to why we asked for you, Miss Emery. It is my impression from Detective Jackson and also officers Vasquez and Carson, whom you met on the scene of the bloody Dumpster, that you have a psychic ability that may be useful to us."

My jaw dropped open and I blinked at him in disbelief. I began to deny this but Jenny was already on her feet.

"Omigod, omigod! You want to see if Tab can use her powers to find the murderer! This is great! She's a kick-ass clairvoyant. When she does that blinking thing with her eyes you just *know* something's gonna happen and— Ow!"

"Sit down," I ordered. "And shut up!"

Jenny rubbed the spot on her arm where I pinched her and sulkily took her seat. One corner of Detective Jackson's lips twitched. He was either about to smile or growl; it could've gone either way.

"Look, Lieutenant, I'm flattered that you think I could help, really I am, but there is nothing I can do." My tone was soft and reasonable. "Sure I admit that sometimes I do get a bad feeling like I did that day at the cemetery and sure I also had one that time behind the building at the Dumpster." I threw in a tight smile. "But my bad feelings or premonitions, if you want to call them that, are not going to help you find your murderer."

Jenny snorted and I shot her a poisonous glare.

"Apparently your friend feels otherwise," Lieutenant McGillvray pointed out. The wide, face-splitting smile was back in place. "All modesty aside, Miss Emery, perhaps you are not giving yourself enough credit. Are there ways to, er, let's say *encourage* your talent?"

I thought of the scrying mirror and got angry. Hell it was *my* head and *my* so-called talent. Why did everybody need to stick their big beaks in it?

I snapped out, "Look, if I could predict the future or read minds, do you think I'd still be a receptionist? I'd've used my powers in Vegas or for a winning lotto ticket! At the very least I would've gotten rich on the stock market!"

"Miss Emery, don't get me wrong, this department does not routinely make use of psychics to solve cases," he said with a chuckle. "But where murder is concerned, we leave no stone unturned. If there was even the slightest chance that you could shed a little more light on this particular case, I would be remiss in my duties if I did not ask you to do so. Perhaps we could go so far as to say that you should consider it your civic duty to help us in this matter."

I paid taxes and not always against my will, so as far as I was concerned I had already completed my civic duty.

"Sorry. I've got nothing." I stood to go and the Lieutenant's face fell.

"Wait a second, Tab, what about your dreams?" Jenny said and dragged her chair sideways out of my kick, slap or pinch zone.

I fired a glare in her direction, then sighed. "Dreams are dreams. I once had one where Tom Cruise and I were sharing a hot tub. I assure you that was not a prediction."

"The ring might mean something, though," Jenny pushed.

I bit the inside of my cheeks to keep from screaming.

"What ring?" Jackson and McGillvray chimed.

I leaned forward with my palms on the desk and gave a brief outline of my dream. "You see? That's it. That's all. So if you find someone wearing a ring that looks like it may be alive and oozing blood, you'd better slap that guy in cuffs 'cause he's your man," I added sarcastically.

Lieutenant McGillvray frowned and triangled his fingers beneath his chin. For a long moment he said nothing. When he did speak I could clearly hear his barely contained anger. "I think you should know, Miss Emery, that if you are withholding information on this investigation I will make it my personal mission to put you behind bars for this murder."

My mouth fell open and Jenny's expression mirrored my own.

"If you have anything further to say to me, you should call my lawyer!" I snarled and whirled out of there with Jenny in my wake.

Back in my car Jenny wouldn't shut up about it. "Do you believe that guy? What an A-1 asshole!"

I turned on Jenny and for a brief moment considered plowing my fist into her eye or telling her mom that she lost her virginity in the back seat of a Buick at fifteen.

"If you had kept your big mouth shut none of that would have happened!"

"Hey, I'm on *your* side in this, remember?"

"Uh-huh, and with friends like you I certainly don't need any enemies." I pulled the Escort away from the curb and squeezed into traffic.

"It's not *my* fault you're afraid to use your God-given talent," Jenny sparred.

"It's not a talent. It's a curse." My hands tightened on the steering wheel. "You're not the one stuck with it. I'm the one who has to live with the dreams. I'm the one who saw her dad die in a vision but wasn't able to do a fucking thing about it! I'm also the one who had the other slide show in her brain that showed her mother humping a neighbor while her dad takes his last breath!" I drew in a deep breath and blinked back tears. A thick, tense silence filled the car.

After a minute I said, "You know, I'm just going to drop you off and sleep at my own place tonight."

Jenny did not reply until I pulled up in front of her building.

"I'm sorry, Tab." She reached to touch a hand to my shoulder. "I know this isn't easy for you. I should've kept my big trap shut at the station. Come on up and stay the night."

I smiled wearily. "I think I need to be on my own. I need to think this thing through."

I was walking into the foyer of my building ten minutes later and was so immersed in feeling sorry for myself that I nearly plowed right into Clay Sanderson, who was leaning on my buzzer.

"Well, hello there," I joked and nudged his shoulder. He whirled to face me. "To what do I owe the honor of another personal visit?" My hopes skyrocketed at the mere thought his answer could be, *Tabitha my darling, I can't resist you any longer! Let's spend the night together! (insert passionate kiss here).*

He fisted his hands on his hips and glared. "You can start by explaining why the hell I'm getting calls from Lieutenant McGillvray stating that he believes you're withholding information on a murder investigation."

"Oh, that." Loud thunderous thud as sex fantasies crash to the floor. I winced. "I guess you heard."

"Yeah. Now I want to hear it from you."

"I didn't think he'd call you."

"You didn't think period," he barked.

My anger sparked sudden, potent and with the force of a woman who hadn't had good sex in a very long time. "I don't need this!" I jabbed my key in the security door and stormed through. When I crossed the lobby I turned, expecting Clay to be gone; he'd done the exact opposite of leaving, he was right behind me.

"I did not invite you in," I reminded him.

"We need to discuss this."

You see, that's where Clay and I are different. He's the type of guy who wanted to discuss a problem until the answer was found. I, on the other hand, liked to ignore my problems until they were so huge they either exploded or solved themselves. I happened to like my way better.

"There is nothing to discuss."

I banged open the stairway door and jogged down to the basement level. Clay did not take the hint and leave. He did the complete opposite of leave.

I stomped down the hall and when Mrs. Sumner's door

opened a crack I snapped, "Yes, I *am* gonna slam my door, so get used to it!"

When I was opening my apartment door Clay was still on my heels.

I turned to face him. "Clay I do *not* want you to come inside my apartment. I want you to go home and leave me alone." I never in my wildest fantasies would have imagined those words leaving my mouth.

He just crossed his arms over his chest and stood stubbornly glaring at me.

"Fine." I sighed and opened the door.

Inky greeted me with a loud and enthusiastic, "Meow!"

"Attack!" I ordered the kitten while pointing to Clay, but instead of attacking, Inky rubbed against my leg.

Clay closed the door behind him and smirked. "I guess I'm lucky you pick up stray cats and not stray pitbulls."

I opened my refrigerator, snagged a couple beers and handed one to him.

"You wanted to talk, so talk," I ordered, leaning a hip against the kitchen counter trying to remain cool and pissed off. But he had those gorgeous azure eyes and that great body and both were in my apartment.

He drank some of his beer. "Why did you go down to the police station without your lawyer? I thought I'd made myself perfectly clear about that."

"And I made myself perfectly clear when I said I do not need a lawyer." At least not representing me. In my bed I could use a lawyer but that was another problem altogether.

"Lieutenant McGillvray feels you know more about this thing than you're telling."

"Lieutenant McGillvray is a lipless wonder and a horse's ass."

"And also a good friend of mine."

Sheesh! "He's still a horse's ass. I am not about to defend your taste in friends."

He offered a world-weary sigh that made him sound just like my mom.

"Look, Tabitha, the Seattle PD are stumped here. They have a murder scene but no body. So far they've kept it quiet but eventually the press will get hold of this mess and when they do, they're going to have an absolute field day. Have you even thought about that?"

"I fail to see how that is my problem." I downed more of my beer and poured fresh water in Inky's bowl.

"It will become your problem because if reporters catch wind of this thing, how long do you think it'll be before they also find out how the cops discovered the murder scene? Are you ready to defend and explain your so-called talent as a psychic visionary to the Seattle public?"

I slumped into a nearby chair and massaged my temples with my fingers. I hadn't thought of that.

"I'm not withholding any information. Honest. I told the lieutenant everything I know."

He walked up behind my chair and put his hands on my shoulders. Even in my sudden state of spiraling depression I couldn't help but wish he'd kiss the back of my neck.

"McGillvray said you mentioned something about a skull ring."

I stiffened. "So? It was a dream." A bloodcurdling nightmare, actually.

"There's a group of Satanists who are known for animal mutilations and they've also been known to wear skull rings," he said softly.

"Let me guess, this group is called the Scarab Sentry?"

He started. "How did you know?"

"There was something in the paper about it."

He rounded my chair and looked me in the eye. "I don't know exactly how I feel about this thing you do. All I do know is that you don't want to be messing with this group. If word gets out a psychic is accusing them of a murder, even one without a body…" He shrugged with palms up. "Who knows how they'll react? It may not be safe for you."

"Oh, great." I blew out a breath. Inky hopped into my lap and I scrubbed him gently behind the ears. He began purring loudly. Suddenly, I felt the sting of unshed tears make my contact lenses float. This sucks.

"Hey, you'll be okay," Clay said. "Next time, just clear any thoughts you have with me first, before sharing them with the police, okay?"

I nodded. Then Clay bent, planted a kiss on the top of my head and left my apartment. I'd gone from receiving sudden sexy full lip locks from him to getting little pity pecks on my scalp. At the rate I was going we should graduate to handshakes within a few more days.

I fell into a restless, thrashing sleep and it wasn't long before the dreams started. They began much like the others, inside the same dim room….

I struggled to focus but my senses were dulled. My vision was obscured, kind of like looking at the world through the bottom of a highball glass after too many drinks. It occurred to me that there was another person in the room with me and, although I was right behind him, he did not know that I was there. I was unable to see his face, or what he was doing. He wore the same dark shroud and was surrounded by not one but dozens of black candles that shimmered shadows around the room.

The air was thick with the aroma of candle wax. The figure exuded a feeling that was simultaneously exhilarating and something more vile and darker. He knelt and murmured unintelligible words in a low chant. I yearned to see his face but I was immobilized by fear. Suddenly, he raised his hands above his head and in a split second I saw first the skull ring on his finger and next the intricately carved ceremonial anthame blade clutched in both hands. The knife glistened with fresh blood….

And that's the moment I ran screaming from my dream.

I tried to go back to sleep, but even after checking all the closets and under my bed for bogeymen, my thoughts would not unravel from the nightmare. It was around one in the morning. Shit. I really needed some sleep but it just wasn't available, so I popped my contact lenses back into my eyes and Inky and I stayed up and watched an infomercial. We also shared a bag of cheese doodles. Afterward, Inky leaped onto the counter and started batting around the box that held the scrying mirror. He managed to get the lid open and then proceeded to pounce on and shred the tissue inside.

"Hey, don't do that!" I got up and picked him out of the box and put him down on the floor. He flicked his tail in irritation and blinked his green eyes at me.

It was our first fight so I tried to reason with him. "Look, just because I don't want this thing, doesn't mean I want you to scratch it up with your claws."

Inky did not look like he was buying it. He gave me a look that said, *Yeah right, lady, we both know you want to try that thing.*

"I do not!" I shouted at him and he swiveled and scampered to dive for dust bunnies under my sofa bed.

I lifted the scrying mirror out of the box and ran the tip of a trembling finger around its pewter edge. Was it possible that I could find out more about this woman's murder using the scrying mirror? Or would the authorities just find me blubbering in the corner of my apartment and send me for shock therapy? I needed to consider all of the possibilities.

I paced while I debated the issue. I had to admit that there was a slim chance I could get some information using this thing. Then again, there was also a slim chance Clay Sanderson would knock on my door and ask me to run away with him.

I guess the question was could I live with myself if I didn't at least try?

Inky returned from his hunt to snake between my legs to show he'd forgiven me for my earlier abruptness.

"So what do you think?" I asked him. "Should I try this thing?"

Inky twitched his whiskers as if he were actually thinking about it and then meowed loudly. This could've been a meow that requested more cheese doodles, it could've been a meow that said, *Hey, I have no idea what the hell you're talking about,* or it could've been a meow that said, *Go for it.* In my current state of sleep deprivation I chose it to mean the latter.

Using the stand it came with, I propped the scrying mirror on my coffee table. When I researched the subject a couple of years ago, with the help of a certain knowledgeable librarian, I'd had her show me her personal technique for scrying but I'd never tried it myself. I found myself wishing I'd paid more attention back then. I remembered something about votive candles but pushed that away. I didn't have any. Okay, so next I was supposed to make the room dark. Easy enough since it was just before two in the morning. I closed the blinds on my small windows, turned off the lights and slammed into a wall on my way back to where the scrying mirror sat waiting.

"Ow!" I rubbed my forehead with my fingers and inched slowly toward the coffee table.

"Here goes nothin'."

I wiped my sweaty palms on the oversize T-shirt I wore to bed then knelt on the floor next to the coffee table. As my eyes adjusted to the dark room, I reached out to position the scrying mirror so that it was about a foot away from my face. I inhaled deeply then slowly released my breath while gazing steadily into the mirror. I tried not to look at it, but through the surface and beyond.

At first there was nothing but steady darkness. Then slowly the blackness shifted, twisted, writhed and did the hokeypokey. Quickly, I fell into a seemingly endless abyss. It was like the worst tequila bed spins you could ever imagine.

My eyes became hot, straining against the dark, but next there was an abrupt explosion of neon color. I gasped as the random shades began to take shape and form images that flashed then faded. I was glad I'd never tried hallucinogenic drugs. First, the abandoned building appeared and that image washed away and was replaced by a vision of a thick black pillar candle. The flame expanded, stretched and evolved into the shape of a skull. Slowly, the skull's gaping grin turned sardonic and its orifices bubbled with thick blood. A woman's horrific screams reverberated in my head, pulling me through the building toward a Dumpster that swayed, beckoned, then squirmed as its shape emerged into a large beetle that twitched its antennae in my direction.

The raspy feel of a kitten's tongue on my cheek yanked me from my trancelike state back to reality. I jolted, disoriented and surprised to find myself sprawled on the floor and with the imprint of shag carpeting on my face. I noticed the scrying mirror had somehow found its way across the room, banked up against the wall. No doubt I'd flung it there.

Inky hopped onto my lap, pawed at my chest and mewed loudly. I couldn't wait to get to bed. It felt like I could sleep for a year but I'd learned there was no snooze button on a cat who wanted his breakfast, so I got unsteadily to my feet. I figured I would feed Inky, then go to bed and catch a couple more hours of sleep before work. Later, I would just have to deal with what had happened. Much later. Like when I retired and had nothing better to do. As I was opening Inky's canned food the phone rang. I snatched it up. Who could be calling at this hour?

"Hello?"

"Hi. Just wanted to make sure you made it to work on time this morning." It was Jenny.

"So you're giving me a wakeup call at…" I glanced at my microwave clock that glowed seven. Since I'd fallen asleep with my contacts in, my eyeballs felt as if they'd been shrink-wrapped. I rubbed my eyes and blinked but the clock still glowed seven.

"What time is it?" I asked, my mouth suddenly filled with cotton. And fear.

"It's just after seven," Jenny stated. "Are you okay? You sound funny."

"I don't feel funny." There was nothing funny about the fact that it had been just before two in the morning when I was last conscious. "I think I'm okay. I'll see you at work."

"More nightmares?"

"I guess." I shuddered as a strong unpleasant visual of a skull oozing blood tickled my subconscious. "Can we talk later?"

"Are you sure you're okay?"

I disconnected with only a curt assurance to Jenny. A blasting hot shower, a quick contact lens scrubbing and two cups of coffee allowed me to slip shakily back to reality.

"Obviously I fell asleep using the scrying mirror," I said.

Inky was sitting on the counter licking the butter off his slice of toast. At my comment, he looked up at me, his dark eyes meeting me with a challenge.

"Well that's my story and I'm sticking to it," I grumbled and offered Inky the rest of my toast, too. My stomach didn't feel so good. Neither did my head.

"I'm gonna go visit Lina after work."

Jenny dropped her pastrami on rye and it landed with a thud on our table. "What do you mean, you're going to visit Lina? She's a loser."

I took a bite of my tuna sandwich and talked around it. "She's not a loser, she's a librarian."

"Not only is she a loser librarian, but she's a host of other *L* words like *loathsome, loco* and *lunatic.*"

"I don't want to spend our entire lunch hour fighting."

"Then don't go see Lina the limp, ludicrous librarian."

"Stop with the *L* words."

Jenny sighed. "She makes you crazy. Why are you going to see her?"

"I want to." Actually *want* was a little strong because I didn't *want* to see Lina any more than I wanted to visit my gynecologist, but sometimes it was necessary.

"The last time you saw her you said—" Jenny drew quotes in the air "—I'll rot in hell before I go see that crazy bitch again.'"

I cracked my knuckles and sighed. "That was different. I was—" irrational and unhinged "—still grieving over my dad."

We ate the rest of our sandwiches and washed them down with hot coffee before taking up the subject again.

"It's 'cause of the dreams isn't it?" Jenny asked.

I hesitated. "I used the scrying mirror last night."

Jenny's eyes bulged. "And…?"

"And…" It was weird, creepy and I can't account for five hours of my night. "And I think I need to see Lina." I changed the subject. "Clay stopped by to give me hell about going to the police without him."

"See…that's a good thing. He's just feeling left out."

"He's feeling lawyerish, that's all."

"So he didn't kiss you?"

"On top of the head."

"Ouch."

"Yeah. At least he's in court again today so I don't have

to face him. But he has called the office a few times to check in with Martha."

"Did he say anything to you? Does he make any remarks about kissing you or about your case?"

"I don't have a case," I corrected. "But no, he doesn't say anything remotely friendly to me. If anything, he's more abrupt than he was even before he ever spoke to me, or kissed me."

Jenny brushed sandwich crumbs from her blouse, stood and grabbed her coat from the back of her chair. "Maybe he's just not comfortable mixing his business and personal life."

I downed the rest of my coffee and got to my feet. "I'm not asking him to screw me in his office."

"Oh, but you'd like him to!"

"Of course, but that's beside the point." We elbowed our way out of the crowded deli and into the tapering drizzle. "I just want him to at least give me a friendly hello or something."

Okay, so the *or something* would definitely not be appropriate for the office but I'd settle for a *Hi there, Tabitha, how are you today?*

Back at my reception desk Martha was sitting big and pregnant munching on a Snickers bar.

"Good to see that you're back on time for once," she snidely remarked. "And I seem to recall you were even on time this morning." She got up from my chair with some difficulty, which I was glad to see. "Turn over a new work ethic leaf, Tab, or are you just vying for my job?"

I ignored her question and stated instead, "I see you're eating for two these days."

"Or is it three," Jenny put in with an innocent lilt. "Are you sure you're not having twins or triplets 'cause, man, you are getting big!"

Martha's lips formed a thin angry line as she waddled out from behind my desk. "Why don't you ask her?" She nodded her head in my direction. "Tabitha's the office psychic who told me I was pregnant before I'd even taken the test."

"She probably only guessed on account of you were getting so fat," Jen reasoned with a straight face before turning on her heel and disappearing into the back offices with an enraged Martha right on her heels.

The elaborate phone system that was my master bleeped for my attention, so I scooted around the desk and planted my rear into my chair—still warm from Martha's big behind.

I trilled into the receiver, "Good afternoon, McAuley and Malcolm. How may I direct your call?"

"Martha, please," Clay stated.

"One moment, please," I replied in my most officey voice, then I hesitated and added, "So, Clay, how's court? Are you having a good day?"

"My day's fine. I still need to talk to Martha," he said in a clipped voice.

"That wasn't so hard now, was it?" I snapped. "It took like two seconds out of your day for me to say *How are you?* and for you to answer *Fine.* I know you're Mr. Busy Lawyer and I'm only Miss Lowly Receptionist but you can still be polite."

"Seems to me," he growled, "that you're the one being rude. Not me."

"I'll transfer you," I said soberly then promptly disconnected him. Take that!

The phone rang again immediately.

"Good afternoon, McAuley and Malcolm. How may I—"

"You did that on purpose!"

"Did what?"

"You cut me off just because I wasn't making nice-nice on the phone with you!"

"If you were disconnected, sir, I apologize. It certainly was not my intention to delay someone as important as you and—"

"Just put me through to Martha," he snarled.

I put him on hold and enjoyed the fact that he was listening to our company's sadistic form of classical Muzak. Then I took two other calls and filed my nails. The phone rang again three minutes later.

"Good afternoon, McAuley—"

"Put me through to Martha, now!"

"One moment please." I hit the transfer button and, feeling rather smug about my power and also unwisely playing Russian roulette with my job, I put the call through to Jenny.

I typed a memo warning staff about wasting the company's time by spending too much of it surfing the Net. Then I e-mailed the memo to everyone three times, just for fun. I wasn't surprised when Clay called again.

"Look," he began, sounding dangerously close to losing his cool. "Before things get out of hand maybe we should have a chat about professionalism on the job."

"Well, quite frankly, I think you're more than professional enough. Maybe too professional."

"Not me. You!"

"Oh." I already knew that. "Okay, I'm sorry about delaying your calls to Martha. Do you want me to put you through to her now?"

"No. Jenny connected me and I already talked to Martha. Now I want to talk to you."

"I have another call coming in so you'll have to wait." I put him on hold and nibbled a hangnail while I debated how to handle our chat. I decided on the poor-me approach.

I stabbed the flashing button. "Sorry about that and I'll say I'm sorry again about not putting you right through to Martha but—" I swallowed and hoped for a sad edge in my voice "—I just don't see why you can't at least say a personal hello to me when you call."

He sighed. "I'll promise to say hello to you when I call, if you promise not to disconnect me."

"Deal."

There was a pause, then I blurted, "I used the scrying mirror last night and woke up on my living room floor five hours later."

"Did you have a few beers beforehand?"

"No!"

"I'd say you were just tired. Look, I'm being called back into the courtroom. Tell Martha I'll check in with her again before she leaves."

So much for sharing my personal life with Clay.

I found Lina pushing a metal cart in the autobiography section of the Emerald City Library. She stood tall, her sinuous form stretched to place a book on the top shelf. Her raven hair fell in a curtain down the length of her back. I saw her posture stiffen briefly before relaxing again and though I stood ten feet away from her and she had her back to me, I knew she sensed my presence.

"Hello, Tabitha," she spoke to the books, then slowly turned to face me. "I'd say it was good to see you, but I'd be lying."

"Don't mince words, Lina, tell me exactly how you feel."

Her wide mouth turned up at the corners before she reigned in her smile. "You've always responded best to the direct approach."

"Can you take a break?" I asked, walking toward her.

"I don't see why I'd need to." She turned back to her cart and rearranged some of the books there. When she turned to face me her fifty-something cognac eyes locked on mine and she reached out and clamped a strong hand to my forearm. Neither of us spoke for a full minute. When her assessment was complete she released her grip and wiped her fingers on her green wool skirt with revulsion.

"What *have* you gotten yourself into?" She tsked.

Before I could answer she nodded for me to follow. After passing aisles hiding avid readers, curious bookworms and bored students, we slipped into the small room that was Lina's office as head librarian. She stepped behind her desk. I closed the door behind me and took a seat opposite her.

A small brass plaque behind her desk was engraved with the words *An it harm none, do what thou wilt.*

I nodded my chin to the plaque. "What does it mean?"

"It's the Wiccan Rede. It means do whatever you wish as long as you harm no one, including yourself."

"Oh." I gripped my hands tightly in my lap and announced, "I used a scrying mirror last night." I let out a whoosh of the breath I'd been holding.

Lina simply nodded, not registering even the faintest tinge of surprise. She templed her fingers under her chin and her shoulders went up and down as if to say, *So what?*

"I don't know what exactly happened. I saw some creepy stuff and it all seemed to happen really fast but when reality hit, hours had gone by. Maybe I just fell asleep but it doesn't feel like I was just asleep."

She nodded slowly. "You forgot your circle of protection."

"My what?"

Hot livid anger flashed across her face. "This is precisely why your visit here is pointless, Tabitha. You do nothing with your gift but occasionally take it out to amuse yourself. This is a complete waste of time. Anything you want to know is easily enough picked up on the Internet or in a book. My days of mentoring you are over."

"I'm not here to ask you to be my mentor." I kept my own fury in check only by reminding myself that Lieutenant McGillvray was just waiting for me to admit to murder. "Look, I just wanted to ask you some questions, maybe pick your brain a little about what's going on and—"

"My brain," she spat, "is not yours to pick."

"It's an expression."

Her tone softened. "The very first time we met I was giving a lecture on clairvoyance at the university, remember?"

"Of course."

"When you approached me you were terrified. You'd been afraid to talk to anyone about the visions you'd had."

I nodded. "Yes, and you were kind enough to take me under your wing."

"All those evenings in my own home while I helped you search for answers."

"Yes." I had a moment of fond remembrance.

She slammed a palm on her desk. "Then when those answers weren't what you wanted to hear, you dropped me like trash."

So much for fond remembrance.

Her eyes shot daggers at me so I got to my feet and held out my hands in a stopping motion. "Okay, okay. Well I guess that's that. Thanks for nothing, Lina."

"I see your problem, Tabitha," she whispered. "I've felt it, seen images of it for weeks but I can't hold your hand this time."

"Can't or won't?"

"It makes little difference does it? I will say this, stay away from the one with the vacant eyes. He's the one who wants to pull you down, if given the chance."

I folded my arms across my chest. "Vacant eyes? That's the best you can do? Sheesh, this is Seattle, *every* man has vacant eyes! It comes from months and months of lots of rain and little sun."

She sighed. "Sorry, I don't know his name or other features, all I see are his eyes."

With that little tidbit and nothing more I stormed back to my Escort. I jammed my key into the lock, flung open my door and slumped into the driver's seat before noticing something on my windshield. It was large, with numerous legs, and it had been intentionally crammed under one of my wipers.

chapter five

I turned on my windshield wipers and a large brown rubber insect vibrated across my windshield. Its legs jiggled like jelly but it stayed crammed beneath my wipers. Obviously someone's idea of a joke. I turned the wipers on full speed and the big wiggly beetle winged its way into traffic and was promptly flattened under the wheels of an SUV.

I grumbled and bitched at myself most of the way back to my apartment. I was stupid to ask Lina the Loser for help. At home, I watched bad sitcom reruns while Inky stalked, attacked, then mutilated my latest issue of *Jane*. He appeared to be having far more fun than I was. Truth was—I was bored. Even though it was a Tuesday evening, I suddenly wanted to go out.

I got on the horn to my friends. I tried Jenny but she had a date. Lara was working at the Megaplex and when

I tried Cathy, Jeff answered the phone. He told me Cathy was out and he had no idea when she'd be back.

"Do you want me to leave her a message?" Jeff asked in his monotone voice.

"Yes. Ask her to call me the second she comes home. Tell her I'm bored to tears and I need to go out. Tell her I'll do anything and go anywhere, but I absolutely cannot be in my apartment one second longer!"

"Um, well, I was just heading over to Jimbo's for a drink. You're welcome to join me."

Yikes. "I don't think so, Jeff."

"Why not? I thought you just said you'd go anywhere and do anything?"

"I know, but—"

"You're thinking it would be strange, just the two of us without the rest of the gang."

"Yeah." It would definitely be strange to go out with my friend's gay roommate with whom I had nothing in common. Strange and possibly even more boring than watching Inky shred my magazine and chase dust bunnies under my bed.

"It would not be strange," he insisted. "I can be quite the conversationalist when not pressured by a crowd."

The very fact that he felt compelled to call himself a conversationalist showed me how dull he really was, but what could I do? Well, I could A) hang up abruptly then later explain how my phone was disconnected, B) fake amnesia and claim to forget what I had just said or C) just say no.

"No, Jeff, I'd just rather—" watch my cat bathe himself, clip my toenails, clean the mildew in my shower… "—not."

"I understand." The pathetic, whiny tone in his voice was the first time I ever recalled truly hearing any emotion in his voice. Guilt swooped over and engulfed me.

"You know what, Jeff? Let's do it. Let's go to Jimbo's and you can just leave Cathy a note to join us whenever she gets home, okay?"

"Yeah? You're sure?"

"Yep, I'm sure." I was just as sure that I would be more likely to enjoy dinner with my mother or a root canal but I'd been raised Catholic. Guilt worked on me every time. "Don't forget to leave Cathy a note."

I had never been to Jimbo's on a Tuesday evening. The transformation was amazing. There was far too much lighting and way too many people who resembled depressed alcoholics hunching at the bar. Our usual table looked like a ridiculous choice considering half the place was empty, but there sat Jeff. He wore a black long-sleeved T-shirt, brown Dockers and his usual obtuse expression. He didn't wave. Or smile. He just stared owlishly at me. Oh, boy, this ought to be a hoot.

I took the seat at the opposite side of the round table. "Hi."

"Hello, Tabitha," he spoke before sliding a martini over to me. "I took the liberty of getting you a drink."

"A martini."

"Yes."

"Why would you get me a martini?"

"Because I've never seen you drink one and you are the one who is always saying that we need to try new drinks."

"Okay, but *you* never try new drinks," I pointed out. "You always order a martini."

"Yes, but I know that *you* don't."

I wanted to argue that the reason I did not order martinis was that I tended to become snookered rather quickly when I drank them, but Jeff looked so pleased with himself I could only say, "Thanks." Then I drank it down. Fast. Being tanked was probably the best way to handle this.

Jeff's brows knit together. "You probably shouldn't drink martinis that fast. They can hit you rather hard if you're not used to them."

"I can handle my booze," I stated flatly and because he had the nerve to look hurt I asked, "Okay, Jeff, so why don't you tell me what it is with you and martinis? Why don't you ever try new drinks like the rest us?"

"It's the purest choice."

I blinked at him. "You said that before but it doesn't really answer my question."

His pale lips formed a slight smile as he took a tender sip from his martini glass. "I don't like to pollute my body with impure choices. You know, every martini drinker has his own idea on how the drink should be made. It's a very personal matter. Some prefer four parts gin to one part vermouth, some prefer less vermouth and more gin."

My eyes began to glass over with disinterest.

"Years ago I discovered, if properly made, a martini serves my needs well," Jeff continued. "When Cathy first brought me here to Jimbo's I explained very precisely to our barkeep *exactly* how I wanted my martini to be made and he always prepares them exactly the way I instructed."

I sucked my olive off its little sword and chewed. "And tell me, dear Jeff, how much vermouth do you prefer in your martini?"

"As far as I am concerned the word *vermouth* should merely be mentioned loud enough to make the gin cringe."

I paused in midolive chew. Was that a joke? "I think, dear Jeff, that you just made a funny!"

I drank another martini and warily eyed my third, then decided to let it sit for a while. Jeff matched me drink for drink and the weird thing was he actually appeared less weird when I was drinking martinis. Maybe that was his secret. Maybe he *knew* his weirdness was toned down a notch by the right mixture of gin and vermouth, or maybe I was just drunk.

I found out quite a bit about Jeff. Like how he'd lived in L.A. before Seattle and had spent much of his time hanging ten. I tried to imagine Jeff, who was whiter than milk, lounging on a beach or riding a surfboard. I couldn't. The thought of his pallid body poured into a Speedo made me shudder, so I changed the subject.

"What about family? Any brothers or sisters?"

"No, I'm an only child, just like you." He grinned. "My mother died when I was young and my dad retired to Florida a few months ago."

"Do you miss him?"

"Not really. We didn't exactly have an amicable parting. He didn't agree with my lifestyle."

"Oh. Speaking of your lifestyle, any new men in your life?" I asked him, braver now that my blood alcohol level was balancing out.

He smiled, showing actual teeth this time. "I could ask you the same question."

I nodded, tossed my last olive in the air and caught it in

my mouth. "Yep, you could, Jeffee boy, but my sex life has been the topic of our Friday night discussions for years. Yours has not."

"I date occasionally but I'm not seeing anyone special."

I leaned across the table and poked him playfully in the shoulder. "You may not be dating anyone special but there is someone you have a fondness for, isn't there? You know who I'm talking about. Lucien Roskell. How long have you been in looove with your boss?"

His pasty skin paled further and he glanced around furtively. "Don't talk about him. He could be around."

I leaned back in my chair, "I find it hard to believe that someone like Lucien would be seen in a place like Jimbo's unless—" I sat forward "—unless you invited him." I narrowed my eyes at him. "You wouldn't do something like that, would you?"

He finished off his martini, "Um, well you and Lucien seemed to hit it off and…"

"Aw, jeez! You invited him to come and used me as an excuse for you to spend some extracurricular time with him!"

Jeff's eyes leveled mine, "W-w-well, he likes you and y-y-you seemed to like him so I thought—"

I held up a hand. "Don't pretend you're doing this for me!" I snatched up my purse and unsteadily got to my feet.

"D-d-don't go," Jeff pleaded. "Please don't go! H-h-he might not even show, h-h-he said he m-m-might be busy."

I rolled my eyes. "I'm gonna visit the little girl's room and while I'm there I'll consider whether or not I'm staying."

After I peed I examined my reflection in the bad lighting of the ladies' room and winced. I dug around in my purse and applied some lipstick to my mouth and some concealer to hide the bags under my eyes. When I stared at myself I realized what I was doing. Damn. I was making myself pretty for Lucien. As much as I hated to admit it, I knew that meant I was attracted to him.

"It's gotta be a sex thing," I grumbled into the mirror.

"It always is," responded the peroxide blonde washing her hands beside me.

Returning to the bar, I was taken aback to see Lucien shrugging out of his leather jacket and edging his way into the seat I'd vacated. He was wearing jeans and a navy cable knit sweater. He should've fit in easily with the casual clientele, but his sharp features and intense good looks attracted the lusty attention of all the females in the place, both sober and smashed.

From where I stood, still in the shadows of the long hall that led to the washrooms, I had three choices, I could A) sneak out the back exit and leave Lucien to Jeff, B) sit down at the table and proceed to wow Lucien with my confidence and wit or C) stumble toward the table and proceed to make a complete ass of myself.

Lucien smiled and got to his feet. "Good to see you again, Tabitha."

Although thinking I'd chosen option B, it was clear after a few minutes that I'd really chosen option C. I managed to get to the table with confidence, but my wits had already been drowned in gin and my nervousness had me drinking my third martini rather quickly. My attempt to wow Lucien with witty banter and snappy comments landed me tongue-tied and stuttering worse than Jeff. I was a disgusting embarrassment to independent women the world over.

"Whatcha drinkin'?" I asked Lucien, who, ignoring Jeff's recounting of last week's inventory at the store, was gazing hotly in my direction.

"Water," Lucien stated, his eyes glittering with humor.

"Water?" I gnawed on an olive. "Thought maybe it was gin and tonic or somethin'. Don'tcha drink?"

"Occasionally, but it became apparent to me that you may need a ride home and I wanted to be available to apply for the job."

Ah, shit. I hadn't even given a thought to the car thing. Usually we carpooled to the pub or shared a cab.

"Um, that's okay. Me and Jeff could share a cab." Jeff kicked my ankle under the table and I winced. "Or I guess you could drive us both home. You could drop me off first, even."

Lucien smiled broadly.

I sat in the back seat of Lucien's red Saab sedan while Jeff rode shotgun and chatted Lucien's ear off. Not that Jeff completed more than a few sentences because of his stuttering. Lucien wheeled his car into a coffee drive-through and picked up three lattes to go. The coffee, combined with the fresh air from the open moon roof, had me sober enough to realize that he was headed in the direction of Jeff's place first.

Jeff was giddy as a schoolgirl when we pulled up in front of his building and he appeared to hesitate at first. I thought, Omigod, he expects Lucien to walk him to the door! But he seemed to figure it out at the last minute and blubbered a thank-you before scampering up the sidewalk to his building.

"He has the hots for you big-time," I slurred.

"I'm not gay." Lucien patted the passenger seat and his eyes met mine in the rearview mirror. "Aren't you going to get in the front seat?"

"That's okay. I'm comfortable where I am." My voice went up an octave and I cleared my throat nervously.

He chuckled. "Well, I'd be more comfortable if you came up front. Otherwise you'll make me feel like a cab-driver. C'mon." He nodded toward the passenger seat. "I promise not to bite." Pause. "Unless you want me to."

Realizing I was being ridiculous and choosing to act like a woman, not a child, I blew out a breath and moved into the front seat.

Lucien leaned over me and I sucked in air through my teeth.

"Just buckling you in." He smirked, obviously enjoying my reaction.

"I can manage, thanks," I snatched the buckle from his hands and completed the job myself.

We rode silently the next few miles to my apartment. All the way there I played in my mind whether I needed to invite him up, or if I needed to get out and run like hell when we reached my place.

"I can only come in for a moment," he stated matter-of-factly while parking the car.

"Oh, um, sure, I guess." So much for thinking I had any say in it whatsoever.

Mrs. Sumner glared at us from the fraction her door was

opened, but she forgot her door-slamming warning when Lucien gave her a hundred-watt smile.

When I opened the door to my place, his eyes scanned my small apartment and he quickly declared, "This place does *not* suit you."

"Thanks. But my ocean view penthouse is being renovated. What can I get you? Coffee? Tea?" *Me?* I stopped the last bit from exiting my mouth just in time. "Beer or wine?"

"Nothing, thanks. Well, at least this is right. This definitely suits you." Lucien scooped up Inky and stroked the length of him. "Although a little cliché don't you think?"

"Cliché? You mean single woman, with a cat?"

"I mean, witch with a black cat."

"Witch." I laughed. "Sorry, not a witch. If I was a witch I would cast a spell for many things, like lots of money, a better job, an understanding mother, regular sex, a flat stomach, a cool car and—" I'd been ticking the items off on my fingers but suddenly realized I probably shouldn't have mentioned one of them.

"I could probably do something about the regular sex thing," he offered through a wolfish grin. Inky leaped from his arms and Lucien turned and walked the few steps to the other end of my apartment.

I noticed my answering machine light was blinking and I pressed the message button. Cathy's voice came into the room apologizing for being too tired to make it to Jimbo's tonight.

While Inky snaked between my feet I watched Lucien bend and pick something up. Damn.

He turned, his eyebrows raised in question with the scrying mirror in his hands.

"Sorry, I don't usually keep it on the floor." I strode toward him and took the mirror from his hands and placed it gingerly on a side table. "Guess Inky knocked it off, or something."

"You tried it." It wasn't a question but a statement.

I wavered, then nodded.

He pushed aside a cushion and took a seat on my sofa bed which, thank God, I'd remade into a sofa before work. He patted the seat beside him.

"Come. Sit and tell Uncle Lucien all about the big bad scrying mirror."

I laughed nervously and plunked myself down beside him. Well, not *right* beside him. I squished myself into the other corner of the sofa so you could have fit another large person between us.

"Using that thing was not exactly fun," I stated, putting my feet on the coffee table. "I don't think I'll be trying it again anytime soon."

He slid a little closer on the sofa and put his feet next to mine on the table. "Did you write down what you saw?"

I shuddered at the strong image. "No."

He moved even closer and put an arm around my shoulders. "That bad, huh? Well, maybe I was wrong. Perhaps a scrying mirror is not the right medium to encourage your abilities."

I felt the heat of his arm resting on my shoulders and my mind went completely blank.

"If you aren't going to write it down, it might do you some good to talk about it."

I began to think back to the image that I'd seen. A wave of panic rocketed through me and I jumped to my feet.

"Sorry, but I've got to be at work early and then I've got the Megaplex at night, so I really need my sleep. You should go."

He slowly uncoiled himself from the sofa and got to his feet. "I understand."

He walked toward me and put his hands on my hips. His eyes lanced hotly into mine. "You're afraid of me."

"No, I'm not." Oh, yes, I was. But I wasn't just *afraid;* I was almost bloody terrified but that does not mean I wanted him to know that. I reached my arms around his neck, pulled him close and kissed him. Tentatively at first. Just a tiny sampling. Then his mouth responded fervidly, one strong arm crushing me to him. I was so close to him I could feel the outline of the amulet he wore beneath his shirt, pressing against my chest. Knowing the pentagram was so close to my skin simultaneously alarmed and excited me. His lips parted mine, his tongue probed and savored and an explosion of heat filled my stomach then spread lower. Searing desire charged through me but beneath the intensity of his embrace I could feel the tension of his restraint. He was the only one holding back. Even as he broke contact only one word filled my head. *Orgasm*.

"I'm afraid of you, too," he breathed. "But I'm not willing to do this halfway and you're not really prepared to take it any further than a kiss. At least, not yet."

Halfway? Halfway would work for me since I figure if he did let loose I'd probably self-combust with the ferocity of it. With just a kiss he'd brought me from zero to a hundred million thousand.

I was unable to plead my case though and ask him to stay because by the time I'd untangled my tongue, he'd gone.

★ ★ ★

I slept fitfully. My dreams were the kind that woke me up in a sweat and not because they were sexual. They were a disturbing fusion of horrific images. The phone woke me. I was relieved to break the control of the dreams. In my disoriented state I dropped the phone twice before getting it to my ear.

After I managed to mumble out a greeting, a woman's voice stated flatly, "I'm worried about you."

"Huh? What?" I sat up and shook myself awake. "Your concern is touching, Lina, but unnecessary."

"I certainly don't *want* to worry about you but my off switch must be broken," she replied dryly.

"Look it's—" I squinted at my alarm clock "—six o'clock in the morning and—"

"You're in danger, Tabitha."

"Yeah, I know, some man with vacant eyes, wooo," I said, making ghostie noises.

"There's also something about bugs or beetles of some kind," she snapped impatiently.

I didn't reply, the memory of a rubber bug on my windshield smacked into me and I shook it away.

"Look, Tabitha," she sighed, trying for patience and failing. Her voice was razor sharp. "I'm only trying to get this out of my head so it can become your problem. Not mine."

"Done," I answered curtly. "I'll keep my eyes peeled for vacant-eyed men and rubber bugs."

"I never said anything about the bugs being rubber but that does help my visions make sense. Where have you seen these bugs? I'll have to do some more detailed research on the significance of insects as an offering from evil."

"What? No! I don't need you doing research on my behalf!"

"Yesterday you needed it."

"Yesterday I needed your friendship and you turned me away."

"The last time I tried to be your friend you were the one who turned away." She barely concealed the hurt in her voice.

"Can you blame me?"

She let out a long breath. "You did not kill your father, Tabitha, and neither did I."

"I gotta go." I hit the off button and shoved the phone beneath my pillow.

Hours later, I showered, tossed a toy mouse with Inky and then took a cab back to Jimbo's to pick up my car. I was behind my desk, the picture of office competency and efficiency half an hour before the rest of the staff filed in at nine.

Pregnant Martha was the first to cross the threshold and she did a double take at the sight of me.

"Now I *know* you're after my job." She smiled smugly. "Well I hope you made coffee, too."

"I don't make the office coffee, that's the job of—"

"Of the first person who arrives in the morning," she put in. "But of course you wouldn't know that."

She hoisted her suitcase-size purse onto my desk and began riffling through it. Finding what she wanted, she thrust a mint-green envelope in my face.

"Here."

I shrunk away. "What is it?"

She rolled her eyes. "It's an invitation to my baby shower."

When I refused to take it from her outstretched hand she dropped it onto my desk.

I slowly shook my head from side to side. "I don't get it, Martha. Why in the world would you want *me* to come to your baby shower. You don't like me and I sure as hell don't—"

"Yeah, well all the more reason for you to come and bring me a gift, right? I mean, you *are* probably gonna end up with my job and all, it's the *least* you can do." She trounced off, as hurriedly as a woman who was eight months pregnant could trounce.

I was still sitting there dumbstruck when Jenny stepped off the elevator with a crowd of other employees.

"Wow, I'm impressed!" She smiled over at me with a look of approval. "Look who's all bright-eyed and bushy-tailed this morning."

I was neither bright-eyed nor bushy-tailed, whatever *that* meant, but it was good to see a friendly face.

"I didn't expect to see you here before noon since you were out at Jimbo's last night." She walked toward my desk and spied the mint-green envelope. "So you got one of those, too, huh?"

"You, too?"

"Yep, but I already told her I had plans and couldn't make it. Are you going?"

"I'd rather—" ice-skate naked, eat live ants, wear thong panties… "—not."

Jenny tapped a finger to her chin in thought. "Well, you may have to."

"What?"

"Well, The Bitch will definitely be asking Martha for her opinion about who would be best suited to take on her job."

"But I thought it was only between me and Muriel and Muriel's moving to Florida so…"

"Sure, that's the normal chain of things but there was talk of hiring from outside."

"What?"

"Well, that was before you started coming in early and looking so professional and all."

Two calls came in in quick succession and I transferred them accordingly.

"See," Jen pointed out. "I bet you didn't even cut those people off."

"Great. So I'll have to go to the dumb shower and buy a dumb gift and act like I'm having a friggin' wonderful time just so I can get a job I don't even know I want."

Jen waved it away with a flick of her hand. "Forget all that. Did you see Lina after work?"

"Yeah, but it was pointless. You were right. She's a loser."

The elevator doors swooshed open and senior partner Ted McAuley stepped off with slow old-man steps.

"We'll chat more at lunch," Jen whispered and made herself scarce.

"Ah, just the young lady I wanted to see." Mr. McAuley offered me a tight smile.

"G-good morning, Mr. McAuley," I stammered. I don't ever recall Mr. McAuley ever speaking directly to me. Here it comes. I'm getting fired by the top boss. "L-look, sir, whatever it is I'm sorry. I'm sure I can do better if you just give me another chance."

"Heh?" the old man looked startled and confused. He lifted his small briefcase as if it weighed a ton and plunked it down on my desk. He opened the case and produced a long sheet of paper that he deposited in front of me. "Our firm has always supported the Run for Awareness."

"Run for Awareness?"

"Yes. It's a five-mile run held every year in downtown Seattle to support endangered wildlife. The run is this Saturday and we'll be raising money to save the Mississippi mud crane."

"Mud crane, sir?"

"Yes. Miss Emery, this is a cause near and dear to my heart. In the past few years our company has never wavered in its enthusiasm." He stabbed an arthritic finger at the page. "I'm counting on you to get signatures on this form, I want people running for this cause and collecting pledges."

"If you don't mind my asking, sir, why me?"

"You were recommended for the job, Miss Emery. Just the other day Mr. Sanderson was speaking highly of your qualifications."

Oh, great. I guess it was better than having Clay tell the boss I was a bad kisser.

"I'm trusting you on this, Miss Emery," he said gravely. "Do it for McAuley and Malcolm. Do it for the Mississippi mud crane."

He left me staring at the pledge form on my desk. I didn't know whom I felt more sorry for, the Mississippi mud crane or me.

chapter six

"Come on, Jen, you gotta help me out here!" I whined across our lunch table.

"Nope. Can't do it."

"Why?"

"Look at me, Tab, do I look like a woman who runs without a fire chasing her?"

I looked over at my friend and co-worker. Her size-sixteen body was bulging out of a size-fourteen business suit.

The begging wasn't working so I tried a different approach. "You know, this could be the year we really do it. We could start training for this run and we could get in shape."

"By Saturday?"

"Well, maybe not by Saturday but by Christmas we could actually be physically fit and we wouldn't get out of breath just doing our shopping."

"I'm sorry, but anything that involves a huge cardio workout and lots of sweating without an orgasm is not for me. I'm out."

She took a bite of her pastrami sandwich and chewed thoughtfully. "Face it, Tab, you got taken. Every year, old man McAuley finds another sucker to take up his cause and this year it just happens to be you."

"Who was in charge of this thing last year? I don't remember."

"Clay. You sponsored him twenty bucks."

Huh. I was beginning to smell a rat.

Back at the office I had no better success rounding up willing participants. The direct approach wasn't working. Perhaps I should go for the tug-on-their-heartstrings approach. In between answering the phones I searched the Internet for photos of the Mississippi mud crane. My plan was to find a sad, pathetic picture of the crane, paste it into the body of a sappy plea-for-its-life e-mail and send it around the office. If done right it could either guilt people into signing up, or at least get them to donate money.

I found a Web site, and slowly a large picture unfolded on my screen. Apparently, the Mississippi mud crane was the ugliest creature on the face of the planet. I let my forehead thunk against the screen.

"It must be really hard to type that way."

I turned to see Clay Sanderson grinning across my desk at me.

I pointed to the unsightly bird. "I understand I have you to thank for this."

He smirked. "For placing a photo of some revolting bird on your desktop?"

"No." I grabbed the sign-up sheet and shoved it under his nose. "The Run for Awareness. Thanks to you Mr. McAuley seems to think it's a job that I can handle."

"Can't you?"

"No. Nobody wants to sign up to save the life of some hideous creature that most people would shoot on sight."

"I'll sign up."

"You will?" I let out a relieved sigh. "That would be great." I handed him a pen and he scrawled his name on the top of the sheet.

"You have to sign up, too," he said.

"I do?"

"Of course you do."

"Okay, sure I can do that." I thought back to the fifty-something heroin addict purse snatcher whom I'd chased after. There's no *way* I could run five miles.

He nodded his chin toward my computer screen. "What were you gonna use the picture for?"

I explained my e-mail plan and he shook his head.

"You gotta hit them where they live. Send out an e-mail but tell people Ted McAuley will personally be reviewing the sign-up sheet and pledge form."

"Good idea, but how do I make sure they actually show up to run?"

"You don't. Nobody actually runs in this thing and especially not Ted. He just *assumes* everyone ran. Everyone brings in about ten bucks each of pledge money and Ted gets to send off a company check to save the damn bird. He's happy. The bird's happy. You get all the credit."

I had a sudden urge to grab Clay Sanderson by his silk

tie and lick his tonsils. I opted for the more PC approach and said, "Thanks."

"Do you want me to help you with wording the e-mail?" he offered.

I clicked out of the ugly bird Web site and back to my e-mail screen. "No. I think I can handle it."

Suddenly, my screen went completely black, then a parade of bugs began crossing it.

"What the f—"

"Uh-oh. Looks like some kind of virus."

Jenny came running out from the back, followed by Martha and Muriel. They all whirled to look at my screen and shouted. "Me, too!"

Cindy, our computer guru, arrived half an hour later. She smiled over at my screen. "Cute. I haven't seen one like this before. What is it? Some kind of beetle? How'd it happen?"

"I dunno. I think I broke my computer. I think I broke the whole office system," I blurted.

She chuckled. "It's a virus. *You* didn't do anything."

She slid her skinny butt into a chair next to mine and her fingers danced around my keyboard for an hour.

Finally, she stood up, her mousy brown hair plastered to her head with perspiration.

"So, it's fixed?" I asked hopefully.

"Nope. You broke it."

My eyes opened wide. "What?"

She shrugged. "I mean the virus was directed to you. You must've opened it and then it went out to everyone in the office."

"I didn't do it on purpose."

She glanced at her watch. It was just coming up on five

o'clock. "I'll come back tomorrow and reinstall all the crucial programs."

I was wallowing in self-pity with only the vague assurance that perhaps nobody would know the virus started with me.

Martha waddled out from her office slipping her arms into a yellow prego rain jacket. She looked like she was wearing a neon circus tent.

"Way to go, Tabitha." She sneered at me. "What's your plan for tomorrow, going to embezzle from the employee pension fund?"

"Actually, I thought I'd arrange for all the doorways in the building to be made an inch smaller. That way you'd be trapped outside."

She snarled at me and disappeared onto the elevator. Slowly, the office began to empty. When Clay stepped into the reception area a call came in.

"Good afternoon, McAuley and Malcolm, how may I direct your call?" I trilled.

"I'd like to speak to Clay, please."

I'd've recognized that whiny, prissy voice anywhere.

"One moment please," I said into the phone then sang across the reception area filled with departing staffers, "Claaayy, your girlfriend's on line one."

There were a few sniggers in the crowd as people stepped onto the waiting elevator. Clay flicked me a lethal glare and walked over to my desk.

"Very mature, Tabitha," he stated. "I'll just take it here."

He held out his hand for the receiver; I handed it to him and engaged line one.

"Yes, honey, I'm on my way," he drawled into the phone.

I squirmed in my seat as I listened to him talk about dinner reservations at an expensive restaurant and theater tickets for later. At that moment, I hated him. What I hated more was the fact that I was not the girl on the other end of that phone line.

During my shift at the Megaplex that night, Lara took me aside and told me to snap out of it.

"You knew he had a girlfriend. Did you *really* think he'd dump her just because he kissed you once in a moment of weakness?" she demanded.

The voice in my head said, *Well, yeah!*

I blew out a breath. "No. I guess not."

She nodded. "Next time the slut calls the office, just disconnect her."

In honor of Halloween being only nine days away, the Megaplex was offering a discount on the newest thriller and slasher flicks. The result was that the place was jammed with teens wanting to watch other teens being chased and mutilated on screen. All of that screaming and necking made for parched throats, so those of us working concession were run off our feet—even more than usual. Harold Wembly had the foresight to call in two extra staff members for the night, but that meant that there were now five people working behind the cramped counter instead of the normal three.

I was just thinking I wasn't doing too bad keeping up with the crowd, when balancing two colossal-size colas, I squeezed between the popcorn machine and a co-worker bending beneath the counter for candy. When he stood up he whirled to get popcorn as well, slammed into me and one of the colossal-size drinks I was carrying flew through the air and landed with a very wet and a very loud *sploosh!* inside the popcorn machine.

Aghast at the horror, I dropped the other cola I was carrying and two employees, rushing to the aid of the popcorn maker slipped, skidded and finally toppled into the sticky puddle. There was soda pop everywhere.

In addition to destroying the entire batch of popcorn that had just been freshly popped, the machine abruptly began sputtering, sparking, smoldering then smoking. The lobby became completely still as customers and employees watched the accident with the kind of silent awe usually reserved for car wrecks.

"Holy shit!" I muttered under my breath.

"It's gonna blow!" somebody shouted and then people began shrieking and stampeding from the theater.

As it turned out, the machine did not blow; it merely caused a power failure when it short-circuited. That was good.

I was fired and told by Harold Wembly that I should be grateful he wasn't calling the cops on me. That was bad.

I arrived home, dragging my feet and if I'd had a tail, it would've definitely been between my legs.

Then I saw Lina. She was standing on the sidewalk in front of my building looking unsure. Obviously she was undecided about whether or not to buzz me. I helped clarify her decision.

"Go away!" I shouted then brushed passed her to the door.

"Have you been in some kind of accident?" she asked, falling into step beside me.

"No. See? Even your premonitions aren't one hundred percent right all of the time."

"It wasn't a premonition. You've got something sticky all in your hair and face and clumps of… Is that popcorn?" She reached and pulled a soggy kernel of popcorn from behind my ear.

"I don't want to talk about it, especially not with you." I opened the door and stomped inside.

Lina, of course, followed.

"I'm not inviting you in. You can go now."

I made shooing motions with my hands but she didn't leave. Instead, she went straight for the stairwell door and made her way toward my apartment ahead of me.

With an exasperated sigh I followed Lina down the stairs and along the hall.

Mrs. Sumner opened her door. I glared and hissed, "Shut up!" and she harrumphed and quickly closed her door.

I stuck my key in the lock.

"I'll give you five minutes, Lina, not a second more."

"Ten."

I closed my eyes and let my head slump forward in surrender. "Fine. Ten minutes."

We walked inside and I kicked off my shoes, dragged my sorry ass to my sofa and plopped down, right on top of Inky. With a loud indignant hiss he squeezed out from under me and ran to Lina for protection. Figures. Even my cat hated me. I began to cry.

When I finally got myself together, Lina handed me a wad of toilet paper from the bathroom and I blew my nose.

"Just so you know, the six minutes you spent blubbering do not count against the ten minutes you promised me," she clarified unsympathetically.

"Just say what you came to say, Lina."

"Why don't you tell me what's been happening with you lately? My visions are jumbled and unclear. I see beetles and Satanists and that man…" She shuddered.

"Oh, yeah, let's not forget Mr. Vacant Eyes," I sneered.

Her face registered hurt before she cleared it. I studied her standing across the room from me clutching Inky in her arms and gently stroking the length of him. I noticed for the first time the touch of gray in her black hair, the thin lines around her eyes. I looked in those eyes that met mine and saw her waver.

Still, I took a deep breath and told her everything. When I was done she let Inky jump to the floor, picked up her purse and took a seat beside me on the sofa. She took a pen and paper from her bag and drew something.

"These so-called pentagrams you saw, did they look like this?" She drew something else. "Or this?" She handed the paper over to me and I looked at the two shapes.

"What's the difference?" I shrugged. "Aren't they both the same?"

"No. You see the first one I drew is an inverted pentagram." She pointed to the paper. "It has two points pointing up, not one. Is this the one you saw?"

I shrugged. "I dunno, Lina, I didn't really pay that close attention."

She shook her head, "It doesn't matter. I *know* the one you saw was an inverted pentagram."

"Oh, yeah? How do you know if *I* don't even know?"

"Because Satanists use it inverted. Practitioners of The

Craft, Wiccans, do not. The cat you saw, the blood from that woman…" Her fingers trembled slightly and she fisted them in her lap. "You read the Wiccan Rede in my office, Wiccans are not allowed to dominate, manipulate, control or harm others."

"Whatever. Lina, I know you take this stuff very seriously and that's fine for you, but I don't want to be dragged down that road again."

"You better start taking it seriously." She took the scrap of paper back again and scrawled a picture on it then handed it back to me. "Do you know what this is?"

"It's a bug."

"Yes. Is this the bug that was on your windshield and on your computer?"

I wasn't sure. All bugs looked the same to me.

Lina huffed. "I think that it must be. It's a scarab beetle."

Scarab beetle? Her words tickled my subconscious but I was tired, miserable and really needed to use the bathroom. I pushed the words aside.

"Okay. I give up. What's the big deal about the scarab beetle?"

"The scarab, or dung beetle, is an ancient Egyptian symbol of reincarnation. It is also a symbol of Beelzebub. Satan. Some occultists wear it to show that they have power, or use it as a source of protection."

"Makes for interesting jewelry I'm sure," I said dryly. "If it's protection, then I've got nothing to worry about, right? I mean if someone's giving it to me, even if they are a satanist or an occultist or a monster with three heads, they're just trying to protect me, right?"

"I don't know," Lina said. Then she got to her feet and

paced. "That's why I'm so worried. There's no hard and fast rules here, Tabitha, people are constantly manipulating these things to suit their own needs."

I inwardly admitted that part of me was really enjoying this reunion with Lina but an even bigger part of me was weary from my destructive day. I yawned, stretched and asked Lina to get up so I could convert sofa to bed.

"We need to get together soon and work more on your protective skills. For now though, I'll give you these." She pulled from her purse two small white cloth sacks tied in purple cord.

"Protection satchets?"

She raised her eyebrows. "Nice to know you haven't forgotten everything."

"Not for lack of trying," I mumbled.

"Here's one for you to keep in your pillow, it'll help with the bad dreams."

She gave it to me and I held the satchet to my face inhaling the fragrance of dried rosemary, cloves and whatever else she'd mixed.

"You should keep the other one with you at all times." She strolled to the kitchen counter and stuck the second one inside my purse. "I'll try my best to see what's around the next corner, Tabitha, but it won't be easy. We're not as connected as we used to be. Whichever evil it is that has you in its sights, isn't letting go easily."

chapter seven

The bogeymen stayed out of my head all night long. Whether I could attribute that to Lina's protection satchet under my pillow or the two shots of medicinal tequila I'd taken before bed was hard to tell. Although I had no nightmares, I did experience a peculiar dream about plunging over Niagara Falls. I abruptly sat up in bed and realized the sound of rushing water was inside my apartment. Aak! And all over my floor. I jumped out of my sofa bed into the ankle-deep lake, ran toward my kitchen and saw the water gushing from under the sink. I lost my footing as I darted forward and fell with a wet splat in the pond that was my floor.

I sloshed out of my apartment, crossed the hall and hammered on Mole Man's door. He answered, glasses askew, dressed in royal blue pajamas emblazoned with a shimmering gold Star Trek logo in the middle of his chest.

"Huh? What?" Mel the Mole Man blinked rapidly.

"My apartment. Water. Come. Now." Apparently seeing a three-hundred-pound man in blue Lycra rendered me incapable of forming complete sentences.

We ran across the hall, waded through the water in my kitchen, then Mole Man proceeded to explain the obvious.

"Your apartment's flooded."

"Do something!" I screamed.

He folded his arms across his chest and looked at me. "You don't have to shout."

"It's getting worse! Everything I own is going to be destroyed!"

"Well, it's not like *I* flooded your apartment. Just because I'm your landlord doesn't mean that I deserve to be yelled at."

I could not believe that my flabby landlord was standing in the sea of my kitchen in his Star Trek jammies demanding that I give him respect.

I squeezed my eyes shut and muttered. "You're right. I'm sorry. Now can you *pleeeaaase* do something?"

"Now you're just being sarcastic."

"Mel!"

He put his hands up in a stopping motion. "Okay, okay." He reached into the cupboard under my kitchen sink and fiddled with something. The water stopped flowing immediately. I sighed with relief until I looked around my flooded apartment.

"Now what?"

"Well, now I'm gonna have to get my shop vac up here to suck up the water. Then I'm gonna have to replace that pipe that broke. After that…" Mole Man's eyes narrowed to become even smaller. "What's that on your bed?"

With a sinking feeling I turned and looked. "What?"

"That *thing*. That black furry *thing*. Curled up in your bed!"

"Oh, my God! Look at that! There's a cat in my bed!"

"Cats aren't allowed in this building."

"It's not *my* cat."

"If it's not your cat, why is it asleep in your bed?" he demanded.

"I left my apartment door open when I went to get you. He must've just ran in here when I wasn't looking."

"You're trying to tell me that in the five seconds you were at my door some cat came down the hall of my building, ran through the water in your apartment and jumped up to sleep in your bed?"

"I never said he wasn't a smart cat."

He rolled his eyes then looked around. "There are pet food dishes on your floor." He walked into my bathroom and shouted from there. "There is a litter box in your bathroom."

He walked back into my kitchen, his feet making sloppy slushing noises in the water.

"That is your cat."

I rushed over and hugged his portly, Lycra-clad frame and whimpered against his chest. "Oh, *pleeeaase* don't make me get rid of Inky. My life is a living hell. I destroyed the computers at work and blew up the popcorn maker at the Megaplex. I'm being hunted by a dung beetle, the scrying mirror didn't help and I am single-handedly responsible for the fate of the Mississippi mud crane!"

Mel untangled himself from my grasp. He looked down at me and clucked his tongue.

"Tsk, tsk, tsk." He slowly shook his head. "I'm gonna say one word to you, Tabitha. Listen carefully…*therapy.*"

I arrived at McAuley and Malcolm just before nine and saw that Cindy was already packing up her things.

"I'm done," she announced proudly. "You'll be happy to know that with the efficient firewall I've installed in your system, Satan's Soldier won't be getting any more viruses onto your system."

"Satan's Soldier?" I asked.

She nodded. "Cute name, huh? As far as I can tell, that was where the virus came from. Was directed to you personally, too."

I could feel the blood drain from my face.

"Oh, don't get yourself all in a tizzy over it." She fluttered her white sparkly nails in the air. "I see this sort of thing all the time." She leaned in toward me and whispered conspiratorially, "Usually the porn sites are the worst for these kinds of viruses but the occult sites can be just as bad. Just try to stay off them when you're at work, okay?"

I shook my head. "But I don't go on any occult or porn sites."

She didn't look like she believed me and I was still looking distrustfully at my computer when Jenny breezed in a few seconds later.

"How's it going, Tab?" she asked cheerily.

"My apartment is flooded. My landlord's evicting me 'cause of Inky and Satan's Soldier is after me."

"Wow, and it's only nine o'clock."

"My life is in the toilet."

"You forgot about destroying the concession area of the Megaplex and creating a stampede of moviegoers."

"That was last night. I'm trying to make myself feel better by taking one miserable day at a time. Work with me here."

"Okay, why did your apartment flood and who is Satan's Soldier?"

I gave her the ludicrous details of both.

"So Mole Man figures it'll take him a couple days to make your place livable again?"

I nodded.

"So after work go and pack a suitcase and your cat and bring them to mine."

"Thanks, but Lara's allergic to cats, remember?"

"Oh, yeah," she shrugged. "So call Cathy."

I winced. "And share an apartment with Jeff?"

"Or you could call your mom."

"Cathy it is."

I reached Cathy on her cell phone and she was thrilled at the prospect of entertaining both Inky and me for a couple of days. She figured it would be just like the slumber parties we had as girls only now we could drink. I reminded her that we'd drunk at the slumber parties we had as teens, too, but we'd had to smuggle the booze in plastic pop bottles. Ah, the memories of youth.

The rest of my morning actually went pretty well. I managed to convince the majority of the staff members to put their names on the pledge sheet and pay cash up front. Of course, I had to use Clay's idea first and send out a threatening e-mail memo advising that Mr. McAuley would be reviewing the list of names personally by the end of the day.

Lina called and I had the satisfaction of informing her that her protection satchets were working like crap. She pointed out that if I didn't have the nightmares, the satchets were doing their job. She seemed neither surprised nor upset about my flooded apartment. Ever a see-the-silver-lining kind of person, she thought it would be good for me to get away from whoever may be pursuing me and stay somewhere else for a while.

Since I was ever the things-are-bad-and-they're-gonna-get-worse kinda person, I explained about Satan's Soldier and the e-mail directed to me. Lina took a moment to think about that one.

"Do you think this person is connected to the Scarab Sentry?" she asked.

Damn. I'd forgotten about them.

"They're that cult group that wear skull rings and have been accused of animal mutilations, right?" I asked.

"Why, yes, that's right. It's nice to hear you're actually doing some research into this."

I did not point out to her that I hadn't done any research into this to come about said knowledge. It had been Jenny's voyage through my landlord's newspaper that had offered the information.

Jenny and I went for our usual deli lunch and returned to find Martha looking more aggravated than usual behind my desk. She picked up the green envelope nearby and waved it in the air.

"You haven't even opened the invitation yet? How are

you going to know when and where the shower is if you don't open the damn invitation?"

"Don't worry, Martha, I already used my psychic abilities, which told me that the shower is this Saturday at noon and that the baby is gonna have this huge birthmark and—"

She paled and nearly ran out of the area.

"How *did* you know when the shower is?" Jenny asked.

"Someone called this morning to say they couldn't make it. I just forgot to give the message to her." I slipped into my chair.

Jenny smiled. "You're mean."

I smiled back. "Yeah, I know."

The elevator doors slid open and out stepped none other than Clay Sanderson's girlfriend, Candy.

I whispered to Jenny, "You're about to find out how mean I can really be."

Jenny stood off to the side as Candy approached the reception desk. Candy was wearing four-inch black slingbacks and her stylish overcoat was opened to reveal a clingy teal-green dress with a plunging V-neckline. When she reached my desk she finally glanced up then visibly cringed at the sight of me. Her plastic smile was immediately readjusted into a scowl.

"Oh. It's you."

Jenny turned to me and said, "Does she mean you, or me?"

"I believe she means me," I answered. "This is Clay's girlfriend. I'm guessing she's still ticked about having to take a cab home while Clay drove me back to *my* place."

"When Clay has to baby-sit a client I don't get in his

way and I'm not ticked." Her pointy little nose jutted into the air. "I just don't have time for foolish chitchat."

Jenny looked at me. "Were we having foolish chitchat?"

I answered, "No, I don't believe we were."

"That's right. We were discussing that important legal matter."

"Yeah." I nodded. "That case where Smith was being sued for wearing inappropriate plunging necklines in an office environment."

"Wasn't Smith also being harassed because of his stupid name?"

"Yes, I believe he was. His name was Chocolate or Marshmallow or something equally stupid like that."

Jenny and I grinned at each other then turned our evil grins into pleasant businesslike smiles and whirled them on Candy.

"Just tell Clay that I'm here for our lunch date," Candy stated, biting each syllable off abruptly.

"Sorry. Can't," I said just as curtly.

She narrowed her eyes. "Why not?"

"Because he's not here. He's actually—" home in my bed buck naked waiting for me to give him a tongue bath… "—still in court."

The elevator doors parted and Jenny skedaddled out of there when Clay strode into the reception area. He held the elevator doors open with one hand and spoke to Candy.

"Sorry I'm late, but we can head straight out to lunch."

"Thank God!" Candy squeaked and stomped toward him. "That girl is such a bitch," she snapped at Clay, as she leaned in and kissed him.

Clay gave me a questioning look and I offered him an innocent *who me?* expression and then the elevator doors slid closed and they were gone.

Jenny darted back out from the hall.

"I can't believe she called you a bitch!"

When I got to my apartment I was relieved to see Mole Man had suctioned the water from my linoleum, but the place still reeked of dampness and Mel's body odor. He'd also covered my narrow windows with tinfoil behind the blinds. My apartment was as dark as a tomb. Inky was curled up asleep on my bed just as I'd left him. Obviously, he'd adjusted well to the trauma of having his home base temporarily relocated out to sea.

Mel left me a large piece of paper with big black letters scrawled on it that said, "Do not turn on the water! Pipe still broke!"

Moving me and all my paraphernalia plus Inky and all *his* stuff over to Cathy's apartment for only a few nights required three trips to the car. It also meant three times I had to apologize to Mrs. Sumner for slamming my door even though I did *not* slam my door. Even though I really wanted to slam it, right on her face.

On my final trip I was carrying Inky under one arm when Mole Man met me in the hall. He had his toolbox in one hand and paperwork in the other. The papers he thrust in my face promptly advised me that I was *breaking the terms of my lease by having a pet and I was going to be re-quired to vacate the premises.*

"What if I get rid of him?" I asked.

He squinted his beady eyes from Inky cuddled in my

arms back up to my face. "You're not gonna get rid of him. You love that black rat."

I gritted my teeth to avoid hissing at him myself and put plan A into action. Through clenched teeth I said, "So happens I am getting rid of him. I'm taking him and all his stuff to my friend Cathy's place and she has agreed to take him and grant me liberal visitation rights, so if he's gone I can stay, right?"

Mel looked skeptical. "I guess that would be okay, as long as the cat was really gone. Of course I'd have to do a number of surprise inspections of your place to be sure you weren't lying to me."

So much for plan A. Plan B wasn't going to be nearly so great 'cause plan B meant I really *was* going to try and get Cathy to take Inky. Sigh.

Just after six we arrived at Cathy's. She hugged me, nuzzled Inky's neck and welcomed us warmly into the bosom of her two-bedroom-plus-a-den that belted the middle of a modern twenty-story concrete tower.

"Wow, your place looks great!" I gushed, and it did. The walls had been painted a soft gray that offset black leather furniture.

"Yeah, it's Jeff's stuff. He had all his own furniture, so when he moved in a few months ago I got rid of my old things. I tried to sell it all first but ended up having to get it hauled to the dump."

Last time I'd been there it had been tag sales meet flea markets. I was surprised they hadn't turned her down at the dump.

"He painted, too?"

She nodded. "He insisted on it. Said something about only being able to move into a place if it was freshly painted because it made it purer somehow."

That was Jeff. Mr. Purity.

Cathy let Inky jump to the ground and he went about sniffing every crevice of the apartment while I unloaded all of our stuff. Suddenly, I noticed I'd forgotten one crucial item. The litter box. Damn!

"No big deal," Cathy reasoned. "I'll call Pepper's and order a large pepperoni and you can pick up the pizza on your way back. You can kill two birds with one stone."

I wasn't into killing any birds, but my stomach began making begging noises at the mere thought of pizza, so I drove back to my apartment.

When I burst out of the stairwell into my hallway I was greeted by a strident blast of rock'n'roll that vibrated the fillings in my teeth. As I continued, it became apparent that the noise was coming from the direction of my apartment. When I passed by the Sumners' door, it whipped open and Mr. Sumner peered out and pleaded, "Please, Miss Emery, would you mind turning the volume down a little? My wife'll have a fit when she gets home from the market if your music is this loud."

I started to deny that the music was mine, but he had quickly shut his door. Besides, it sure sounded as if the music was coming from my place. I walked a bit farther and outside my door I paused with my keys in my hand. It *was* coming from here. Mole Man must be doing his repairs to Led Zeppelin. Weird.

I stuck my key in the lock and turned. Flinging open

my door, I gaped at Captain Kirk boffing an alien life force doggie-style on my kitchen floor.

"Aaaa!" I screamed and covered my eyes with my hands.

There was the rustling of clothing, then the music was turned off.

"Ah, um, well, sorry, Tabitha. Thought you were out," Mole Man said gruffly.

I tentatively looked around and saw Mole Man in his Star Trek jammies, Beside him was Mrs. Sumner, wearing a green warm-up suit, holding a rubber mask. I stared in shocked amazement, then shifted my gaze from one to the other. Finally, I shook my head to try to recover my sanity.

"Would you like a glass of wine? It's the good stuff," Mrs. Sumner offered quietly, nodding toward a dark bottle on my coffee table.

"No, I'd rather—" shave my head, run naked through thorny rosebushes, suck down an entire bottle of Tabasco sauce… "—not!" I hollered.

I stormed into the bathroom, picked up Inky's litter box, then stomped back to my kitchen where the two evildoers had at least the decency to look shamefaced.

"Okay. This is how it's gonna be," I began in an authoritative tone. "First, I'm keeping my cat. Second, I'm not moving out. Third, you will no longer use my apartment for your—" I swallowed with revulsion "—sex thing. And fourth—" I walked over to my apartment door, balancing the litter box in one hand "—I'm going to slam my fucking door any time I want!"

With my little speech completed, I walked out and made sure that I slammed the door hard enough behind me that it nearly split the frame.

chapter eight

Cathy had tears streaming down her face. Apparently she found my recounting of Mole Man and Mrs. Alien Sumner amusing.

I picked off some stringy mozzarella and shared it with Inky. "I guess it *is* pretty funny, in a disturbing, sick kind of way." I swigged a mouthful of beer and chuckled. "It did work out in my favor, though."

"Well, sure." Cathy giggled. "You can keep Inky without moving and I bet Mrs. Sumner will be keeping her nose inside her apartment from now on. Now, if only you could solve your financial problems and get a date with some sexy guy you'd be all set."

I agreed. I still needed to find a way to come up with the extra cash to pay for my car repairs. "Do you think Mole Man will let me get behind in my rent now that I've got something on him?"

"I wouldn't push it," Cathy advised.

I sighed. "I don't suppose they're hiring any part-timers down at the box office?"

She had a primo job at Ticket Mania that sold tickets for all the best events in Seattle. It got her great tickets for personal use as well and a bunch of us were able to be front and center at last year's Sting concert. True, we hadn't been able to hear a thing for two weeks afterward, but it'd been worth it to be that close to the singer's tight Levi's.

"Sorry," Cathy said. "Nobody ever leaves Ticket Mania unless they die. I'll keep you posted if anyone comes down with a terminal illness."

The phone rang and Cathy picked up. She talked for a couple of minutes then handed the phone over to me.

"It's Jeff."

I offered her a pained expression but took the receiver anyway. "Hello?"

"Hi. Cathy says you're bunking with us for the next couple of nights."

"Yeah. My place got flooded. I hope that's not a problem." And if it *is* a problem, then that's just too bad.

"No problem, I was just going to offer you my bed."

Yuk! I coughed and choked on a mouthful of beer. "Your bed?"

"Sure. I was just telling Cathy that I'm heading down to Portland to make a delivery and I'm going to bunk with a friend overnight. You're welcome to make my room yours until tomorrow."

"Um, thanks, Jeff, but that's—" very odd, awkward, creepy… "—unnecessary."

Just then the other line beeped.

"Can you hang on, Jeff? There's another call coming in." I clicked him off and answered. "Hello?"

"Hi, Tab! You're all settled with Cathy for the night?" It was Jenny and I told her that, yes, I was all settled, then I told her all about catching Mole Man and Mrs. Sumner playing hide the salami. While she laughed hysterically I remembered I still had Jeff on hold.

"Hold on a second, Jen, I gotta let Jeff go."

Click.

"Sorry, Jeff, I've got Jen on the other line. Was there anything else you wanted to say?"

"Well, actually, there was another thing and it may take a while so…"

Sigh. "Okay, just a second then."

Click.

"Jenny, Jeff says he still wants to talk, are you okay holding?"

"Yeah, okay, if you're too long I'll just call back. I have to get ready for my date tonight."

"Okay," I said. "I'll find out what he wants and get rid of him."

Click.

"Okay, Jeff, what else do you want?"

"Lucien was wondering if he could talk to you," Jeff said stiffly.

Yikes! "Hang on a second."

Click.

"Hello?" Nothing. Dead air. "Hello, Jen? Jeff is on the other line and he says Lucien wants to talk to me, what should I do?"

Pause, then a deep male chuckle. "I say, you should take the call and stop being such a scaredy-cat."

Damn! "Um, hold on a second, Lucien."

I glanced over at Cathy who had renewed tears of laughter brimming in her eyes. I hate fucking call waiting!

Click.

"Jen?"

"Yeah?"

"I gotta go. I've humiliated myself on the other line because I was talking to Lucien when I thought it was you."

"Lucien? Wow! Call me right back after you find out what he wants."

I took a deep breath and really wanted to hang up, but then I'd have an even harder time convincing Lucien I wasn't a chicken, so I took two deep cleansing breaths and clicked over to Lucien.

"Hi. Sorry about that. I'm not usually a scaredy-cat."

"That's all right." I could hear him smiling. "It does my ego good to know I unnerve you."

Somehow I doubted his ego needed any boosting.

"What can I do for you?"

Pause.

"Oh, I can think of about a hundred things in various positions," he drawled, then added, "but for now you can agree to let me take you to dinner on Saturday night."

"Dinner? Saturday?" I glanced furtively over to Cathy for guidance. She just grinned broadly and shrugged. Big help. I quickly figured out that I had three choices. I could either A) turn him down flat, B) accept his offer now and then cancel later by feigning injury, illness and/or death or C) accept his dinner invitation and deal with the possibility that it may lead to mind-blowing, multiorgasmic sex for the first time in my life.

"Okay. Sure. Dinner sounds—" I groped for a word and only could come up with "—interesting."

When I hung up the phone Cathy raised her eyebrows at me. "I can't believe you accepted dinner with Lucien Roskell. Jeff is going to be positively green with envy."

"Lucien may be a lot of things but gay is not one of them," I stated matter-of-factly.

"Are you sure you're attracted to the guy? Seems to me you're just scared of him."

"I'm *not* scared."

She leveled a disbelieving gaze in my direction and I caved.

"Okay, I am a tiny bit scared of him, but that's probably because I'm so attracted to him. Jeez, you'd have to be dead not to drool just looking at the guy." I thought back to the bone-liquefying kiss he'd planted on my lips then popped the tab on my next beer and drank deeply. "Maybe that's it. The guy just oozes sexuality. Just being next to him is orgasmic. I'm scared I won't be able to handle him."

Cathy smirked. "Jeff says the same thing."

Gross.

"Well," Cathy said, "you've got two days to build your confidence so you don't spend the entire night trembling with fear."

We called Jenny back and I told her about my upcoming date. She was even more excited than I was but she needed to leave for her date so we made plans to discuss it further over lunch the next day.

Cathy and I tidied up our pizza and beer mess and

watched an *X-Files* rerun. Afterward we painted our toenails.

"I need to check to see what our booze theme of the week will be at Jimbo's tomorrow," she said.

"Check? Check where?"

"I have a Web site that I check every Thursday. That's how I come up with all those neat drink ideas for Friday nights."

The fact that she actually researched our weekly booze up surprised me.

"Web site?" I glanced around. "I didn't know you even had a computer." I stuck the tip of my tongue out of the corner of my mouth and tried valiantly to apply a dollop of salmon-pink color to my puny baby toenail.

"I don't." She got to her feet. "Jeff does. He's got a million rules about allowing me to use his computer but he doesn't mind me checking out the booze site."

I got up and followed. The two of us waddled on our heels so as not to smudge our toenail polish. We entered Jeff's room, Cathy flicked on the light switch and we duck-walked over to his computer desk.

Jeff's room was white. Really white. White walls with white curtains. White furniture and white bed covers. Inky had followed us in and jumped on the bed. I shooed him off fearing the black hairs left behind would offset Jeff's strange color scheme. I couldn't believe Jeff had offered to let me sleep in his room. I couldn't believe *anyone* could sleep in this room.

Cathy slid behind Jeff's white desk and tapped away at the computer while I stood staring around the room.

"Jeff is weird," I stated.

Cathy nodded. "Yep. The weirdest."

"How do you stand it?"

"Remember all my other roommates? The hippy broad who burned all that incense, the fatty who tried to squeeze into my best outfits and the neurotic one who squealed like a pig in her sleep?"

"Yeah, I guess I see your point."

"Jeff is weird like the others but it's a contained weird. He has a thing about never taking his shirt off around me but I don't have a problem with that 'cause he doesn't have a bod I want to see. He's also obsessively neat. I like that 'cause he'll clean up after me. He's quiet, keeps to himself and pays over half the rent. You can't beat that. Plus, he also gets gay porn delivered regularly and although that kind of graphic coupling is not my thing, I've never been opposed to seeing a centerfold of a nude buff male. That even makes up for his strange friends."

"Weird friends?" The idea of Jeff having *any* friends, strange or otherwise, was news to me.

"You know the type, long dark coats, dark clothing and white pancake makeup." She shrugged. "That kind of nerd-goes-gothic look. He says he met them when he worked for his father. They don't come around often anymore, I think they had a falling-out. Anyway, I think Jeff mostly met with them for Dungeons & Dragons or some other stupid game."

Cathy clicked the keyboard and the printer hummed out a couple of pages that she snatched up and read. "Looks like Friday will be melon liqueur night."

I was all atremble at the thought.

★ ★ ★

I woke up Friday morning with my back aching from being pretzeled on the sofa. My head was still in a hazy dream state and Inky's butt was in my face so it took a while to orient myself to my surroundings. I pushed back a vague nightmare that was trying to crystallize and I also pushed away Inky who mewed loudly at the intrusion. The aroma of fresh-brewed coffee wafted over and I could hear Cathy humming softly to herself in the kitchen. I was seriously thinking of offering to become her next roommate.

"Here ya go," Cathy said, handing me a mug of coffee.

I sat up and gratefully took the cup.

"Sorry. No time for chitchat this morning." She winced down at her watch. "I'm already late."

I managed to get to the office only a few minutes late myself. Jenny was holding the fort behind my desk looking bleary-eyed and rumpled.

"Didn't make it home last night, huh?" I smirked.

She yawned. "Nope." She got to her feet and stretched. "You know, I think he might be the one."

I plopped my butt into the chair Jenny vacated. "The one, huh? Which guy are we talking about?"

She placed a hand over her heart. "Gerry. He's just dreamy."

"Gerry. Isn't he the one who pumps gas in Renton?"

"No, that's Joe."

"So he's the one that does lawn maintenance at Discovery Park?"

"No, that's Gavin Furly. Gerry's the security guy I met at the food court in the mall."

I shook my head. Between Gerry, Joe and Furly it was hard to keep all of Jen's stooges straight.

"So what makes you think this guy's *the one*?"

She leaned into my ear and whispered details that are better left unsaid at nine in the a.m. to someone who has not had sex in a year.

I fanned myself with my fingers. "Okay, you can go now," I said dismissively.

She grinned and started to turn then looked back, "Oh yeah, Lina the Loser called. Twice. I told her to go to hell both times but she insisted I leave a message for you."

Clay walked in half an hour later. He paused to offer me a sappy and sucking-up *Hello* and *How are you this morning, Miss Emery?* but the mocking look in his eye and the sarcasm in his voice told me he didn't mean it. I wanted to return his sarcastic tone with an attitude of my own that would've been, acerbic, glib and downright flippant, but I had to swallow my flippin' urge to be flippant because he was with a client.

Then, because Martha was away for the morning at some prenatal appointment, Clay asked me to hold all his calls and then kept checking in with me for messages always with the same sickening sweet tenor in his voice. By the time my lunch hour rolled around I had big-time indigestion from all the bitter words I'd been swallowing that morning.

"So did you call Lina Lumphead?" Jenny asked as we elbowed our way from the deli counter to a corner table.

I glowered at her. "No. I didn't have time to call her and I'd appreciate it if you would not call her names," I snapped.

Jenny paused in midchew and narrowed her eyes at me. "What crawled up your butt?"

I ripped off a corner of my tuna sandwich and chewed angrily without answering.

"It's Clay, isn't it?"

I washed down my sandwich with some scalding coffee. "Yeah. He comes in this morning and is all pleasant to me and stuff."

Jenny looked askance. "Well I can see how that could mess you up, wouldn't want him to try and be nice now would we?"

I stabbed my finger into her shoulder. "That's exactly the kind of attitude he has, sarcastic to the hilt. He's says 'Thank you for the messages, Miss Emery.'" I sang the words out in an exaggeration of Clay's sappy tone. "Geesh, all I asked was that he say a few kind words to me when he called."

Jenny was quiet for a moment.

"You know what your problem is," she began, "you're never satisfied."

My jaw dropped open. "What the hell is *that* supposed to mean?"

"It means that you've got this sexy guy, Lucien, hot on your trail but all you can think about is Clay. Clay this and Clay that." She snapped her fingers in my face. "Wake up, Tabitha, Clay's got a girlfriend named Candy who looks like a model and he's probably not gonna dump her for you."

I sulkily pushed the rest of my sandwich away. "You're just being nasty."

Jenny sighed. "Love ya like a sister, Tab, and that's the only reason why I'm telling it like it is."

"You're right." I downed the rest of my coffee. "So you're thinking I should be forgetting all about Clay and taking a closer look at Lucien?"

"Honey, I think if you don't look closely at Lucien you're either blind or stupid."

Jenny's rough pep talk worked. I returned to my desk with determination to forget looking at Clay as a sex god or a potential lover. From now on I was going to be Miss Professional. I'd be so damn professional I'd rock his world and one day when he got tired of Candy and wanted me I'd be like, *I'm sorry, Mr. Sanderson but I'm marrying Lucien Roskell tomorrow. Na na na na na na.*

What really hurt was that even though I was being Miss Professional, Clay did not notice and when Candy called and I put her through to him without even cutting her off once, he failed to even congratulate me. Men!

Later, I was waiting for the FedEx guy who usually arrived at four-forty-five. I was hoping to sneak out with him after I signed for the day's deliveries but he was late, so all I could do was sit there until five o'clock. The phones were dead and everyone else in the office was leaving early because it was Friday. Friday meant there were happy hour cocktails waiting and hot wings and nachos to be consumed.

Finally, Jenny came out and said, "Guess what? I've decided to go shopping with you!"

"Shopping?" I shook my head. "I've got no money to shop, remember? I've got to save my pennies or I'll be dating your no-neck cousin, Doug, to pay for my car repairs."

"Oh, but you must shop."

"I must?"

She nodded, "Baby shower tomorrow, remember? I bet you haven't bought a thing for Martha yet."

I slammed the palm of my hand to my forehead. "Damn. I forgot all about the shower!" I riffled around in my desk until I found the mint-green envelope and ripped it open. "Tomorrow, from noon to four at someone's place in Fremont," I moaned. "I don't wanna go. I'd just rather—" get a bikini wax, watch the shopping network, drink dealcoholized beer… "—not."

"You have to," Jen said firmly. "But I'll help you pick out the perfect gift so she'll be so distracted by your wonderful, amazing taste in baby stuff that she won't even notice you skipping out two hours early."

Empowered by that thought, we hit the mall. Once you started looking for it you couldn't help but notice that baby crap was *everywhere.* I couldn't find blue jeans to fit my size-seven ass but I could buy ten in a dozen shades for a six-month-old for the same price. It was downright depressing. We had our dinner at the food fair where I convinced myself that what I really needed was to blow my money on bad Chinese and a huge slice of greasy pizza.

"I thought you said you were going to help with this shopping thing," I accused.

"After we finish eating we'll get serious," Jenny said.

I glanced down at the half-dozen shopping bags surrounding Jenny's legs and pointed out, "You've been serious, just not about finding a baby gift." Spending hours watching Jenny wriggle her size-sixteen body into a rainbow of outfits in size fourteen was not the way I wanted to end my week.

Jenny pointed a finger in the direction of a woman at the next table. "Now see? That's exactly what you need!" She jumped up from her plastic chair and marched over to the woman holding up a large gift basket filled with baby gunk.

Jenny returned and stated proudly, "See? Now I know what to get and where to get it."

I slid my eyes over to the bulging basket at the next table. "All that stuff probably costs a fortune."

A few minutes later at a cute baby boutique my fears were confirmed.

"It's a hundred bucks!" I put the basket back down. "Now what, genius?"

Jenny picked the basket back up and examined it closely. "You know what? We can do this."

"We can?"

"Sure. We buy a basket, cellophane wrap and a pile of baby stuff at Wal-Mart and throw it all together. I bet we could do the same thing for under thirty dollars."

"I don't know," I said doubtfully. "I'm not very good at crafts."

"It's not a craft," Jenny explained patiently. "It's a friggin' basket. Come on, it'll be easy."

She was right about it being easy. It was perfectly easy to create a disaster when you had no idea whatsoever what you were doing. Two hours later, Cathy's living room looked as though a gift shop had exploded in the center. We had assembled a massive three-foot-high gift basket wrapped in a dozen feet of clear plastic wrap and tied together with a large yellow bow.

I shook my head. "It looks like crap."

"It looks great," Jenny insisted.

Cathy strolled in from her bedroom where she'd been dressing for our night at Jimbo's and said, "It looks like crap. You used far too much wrap and all the stuff is just crammed in there."

Jenny got to her feet and dusted her hands together. "Well, I'm not redoing it, especially not for Martha. I need a drink so I say we move our asses over to Jimbo's for—" she looked at Cathy "—what's our theme this week?"

"Melon liqueur."

"For Melon Liqueur Night." Jenny licked her lips in anticipation.

Cathy and Jenny cleaned up the extra tissue and cellophane wrap while Inky did his part and shredded whatever he could find to ribbons. During that time I prepared myself by applying an overload of mascara and lipstick. We split a cab to Jimbo's where Cathy handed over the recipes for two melon liqueur drinks to the bartender. One of these drinks was named Alien Secretion and the other was Alligator Bait. Despite their ridiculous names and colorful umbrellas, the drinks were not as quick to induce vomiting as one might think. In fact, by the time I'd consumed my second of each I was even convincing some young Washington State boys to try a drink or three.

"Get your arse back in your chair before you humiliate yourself," Jenny whispered in my ear and yanked me over to our table.

I plunked my butt back in my chair with reluctance.

"You gotta admit, Jen, they didn't make 'em like that when we were in university."

"Don't be fooled by the outside package." Cathy grinned. "They were *exactly* like that when we were in college and they didn't look at us *then* either."

Jenny tsked and shook her head. "Your date tomorrow would blow the socks off any one of them. What are you going to wear?"

I frowned into my Alien Secretion and admitted I had no idea. "I don't know where he's taking me so I guess it'll have to be my little black dress."

Both Jenny and Cathy moaned.

"What?" I asked.

My two friends shared a look then turned to me.

"It's just that it's…" Jenny began.

"Ugly," Cathy finished.

"And it's…" Jenny started.

"Out of fashion," Cathy added. "And it's got that…"

"Snag in the back of the skirt," Jenny complained.

I held up a hand in surrender and then downed the rest of my drink. "Fine! What do you two suggest, huh? I've got no money and with the shower tomorrow I've also got no time to shop for new even if I had the cash."

"You could borrow something of mine," both girls chimed.

I looked from Jenny, size sixteen, to Cathy, size five, and laughed until melon liqueur came out of my nose.

The thick perfume of candle wax filled my senses. Even as the sane part of me resisted, I found myself struggling to illuminate the opaque images before me. A mumbled mantra, muted and rough, reverberated in the haziness. The vision faded to black only to explode in intense white light a second later. A ceremonial knife plunged into both flesh and bone repeatedly in a crazed frenzy. The sound that fractured the night was my own scream.

chapter nine

The sting of the slap was still ringing in my ears when my eyes snapped open.

"Why the hell did you hit me?" I demanded, blinking in the light that flooded the previously dark room.

Cathy stood staring at me, her face ashen with worry. "Because, you twit, you wouldn't stop screaming."

"Oh." Movement in the corner of my eye startled a small squeak from my throat, then I realized it was only Jeff. Still I placed a hand over my heart to steady it. "Jeff, my God, you scared me."

"I—I think your d-d-dream did that," he said.

"Actually—" I blew out a long breath "—I think it was your glow-in-the-dark pj's."

Even in the dim light I could see him blush.

"Not that they're not perfectly nice," I added hastily, recovering my manners. I was in his apartment, after all. "I've just never seen black pj's with white glowing stars on them before." At least, not on a grown man.

"Jeez, Tabitha, you scared the life out of me," Cathy breathed. She stumbled forward and wrapped her arms around my neck in an awkward hug. "You just kept screaming *Finger! Finger!* Over and over." I felt her tremble before she pulled back.

"Finger?" I smothered a giggle with the back of my hand. "Really?"

"M-m-must've been some dream," Jeff commented. "Do you want to tell us about it?"

I shook my head violently from side to side. "No. It's gone. I've already forgotten all about it." Or at least I was *hoping* to.

"Are you sure you're going to be okay? Can I get you a drink? Warm milk? A Valium?" Cathy asked.

"Nah, just go on back to sleep. Sorry I woke you up."

"Well, if you're sure…"

I nodded and they left me to snuggle back down on the sofa. The sheets were still damp from my perspiration. Inky stared at me from a chair across the room and I was sure he was thinking, *Of all the women in Seattle I had to end up with a lunatic.*

The rest of the night I slept like the dead but at least I didn't dream about them. My eyes blinked open in the morning with two gleaming thoughts. I had a hot date tonight and I had a dreaded baby shower to get through first.

Both Cathy and Jeff had to work so there was a lot more activity in the apartment at eight-thirty on a Saturday morning than I was used to.

Before he headed for the door, Jeff presented me with the gift basket that I was bringing to the shower. He carefully planted the huge basket on the coffee table in front of me. I couldn't believe it. He'd totally fixed it. The blankets, bottles, booties and other *B-is-for-Baby* items had been somehow suspended and arranged tidily inside the basket so that it now appeared full and tastefully done. The wrap had been stretched tightly over the huge basket and tendrils of ribbon curled delicately down from the large bow.

"Wow. I don't know what to say." I reached out to tentatively touch the cellophane wrap. "You must've worked all night on this."

"Not all night." Jeff grinned sheepishly. He reached out and straightened the bow with obvious pride. "When I lived in L.A. I used to earn extra bucks at a mall gift-wrapping at Christmastime. Guess I learned a few things."

"Well, thanks." I flashed him the biggest smile I could muster before my morning coffee. "I'm actually looking forward to going to the baby shower now." *Not!*

He waved my thanks away with a flutter of his effeminate hand and made his way out the door to head for the Scrying Room.

Cathy scooted over to me, stainless steel travel coffee mug clenched tightly in her fist.

"Gotta go." She glanced at her watch. "There's coffee made, turn off the pot when you're done." She pecked my cheek and I guiltily noticed the dark circles under her eyes as she patted the top of Inky's head. "It was fun having you stay for a two-night pj party, but next time leave Inky with me and you bunk with Jen, okay?"

"Deal."

"Oh, by the way, when I couldn't get back to sleep last night, I solved your wardrobe problem for your date with Lucien."

"You went out shopping at 3:00 a.m.?"

"No, I went through my own closet." She held up a hand in a stopping motion to halt my protests. "I know my skirts won't fit you but I'm pretty sure a couple of my blouses will because…" She glanced obviously from her C bust to my A and shrugged. "Anyway, you have that nice black wool skirt, right?"

"Yeah, but it's an *office* skirt, not a *date* skirt."

She shook her head, "Take the blouses I laid out on my bed and try them on with that skirt. One of them is bound to work. Open an extra button and show a little cleavage." She glanced back to my chest. "Wear your WonderBra."

I was glad to return to my own building to find that my apartment looked great and smelled great. Mole Man had done a superb job of repairing the leak and cleaning up afterward. He'd even left me a note stating that he'd also discovered a problem with my showerhead and had replaced it. I checked. It was one of those detachable shower massages that made a man optional. It was almost enough to make me feel guilty for blackmailing my landlord.

It was a soothing feeling to make the three trips from my car to my apartment carting in all my stuff without worrying about Mrs. Sumner poking her head out her door to give me the evil eye.

I hung up the blouses that Cathy loaned me and although I was tempted to try them on, they'd have to wait until after the baby shower. I fed Inky and asked him his opinion about what to wear to the shower. His answer was to give himself a tongue bath so I took a guess and changed into navy pants and a cream sweater. I brushed my hair, refusing to attack it with a curling iron before my date.

I noticed the light on my answering machine was blinking angrily. The message was from Lucien, who stated he'd pick me up at seven for our dinner. I would've had to do deep breathing exercises to calm myself, however, after his message there was a blast of angry messages from Lina. I sighed and dialed her number.

"Where the hell have you been?"

"My apartment was flooded, remember? I've been bunking at Cathy's while it got deflooded."

She blew a long breath into the receiver. "Don't you check your messages? Okay, I'm not going to nag, I'm just glad you're okay."

I felt a pinch of guilt. "I'm sorry you were worried. I'm fine."

"I know a little about that group that calls themselves the Scarab Sentry. They tend to mark themselves with tattoos in the likeness of the scarab beetle. From what I understand the tattoo is usually between the thumb and forefinger of the right hand so it'll be obvious," she blurted nervously.

"Okay, so you want me to watch out for vacant-eyed guys who have tattoos of bugs on their hands. Got it," I joked.

Poignant pause. "Tabitha, this is not funny. You're in danger."

I could hear the distinct flutter of cards being pressed to a table and had an image of the Tarot arranged before her.

"Put your cards away, Lina, they don't solve anything."

"I don't have my cards in front of me but I used them earlier." Another pause. "But you can see them, can't you? The Devil card? The Tower?"

I pinched the bridge of my nose and squeezed my eyes shut to stop myself from seeing anything.

"I gotta go, Lina, I'm late for a baby shower. Unless you want to tell me I shouldn't go because a pregnant woman with vacant eyes is gonna get me." I drew in a breath and let it out. "Sorry. I know you're just trying to help. I promise I'll be careful but I do have to go." I hung up the phone and waved goodbye to Inky.

It was just after twelve when I made it to Fremont. I drove past numerous funky shops, microbreweries and street artists displaying their wares in a rare moment of October sunshine. I found myself wishing I was there in June to watch the annual Solstice Parade that featured stilt walkers, colorful floats and, of course, nude bikers. Instead, it was fall and I was hunting for a parking space in an area of expensive condominium apartments that rented monthly for a third of my annual salary.

I sat at a red light in my small Ford Escort squeezed in between a HumVee and a Suburban. One swerving motion from either vehicle and I'd be a pancake. The light turned green and I punched the accelerator to move ahead in traffic. After circling the block three times I saw a black Honda nosing out of a spot ahead. After cutting off two sports cars and receiving a retort of horns and hand gestures, I wedged my small car into a spot only a block away from my destination.

I hefted the immense gift basket from the passenger seat and trudged up the street. I buzzed the trendy condo security button and was greeted by a woman's flat voice telling me to "Come on up."

Up I went, cursing the fact that I'd chosen the stairs while clumsily hauling this behemoth basket. If it was not for the clear plastic wrap, I would not have been able to see in front of me. Since my hands were occupied I kicked softly at the door to number 302.

"Oh, my God, is there someone behind this thing?" a voice blurted, then the basket was tugged from my grasp and I was looking up into the birdlike face of a tall stern woman of about sixty. She wore a linen suit and an expression that looked as though someone was holding a small turd under her beak of a nose.

"Hello, I'm Tabitha Emery. I'm here for the shower."

"Oh, is that a fact? I guess that would explain this thing." Bird Woman turned and grunted under the weight of my gift, choosing to plunk it down on a mahogany hall table.

I noted her slurred speech and it occurred to me that Bird Woman was royally tanked.

"Tabitha!" I heard Martha's voice followed by the clickety clack of her heels as she waddled high-speed toward me wearing a fuchsia-colored tent that billowed around her. She embraced me in a suffocating hug and breathed in my ear, "I'm so glad you could make it."

"Well sure, I told you I'd come."

She dragged me by the hand to the living room that was a large airy space with an entire wall of windows. Light flooded the room through the opened drapes and shone on a sofa sectional, a dozen folding chairs, a table heavily laden with food and only one other person. A smaller, younger version of bird woman. I glanced down at my watch. It was twelve-fifteen.

"Am I early? The invitation did say twelve, didn't it?"

Martha's smile was wide and strained. "No. You've got it right. The shower started at noon. Unfortunately we've had a number of last-minute cancellations. People are just so busy these days, you know?"

Oh, this ought to be a ton of fun.

Martha clapped her hands loudly and I jumped.

"Okaaay," she began, her voice a pitch higher than I was used to. "Let's start with some introductions, shall we?"

She pulled me by the hand again and brought me toward Short Bird Lady and Tall Bird Lady who were now standing at the buffet filling their plates.

"This is my sister-in-law Sandra Martel," Martha said to me. "And my mother-in-law Gina Martel."

"Mom, Sis, I'd like you to meet my best friend in the world, Tabitha Emery."

Her what? I stared at Martha who gave me a pleading, please-play-along-with-this look.

Both ladies offered me identical dismissive glances before returning to load their plates.

"Help yourself," Martha trilled, handing me a china plate. "We've got a pile of food just waiting to be eaten."

"And booze," Sandra the bird lady said with a mean giggle. "Thank God for the booze."

"Oh, yes." Martha nodded her head bobbing forcefully on her neck. "There's wine, fruit punch and if you want something stronger I've got a liquor cabinet filled with more."

"So this is your place?" I asked.

That got a guffaw and a snigger out of Gina Martel. "She's your best friend and she hasn't even seen where you live?"

The way I saw it I could either jump on the obvious we-hate-Martha bandwagon, or rescue my co-worker and possibly even simultaneously secure my promotion.

I never thought I'd feel this way, but I actually felt sorry for Martha. "So happens Martha here usually comes over to my place. It's just more convenient. That way we don't have to bother…" I looked to Martha for help.

"Dave," she offered.

"Right. Dave. That way all our noisy girly talk doesn't bother Dave." I snagged Martha by the elbow. "Could I talk to you in the kitchen for a second? You can show me that new thing you said you bought."

"Sure," Martha said, her happy voice nearly cracking under the strain.

I steered Martha in the direction of the kitchen and once we were behind closed doors I started in.

"What the hell is all this?"

She let out a snort that sounded dangerously close to turning into tears. "It's my baby shower."

"What happened to all the other guests?"

"I don't have a lot of friends," she stated, playing nervously with a strand of hair. "This was supposed to be a surprise for me thrown by Dave's family but when I found out about it, I invited a couple of my friends just in case this happened."

"You *expected* nobody to show?"

She looked defeated and wearily leaned against the kitchen counter. "His family doesn't like me very much.

It all kind of started when I refused to change my name when we got married."

My lips tugged up into a smile. "You mean they don't get why you wouldn't want to be called Martha Martel?"

She giggled. "No. They don't get that."

We were quiet a moment. "So, you're not expecting anyone else?"

She hesitated and shook her head. "Well, Jen couldn't come and the only other person I invited was Sonya Suderman from the office and she called to say there was a sale at JCPenney that she couldn't miss."

"You invited The Bitch?" I asked, dumbfounded.

She smirked. "Yeah. You must think I'm pathetic, don't you?" Her eyes were brimming with tears and suddenly I did think she was pathetic and I didn't mind so much that I hadn't had good sex in a long time. That's the good thing about being in an extremely awkward situation like this—it made you believe that your own wretched excuse of a life wasn't nearly so bad, after all.

"I've got an idea and we're getting out of here." I nodded toward the living room. "Grab your coat and wait for me by the door."

With determination I strolled in the direction of the two bird ladies and announced conspiratorially, "I'm sorry, ladies, but there seems to be a bit of a problem. You see, I'm actually throwing a baby shower for Martha at my place. I was just coming to pick her up. At this very moment my apartment is filled with a dozen women waiting to jump up and scream 'Surprise.'"

Sandra narrowed her eyes. "Then why did you bring that big gift over here?"

I shook my head. "To throw her off, of course, if I brought her a baby gift the last thing she's going to suspect is that I'm taking her to a baby shower."

Gina looked skeptical. "Well then, where does she think she's going?"

Good question. "Um, I told her we had a big emergency at the office that only she can solve and that I'll bring her right back." I may not be quick on my feet but I can lie like a champion.

"Okay, Martha," I said loudly. "We'd better go take care of that office emergency. I'll bring you back as soon as possible." I gave an exaggerated wink to the ladies staring after us and we were gone.

While on the way to my car I explained the line I'd given to her in-laws about a baby shower at my place.

Snuggled cozily into the passenger seat of my car Martha asked the obvious. "Now what?"

"I have no idea." I turned my key in the ignition. "Where would you like to go?"

She considered this a minute then answered firmly, "Your place."

"My place?"

"Yes. We can sit around. Have some girly talk—that kind of stuff."

"You know, Martha, my place may not be such a good idea. It's small. As a matter of fact, compared to your condo there, it's a dump."

"That isn't my place. It's Dave's. He had it since before we were married and we have a prenup that says he gets it back if we ever divorce. Before we were married I lived in a basement suite in Renton."

"My place it is."

It wasn't nearly as awkward having Martha in my apartment as I thought it would be. She made herself comfortable on my sofa, put her feet on my coffee table and held Inky on her lap. It was strange to think that a person I despised from nine to five Monday to Friday could actually be someone I almost liked outside of that time slot.

"So can I get you anything?" I thought back to the huge amount of food at her place and wished I'd eaten there. I began rifling through my cupboards. "How about some microwave popcorn?"

"Sure."

A few minutes later we were sitting in my living room munching popcorn and sipping soda. The telephone rang and it was Jenny.

"You managed to escape the shower early, good for you," Jenny cheered.

"Yeah, well, I've actually got Martha here with me."

"Kidnapping is a federal offence, Tab, and so is murder."

"The kidnapping was mutual. Her shower was bumming us both out, so we left."

"She's not holding a gun to you, is she?"

"No!"

"Oh. I guess since she's sitting right there you can fill me in on the details tomorrow when you're also telling me all about your date. Have you decided what to wear yet?"

"Cathy loaned me a couple blouses to go with my black skirt."

"Good idea. I'm only going to say one word, Tabitha...*cleavage.*"

I hung up and said to Martha, "I've got a date tonight

and no idea what to wear so would you mind giving me your opinion on a couple outfits?"

"I'd love that!"

And because she looked like she meant it, I grabbed a few things from my closet and began a fashion show. Half an hour later, Martha had decided on my black skirt and a sheer style black blouse that was one of Cathy's. I wasn't so sure about the shirt.

I glanced down at my chest. With the help of my WonderBra, my cup and cleavage now runneth over. "Don't you think it's a little snug?"

Martha said seriously, "Yep, I'm sure that's the first thing this Lucien guy is going to complain about. He's definitely going to say, *Honey, you've got far too much of your breasts showing.* Why, I'll bet he'll march you right back home to put on a turtleneck!"

We laughed until we cried.

Just after five Martha had to go on account of she needed to cook dinner for hubby. Though she would've taken a cab I didn't mind driving her. It helped to kill some time that I would've normally spent agonizing over my upcoming date. I managed to secure a parking spot directly in front of her building.

"Look, Tabitha, I don't think I'll ever be able to thank you for today."

"For what? Kidnapping you from your own baby shower and forcing you to come to my dump and eat microwave popcorn?"

"You know what I mean. It was nice of you." She smiled and then her smile turned to wonder as she placed a hand on her ample belly. "She's doing the wave or something."

"You know it's a girl?"

"Nah, I refused to let them tell me when I had my ultrasound. I want it to be a surprise, you know?" Her eyes opened wide. "Oh, that was a good one! She's a real kicker. Here." She grabbed my hand and placed it on the side of her abdomen. "If you keep your fingers right there, you'll feel it."

I felt it all right. My head went woozy and a horrible picture flared in my mind.

"Is there something wrong with your eyes?"

"Huh?" I yanked my hand back from her stomach. "Um, Martha, you see a doctor regularly, right?"

"Yeah, of course. Now that I'm only a few weeks away I have to see my OB-GYN every week." Her eyes flew to search mine. "Wait a second, was that one of your premonition things? Is there something wrong with my baby?" Her arms wrapped protectively over her stomach.

"Look, Martha," I faltered, "sometimes I get a feeling about things but they're not always accurate or anything." Lie number one. "I'm sure everything is just fine with the little guy." Lie number two.

"Are you sure?"

"Of course." Three strikes and I'm out. "But to be on the safe side, will you promise me you'll see your OB-GYN right away? Get him to do another one of those ultrasound things."

She all but tripped over herself running from my car and into her building.

"You really know how to end an afternoon, Tabitha." I admonished myself with a heavy sigh.

★ ★ ★

At five minutes before seven, it was time to take stock. I'd brushed my teeth once. Changed my clothes twice. Reapplied my makeup three times. Checked the black skirt, black sheer blouse and black sling-backs for the umpteenth time. As far as I was concerned if I could keep myself busy right up until Lucien arrived I wouldn't become a nervous wreck. I caught a glimpse of my panicked reflection in the bathroom mirror and sighed. Too late. I was beyond panicked—I was terrified. And now that I was dressed I couldn't even sit down for fear of attracting every cat hair in the place.

I called Jenny.

"Help, I can't sit down!"

"Why, is your ass broken?" she asked and laughed.

"No, there's cat hair everywhere and if I sit it'll stick to me like glue."

"So stand."

"I feel like I'm going to pass out."

"How long has it been since you had a date?"

"Um, well, um…"

"That long, huh? Don't worry, you'll be fine. He's just a man. Remember that and you'll do fine. How do you look?"

"Fine."

"Fine or hot?"

"Not sizzling hot but I'd say marginally warm."

"Okay, take a deep breath. Did you remember your lucky purse?"

"No! Oh, my God, I almost forgot my lucky date purse!" I yelped. At my outburst Inky dived for cover under my sofa bed. Obviously, he had no concept of the importance of my revelation.

"Get your lucky purse and you'll be fine."

I reached up into the far recesses of my closet and pulled down the slim black leather Ferragamo knockoff, sighed and hugged it to my chest.

"Okay, I've got it."

"Sounds like you're ready to go. If anything goes wrong or if you end up in the sack with this guy, call me!"

"Are you going to be at home?"

"Tab, it's Saturday night. I'd have to be dead to be at home. I'll keep my cell on vibrate. If you can't reach me, call Lara, she's got a night off from the Megaplex tonight."

"Where are you and Gerry going tonight?"

"Who said anything about Gerry?"

"But I thought he was *the one.*"

"He was *the one. The one* I caught stealing twenty bucks from my purse on our last date."

"Oh. Sorry to hear that. So who's your date for tonight?"

"John."

"The dentist?"

"No, that was Nick."

"I thought Nick was the shoe salesman."

"That was Harry. I haven't told you about John. I just met him in the laundry room."

I paused. "Jen, don't you ever get tired of dating every John, Nick and Harry?"

"No. It's far better than the alternative."

"What's the alternative?"

"Being alone."

We said our goodbyes and I transferred the necessities from my work purse to my lucky date purse—lipstick, tissue and forty dollars emergency cab fare. Then I spotted the empty bottle of painkiller meds with a smile. That empty bottle had been my escape on more than one bad date.

Act one, scene one…riffles through handbag with pained expression. Line one, *Oh, dear, I've run out of migraine pills, I'm afraid you'll have to take me home.* Disappointing pout followed by, *Just when we were having such a wonderful time, too. I'm so sorry.*

With a smile I tucked the empty bottle in the corner of the small handbag and then it hit, the faint aroma of tobacco. I brought the handbag up to my face and sucked in the cologne of Virginia Slims. This was going to be my first official date as a nonsmoker. How would I survive it?

A sharp rap at the door made me jump. I walked across the room repeating the mantra, *He's just a man. He's just a man. He's just*—I opened the door—*a very, very sexy man.*

He wore charcoal-colored pants, a cream linen shirt that exposed a thatch of dark chest hair and a grin that made me want to drag his ass directly to my bed.

"Hi, Lucien."

"Hi, yourself." His eyes raked over me. "You look great."

He handed me a single red rose and I brought the bloom to my nose and inhaled. It was almost as nice as the smell of tobacco in my purse.

"Thou art fairer than the evening air clad in the beauty of a thousand stars."

I composed myself and found I still had the ability to speak.

"Thanks. I think. I'll just put this in a vase."

"Oh, and I didn't forget about you," Lucien said, crossing my apartment to scratch Inky under his chin. He pulled out a small red ball that had a tiny bell inside and tossed it to the floor. Inky promptly sprang forward and enthusiastically hunted his new toy.

"You wouldn't be trying to get me into bed by bribing my cat, would you?"

"Is it working?"

Oh, yeah, baby. I just smiled.

"If it's that easy, then I believe it was definitely worth the dollar-fifty and the trip to the pet shop." He snagged my sweater from the coatrack and held it out for me. When I put my arms inside his fingers brushed against my neck and made me shiver.

I don't know why being around Lucien made my nerves ping and my stomach clench but it did. My reaction to all the pinging and clenching was to start chatting. By the time Lucien had pulled his red Saab away from the curb my mouth was already moving at fifty miles an hour with gusts of up to one hundred. I had verbal diarrhea and though I realized it, I couldn't seem to stop it.

While my tongue wagged on I was aware we were driving into the area of Seattle known as Capitol Hill. As my tongue sprinted out trivia we drove down bustling streets. When my mouth spilled out nonsense we were passing cafés and markets and when my lips prattled out endless small talk we were driving by quaint cafés. However, when the Saab came to a stop on the interlocking brick driveway of an older home on a residential street my mouth froze, at least for one full second.

Lucien came around to the passenger side, opened my door and I stared up at him.

"What is this place?"

"This?" He turned and glanced at the house as if seeing it for the first time. "This is a 1909 Dutch colonial."

"I can see that." Well, actually I couldn't see that because I didn't know a Dutch colonial from a vintage Victorian but that was beside the point. I got out of the car and nodded toward the house. "What I mean is, why are we here?"

He cocked his head to one side. "For dinner. I *did* invite you to dinner, remember?"

I blew out an exasperated breath. "This is *your* house then?"

"Of course it's mine." He wrapped one of his warm hands around mine and tugged me up the walk. "I wouldn't bring you to someone else's home. At least not on our first date."

"You never mentioned we were going to your place," I stated and nervously nibbled my bottom lip. "I thought we were going to a restaurant." He'd obviously tricked me.

We reached the solid oak front door and he dug out his keys. "First of all, I am a far better cook than most you'll find at any local restaurants." He placed his key in the lock and turned. "Second, you didn't exactly give me a chance to tell you where I was taking you." He placed a hand on my lower back and guided me inside. "As a matter of fact, I do believe you've done more than enough small talk for both of us."

"You're right. I'm sorry."

"Don't be." He lifted my chin with a tip of a finger.

"With all that small talk out of the way we can get down to much more serious matters."

I swallowed. "Like what?"

"Like can you toss a salad or are you better at pouring the wine?"

I smiled and felt a few drops of tension evaporate from my body.

"I can pour wine like nobody else."

He winked. "I figured."

The older home was spacious with lots of dark wood and vaulted ceilings. The furniture was an eclectic mix of antiques and overstuffed comfortable sofas and chairs. I followed him through the living room and into the kitchen. Here I was totally out of my element. It was a cook's dream with a Sub-Zero refrigerator, gas range and slab granite counters. This was no wimpy, macaroni-and-cheese or microwaved dinner kitchen. This was a chicken cordon swiss or roast pheasant under glass kind of kitchen.

"You weren't kidding about being a good cook, were you?"

"Tabitha, there are two things I never joke about, cooking—" he handed me a bottle of chilled white wine and a corkscrew "—and sex."

"Oh."

I stared at the bottle and the corkscrew. "Hey, I said I could *pour* wine. I never said anything about opening the bottle."

Lucien popped the cork and I poured us each a glass. Then I pulled up a stool to his counter and proceeded to watch him slice, dice and stir with the fluid movements of a dancer. Watching his body move and smelling the fragrance of whatever he was making made me crave both food and sex in a way that was making me more than ravenous for both. Of course, it didn't help that I had only eaten microwave popcorn that day and was quickly making my way through my second glass of wine.

While he slid a small roaster of something in the oven he asked about my life. He picked and probed for details in a way that didn't feel like he was being nosy, even though he was. When he looked at me he seemed to absorb everything I told him, making it all the easier for me to spill out the dirty bits of my life to him.

While we ate he commented, "I don't believe you really hate your mother. You're angry with her because she had an affair that took her away from your father when he needed her most. You also feel guilty that you couldn't save your dad, even though you had a premonition of his death. Your mother is a reminder of that guilt." Lucien offered me another warm roll which I turned down because I didn't want him to think I was a pig. Even though I'd already scarfed down a Caesar salad and two helpings of seafood lasagna.

I washed down the last mouthful of my lasagna with a slurp of dry wine and smiled at him over my glass.

"Okay, Dr. Freud, I've played your game and answered your questions long enough. Now it's your turn."

He got up from the table, took my hand and led me to the living room. He gently pressed me into a comfortable sofa while he began building a fire in the fireplace.

"Make yourself comfortable," he said smoothly.

I sank back into the sofa opposite the fireplace and tried to relax but just watching Lucien bend at the waist while he got the fire started already had me overheated. I tried looking at the ceiling then at the walls to distract myself.

"You've got interesting decorating tastes," I remarked noticing the mahogany shadow boxes that held an assortment of items that lined a wall to my right.

"I also have a fascinating taste in women," he javelined back while slipping dangerously close to me on the sofa.

"Don't change the subject," I chided, nervously inching back to my corner of the couch. Sheesh, I really wanted to have his hands on me one minute and the next I cowered like a virgin. "Um, you're supposed to tell me all about yourself. It's your turn, remember?"

"What do you want to know?"

"Well, how did you get interested in opening a metaphysical store for starters?

He walked to the kitchen and returned with our wineglasses.

"I've been running the Scrying Room for just under a year. My brother had it for five years before that. When he died of cancer last year he left it to me."

"I'm sorry to hear about your brother."

"Thanks."

"What did you do before that?"

"I'm a carpenter by trade."

"Did you ever consider selling the store?"

"At first, but the clientele intrigued me and the longer I was there the more I enjoyed it. Besides I still get to do carpentry, I just do it as a hobby instead. Like remodeling this house. What else would you like to know?"

How about whether that package in your pants is as impressive as it looks? I gulped some wine from my glass.

"How about the rest of your family?"

"My mother lives in San Diego, where I grew up. I've never known my father." He slid a little closer to me on the sofa and rested a hand on my knee. "What else?"

My heart skipped in my chest at his touch. "Um. Have you always had an interest in the paranormal and pagan rituals?"

"Have you?"

"I don't."

Lucien only smiled and moved his hand from my knee to tuck a strand of hair behind my ear. He took the wineglass from my hand and put it next to his on the coffee table in front of us.

Alarm bells began to jangle inside my head as he leaned closer.

I blurted out, "What about school?"

"What about it?"

"Well, did you go to college? If you did, was it in San Diego or did you—"

"No more talking," he whispered hoarsely and bent toward me.

Out of fear and panic my hand went to his chest to stop him but his fingers simply linked in mine and brought my hand to his lips. He kissed every finger while his hot carbon eyes drilled a lusty gaze into mine. The fear was still there but it was quickly being engulfed by desire. I wanted him to kiss me. Hell, who was I kidding? I wanted him to drag me to his bed and make me forget my name. Then I wanted to make him forget his name.

He released my hand and it dropped to my lap while he lowered his lips to mine with painstaking slowness. I'd been holding my breath so long there was a ringing in my ears. When it persisted, the clamor began to cut through my haze.

"Your phone is ringing," I breathed against his lips that were a scant inch from mine.

"Let it ring."

I pulled back. "It could be important."

He sighed and got up from the sofa. His feet impatiently ate up the floor in the direction of the kitchen where I heard him snatch up the receiver and bark out a hello.

I uncoiled myself from the sofa and shook off the fog of lust. Slow. We had to go slower. I couldn't just jump in bed with him on our first date, could I? I shook my head. Of course not. No matter how much I wanted to.

His words drifted in from the kitchen. The tone was heated, insistent and cutting.

"No, Heather, I can't talk now I'm busy. I'll call you tomorrow."

I got up and paced in front of the fireplace.

"There, now you see?" I whispered, reprimanding myself. He probably has an entire chorus line of other women calling him. Heather on the other end of the line was probably a tall sexy blonde with big boobs and sex toys.

I pushed the thought aside and roughly focused my eyes on the shadow boxes that hung in decoration along the wall. The first displayed two decoratively carved wands. Apparently, Lucien believed in taking work home with him.

I heard him hang up the phone and I sidestepped to take a look at the next shadow box. I folded my arms in front of my chest and tilted my head to appear casual. I posed myself in a relaxed stance that said I didn't care that he was talking to another girl while my body still ached for him to kiss me. Nope. I didn't care. In fact, I was just standing here staring with fascination at this bronze-handled Wiccan ceremonial dagger. The knife was nestled against black velvet inside the shadow box and its ornate handle and scabbard were adorned with ruby inlays. My eyes locked on the sharp double-edged blade.

I sensed Lucien was beside me and vaguely knew he spoke just as my world slowly oozed to black.

chapter ten

Dark slid back to dim light at the cool, damp touch of a cloth to my forehead and I startled upright.

"Whoa, take it easy," Lucien said, his voice etched with concern as he eased me back to a prone position on the sofa.

I shook my head slowly from side to side trying to clear the cotton from my brain. "What happened?"

"You fainted."

I chuckled and sat up again slowly. "I do not faint. It was the wine. Too much wine." But even as I said the words my gaze slid uneasily to my right and I let out a whoosh of a relieved breath when I saw that the framed box containing the knife was no longer on the wall. I sat up more gently this time. "So how'd I get to the sofa?"

"I carried you."

"Don't suppose you got that on videotape?"

His lips twitched a little at the corners but still Lucien stood there intently studying me.

I stood up. "I'm sorry. I should go."

He took my hand and pulled me down, next to him, on the sofa. "Tell me about it," he said softly.

My shoulders did the up and down thing. "What's to tell? Too much wine and the heat of the fire…" My voice trailed off.

"And the ceremonial dagger?" he coaxed.

I shuddered involuntarily and it was not the orgasmic or near orgasmic shudder I had hoped to achieve on our date.

"You're safe here, Tabitha, with me. I may not understand everything you're feeling but I'm willing to bet I've got a better comprehension than most."

He was right about that. This kind of stuff was exactly up his alley. That should've made it easier to talk to him. It didn't.

"I put the dagger away," he soothed, "but maybe you should take another look at it."

"No way!"

"I'll be right here beside you. I'll help you, if you need it."

I leaned forward with my elbows on my knees and rested my face in my hands. "Today I spent the afternoon with a pregnant friend. When she put my hand on her belly to feel the baby kick I had a clear, distinct vision. I saw that the baby had something wrong with him. Only half of his heart was working." I swallowed thickly. "Now here I am out on a date. I take one look at that thing hanging on your wall and I pass out. It's getting harder and harder…"

"What?" he asked softly, laying a hand on my back. "What's getting harder?"

"To be normal," I whispered and felt hot tears slide down my cheeks. I bit the inside of my mouth to stem the flow of tears and got rigidly to my feet. "I need to use your phone."

When we pulled behind the abandoned stucco building there were already two vehicles parked. Both Detective Jackson and Lieutenant McGillvray were there, waiting expectantly. Lucien wordlessly parked his Saab near the dreaded Dumpster and I felt my stomach clench and roll.

McGillvray and Jackson were at my door before I could even open it.

I introduced McGillvray and Jackson to Lucien and there were manly nods and gruff handshakes to be polite.

"Okay, Miss Emery," McGillvray began, his thin lips disappearing in a tight smile. "Could you please bring Detective Jackson up to speed about what you told me on the phone, the reason for our visit here this evening? I have a phone call to make."

Lucien stood shoulder to shoulder with me and, at this point, he put an arm around my waist. He was obviously meaning to comfort me but the way I was attracted to him the only comfort he could provide would be in the sack. I looked from Lieutenant McGillvray's strained face a few feet away with a cell phone glued to his ear, then I switched my gaze to Detective Jackson's look of mocking disbelief. It was safe to assume I would be sack free in my near future.

"I had a vision. I saw the murderer using a ceremonial

dagger to stab a woman repeatedly." I sucked in air through my teeth and spat out the rest. "During his frenzy he sliced off a finger and it rolled down an open grate. I think it's still there."

"A finger?"

I nodded. "The heat vent didn't have a cover on it. When I was in there I got my foot stuck in the same vent."

Detective Jackson narrowed his eyes. "When were you inside the building?"

"Look, Detective, are you going to go and look for this finger, or not?" Lucien snapped.

Detective Jackson sighed, then shrugged. "Guess we're on a finger hunt, then."

He trudged to his unmarked car, opened the door and routed around until he pulled out a long black flashlight. Next, he made his way toward the back door of the building where Lieutenant McGillvray was waiting for him.

"Um, if it helps," I shouted after them, "it's a pinky!"

I paced alongside Lucien's Saab for a couple of minutes while he leaned up against his car and watched me warily.

"You know, I think I'll go inside and see if they need me to point out the right vent," I announced.

"You're the boss," Lucien joked and linked his arm in mine.

I didn't feel like the boss. I felt more like a puppet on a frayed string.

We walked in through the back door of the building and followed the flicker of a flashlight and the sound of lowered voices into the larger room. Detective Jackson stood with a little plastic bag in his hand facing Lieutenant McGillvray. They turned in unison to face us.

"Miss Emery, I don't know if you should be in here. This is a crime scene," Lieutenant McGillvray explained.

Jackson retorted, "It won't make a difference since she's already admitted to being inside the building." A look passed from Jackson to McGillvray that made my stomach roll, almost as much as the small piece of flesh inside the bag that Jackson held.

I glanced in Lucien's direction and saw him staring, obsidian eyes slitted and furious, as a yellow sliver of light from a street lamp illuminated the crude drawings on the wall.

"Eerie, aren't they? Gave me the creeps but I don't know why," I said, softly locking my gaze onto the drawing of an angel with the strange crescent on its head and then the circle with the cross inside. "Do you think the murderer took the time to draw those after mutilating that poor woman?"

Lucien pointed a finger at the drawings. There was a visible tremor in his hand. "These symbols are Satanic. They indicate a Black Mass has taken place here."

Detective Jackson nodded. "That's what the head of our gang unit said." He turned his hard eyes on me. "But we've known from the beginning this wasn't a run-of-the-mill murder."

I shook my head. "Run-of-the-mill murder? You mean to say some murders are normal murders? I guess you mean the everyday-walk-in-the-park-and-say-Oh-look-there's-a-dead-body murder? I'm sorry, but I guess I'm not as experienced as you are in that sort of thing."

I stomped out of the building. Outside I looked up at the dark sky and watched the clouds sliding in from the Pacific to blank out the stars. I felt, rather than heard, Lucien come up behind me.

"It's going to rain."

"Yeah."

"I'd like to go home now."

"Good idea," Lucien agreed.

When we reached the car I noticed McGillvray and Jackson shared a few words before parting company. McGillvray hopped into his own car while Jackson headed toward Lucien and me. Lucien had already started up his vehicle and I pressed the button to roll down my window.

"Yeah?"

"I'll be taking this to our crime-scene guys," Jackson stated flatly, leaning into my window and holding up the bag containing the severed finger. One end of the digit was festooned with a long nail painted hot pink. The other end was jagged and jellylike. I may never eat cherry Jell-O again.

"Is there anything else you wanted to say, Detective?" Lucien bit the words off angrily.

"Just one more thing." His granite stare fixed on me. "I told you before that I don't believe in coincidences. Yet, there seem to be an awful lot of them surrounding you. Right now my lieutenant seems to believe this psychic thing you have going on and, right now, that's the only thing in your favor."

I gave him a bite-me glare. "I don't care whether or not you believe I had a vision, Detective, but just how do you explain how I knew about the finger?"

"Personally, I believe that you're in this murder up to your pretty little neck. Not only do I believe it but I plan on proving it and—"

I didn't hear the rest of what Detective Moron had to

say because Lucien stomped on the gas pedal and we sped out of the lot.

"I don't trust that guy," Lucien growled a few minutes later as we cornered into my neighborhood. "He's looking for someone to pin this on and right now he's got no one but you."

I combed my fingers uneasily through my hair. "I didn't do a damn thing and he's got no proof that I did."

"I don't mind telling you that this Black Mass thing scares the hell out of me. It looked to me like some satanic sicko sacrificed someone in that building. Who knows," he went on, "maybe even more than one person."

"Thanks, Mr. Sunshine," I grumbled and instantly the revulsion of the evening combined with a stomach still full of seafood lasagna and wine caused me to reach my nausea limit. "I think you'd better pull over."

I didn't actually lose my dinner and for that I was massively relieved. I could think of few things worse than puking on a first date, especially in front of that first date. Mind you, I'm pretty positive that going on a scavenger hunt for a severed pinky finger was not up there with Lucien's favorite things to do on a first date, either.

A couple blocks later Lucien stopped the Saab in front of my building. He turned to me and offered a tentative smile. Then he reached over and stroked the side of my cheek with the back of his hand. "You look beat."

"Thanks again," I chuckled lightly and leaned in to his caress. "Sorry for screwing up our date. You're welcome to come in." I nodded toward my building. "I can't offer any fancy dessert to go with the great meal you prepared, but I've got potato chips and cold beer." *And a bed that would look superfantastic with your naked body in it.*

He pulled his hand away and I felt his unease.

"Maybe we should just call it a night."

Strike one.

"You're tired. I'm tired."

Strike two.

"This Black Mass thing has me a little freaked."

Strike three. Sigh.

I offered him a brave smile. "Sure. Fine. No problemo. I understand perfectly."

"I'll give you a call sometime."

Ouch. That hurt. I guess I had three choices. I could either A) act cool and aloof like I didn't care, B) I could try to change his mind with a steamy love session in the car or C) I could chalk this up to bad date number one million for Tabitha Emery.

I flung open the car door and narrowly missed smacking it into a person who'd approached the curb.

"My God, what are you doing here?" I offered Lina a quizzical look while slamming the passenger door behind me.

She scrubbed a hand over her face roughly. "I've been calling you all night and I just couldn't sleep until I knew that you were okay."

I heard another car door slam and turned to see Lucien's long strides rounding the back of his car.

"This may come as a surprise to you," I said to Lina, "but I was out on a date."

"You have got to be kidding." She shook her head incredulously. "Not with this idiot?"

My mouth fell open. "Lina, what the hell's your problem?" My eyes bugged in disbelief.

"Yes, Lina, why don't you explain it to both of us. I've always wanted to know if your exact problem could be narrowed down to one particular thing. I always imagined it to be an entire variety of problems."

"The only problem I have, Lucien Roskell, is *you*." Lina hissed.

"Apparently you two know each other." I flicked a look from one to the other. "And apparently you also hate each other."

"Come on, Tabitha." Lucien placed a firm hand on my elbow. "Let's go inside."

I tugged my elbow from his grasp. "I seem to recall you were too tired to come inside."

"And I seem to recall an offer of cold beer and potato chips. I've changed my mind." The smile he offered was forced.

"Send your boy toy home." Lina sneered. "He's not worth your time or your energy."

Part of my mind was listening to Lina and Lucien exchange insults. The other part was weighing my options. I could either A) invite only Lina into my apartment and satisfy my curiosity about her history with Lucien, B) invite both Lucien and Lina inside and have them finish scratching each other's eyes out in my apartment or C) ask Lucien to come inside and release my secret sluttiness and seduce him into having wild monkey sex with me. Of course, since he hadn't agreed to come in with me in the first place, there was a very good chance he had no desire to have even polite sex with me.

"Well?" they asked in unison and it snapped me from my revelry.

I glanced from one angry face to another.

"Here's my plan. I'm going into my apartment now. Alone. I'm going to play with my cat and then go to sleep. While sleeping, I'm going to do my best not to dream about slaughtered women and their detached body parts. What the two of you decide to do with the rest of your evening is up to you."

I whirled on my heel and trounced up to my building feeling proud but in a lonely, wish-I-could-just-get-laid kind of way.

Inside my apartment Inky appeared to be pouting and had no desire to play. In fact, he was choosing to ignore me altogether. I unfolded my sofa into the bed position, turned off the lights and tried to sleep. Then the phone rang.

"Hello?"

"How could you actually go out with someone like that?"

"Someone like what, Lina?"

"Someone like Lucien." She spat his name across the line.

"Actually, he's quite nice. Sexy. Successful. He can cook a half-decent meal and…"

"Oh, and I'm sure he's a fantastic lover, as well."

"I assume so, but I don't know for a fact since this was our first date and I'm not a slut." Although earlier I really wanted to be a slut, for at least one night.

"You mean you've only just met? Thank God!"

I sighed. "What's up, Lina? How do you two know each other and why do you despise each other so much?"

"We've known each other for about a year. We met when he first took over that absurd shop of his. You know that I belong to a group of Wiccans and Druids who get together occasionally?"

I searched my memory and shrugged. "Sure. I guess I know that."

"Well, when Lucien Roskell first replaced his brother as proprietor of the Scrying Room we asked him to speak to our gathering. It became apparent from that first speech that he is a nonbeliever, Tabitha, and don't let him try to convince you otherwise. His brother was open to many interpretations of pagan beliefs, but not Lucien. He is the vile of the most vile. He uses others' beliefs for his own financial gain. Of course, it works for him since many members of my group continue to purchase their supplies from him."

I waited for her to continue and when she didn't I coaxed. "So you hate him because he doesn't share your beliefs and he's successful?"

She blew out an exasperated breath. "Of course not! It is because with him it is all pretense. He puts on a huge show of being supportive of alternative beliefs, but he is not. I repeat, Tabitha, he is *not*. I just don't trust him."

"Okay. Whatever." I yawned. "I'm touched by your concern, Lina, really I am, but you have to stop being so worried about me. I'm a big girl and I can take care of myself." I thought about sharing the information about the Black Mass and the finger, but didn't feel like reliving it. We hung up and seconds later the phone rang again.

"Hello?"

"I owe you an apology."

My heart skipped a beat at the sound of Lucien's voice.

"You do?" I asked innocently. "What for?"

"For making you think that I didn't want to take you inside your apartment and kiss every inch of your body good-night."

I closed my eyes and pressed a hand to my heart. "You did?"

"Yeah. I did."

"Oh." Then why the hell didn't you?

"I didn't want to have memories of our first time in bed to be tied with bad things."

"Oh." How sweet is that? "I can understand that."

Silence.

"How long have you known Lina, Tabitha?"

"A while. We just recently mended fences."

"You should've let them stay broken."

"You don't like her."

"I don't trust her."

"There's a lot of that going around."

Just after ten the following morning I met up with Jenny, Lara and Cathy at Michael's Diner. The counter was filled so we settled for a cramped corner table. It had taken two cups of scalding-hot coffee and a jumbo sticky cinnamon bun in my stomach before I could relay the details of my date.

"So the guy takes you to his fabulous house in Capital Hill," Lara started.

"Makes you a superb meal," Cathy added.

"And you reward him not with sex, but by fainting, some horrific severed finger trip, nearly puking in his car and then meeting up with Lina?" Jenny concluded, her mouth agape in shocked disbelief.

"Yeah," I agreed. "That just about sums up my night." I motioned to the waiter for more coffee.

My three friends all shook their heads at me simultaneously.

"You blew it," Lara announced.

"He'll never ask you out again," Cathy stated.

"Oh, God, she's going to be back to mooning over Clay," Jenny concluded.

"I obviously forgot to mention that he called last night after dropping me off."

"He did?" they chorused and leaned forward in astonishment.

I nodded. "He said that he needed to apologize—" I drew quotes in the air "—for making me think that he didn't want to kiss every inch of my body good-night."

My three friends simultaneously sank back in their chairs and sighed.

"Fuck you, Tabitha!" Jenny blurted ferociously. "If you don't at least get into the sack with this guy I'll personally beat you to a pulp!"

I returned to my apartment feeling fulfilled by sweet buns, caffeine and friendships worthy of receiving beatings only to find Clay Sanderson pressing on the buzzer to my apartment. It was becoming painfully evident to me that people felt that I should never leave my apartment in case they just happened to drop on by. I could see Clay's expression crystal clear from my spot a few feet away and it was also painfully evident that his appearance did not exactly say that this was a social call. Hands fisted at his side. Posture rigid. He looked pissed.

Could it be that he'd already heard about my rendezvous

with Seattle's finest last night? Clay turned. His eyes locking onto mine, he mouthed a curse. Yep. No doubt about it, he'd already heard the news.

I sighed and closed the gap between us.

"I was going to let you know. Really."

"Oh, you were, were you? When? Tomorrow at work while you were passing me my other messages?"

Actually, yes.

"No, of course not! I was going to call you this afternoon and tell you all about it."

He fell into step beside me as I passed through the lobby and down the stairwell. We exited into my hallway.

"I don't get it. Why didn't you call me last night? We've been all through this and I thought I made myself abundantly clear that you were not to meet with the police without having me present."

We both turned suddenly when it became clear there was all sorts of activity at one end of the hallway. Detective Jackson was talking to Mole Man just outside my apartment and my apartment door was wide open.

"Well, you're getting your wish, aren't you?" I said to Clay sarcastically. "This time you get to be right at my side while I talk to the police."

We trudged down the hall together.

"What the hell's going on here?" Clay spat out before I could gather words to speak.

Mole Man, knowing a good moment to run when he saw one, dived into his own apartment.

"We have a warrant to search these premises," Detective Jackson proclaimed, holding up the white papers with a touch of triumph.

Clay snatched the paperwork from his hands and scanned their content with a scowl.

"You're looking for a murder weapon? This is ludicrous!"

Yes, it was ludicrous, ridiculous and preposterous, not to mention embarrassing to think Seattle's PD were at this very moment rummaging through my panty drawer in search of a knife. Still, all I could think of when I walked into my apartment and saw four uniformed officers going through my personal belongings was, where is my cat?

"Where's Inky?" I shouted at Detective Jackson.

"Where's who?"

"My cat! Where's my cat?" I felt hysteria bubbling in my blood when he only shrugged.

"I didn't see a cat. Maybe he went out."

"Tabitha, with all due respect we've got other, more important things to contend with," Clay said in his most official lawyer voice. At that moment I hated him. Lots.

"I happen to love that cat so I think it *is* important!"

He actually had the nerve to roll his eyes like I was some hysterical female. So I did what any normal ticked-off woman would do, I punched him in the stomach.

While Clay was doubled over in either shock, pain or both, the Mole Man appeared in my doorway.

"By the way, I've got Inky over at my place. I didn't want him to get all freaked out by all these people."

"Oh. Thanks, Mel." I glanced over my shoulder at Clay who, although a little pale, seemed to be recovering quickly enough to look as if he really wanted to slug me back.

"I'll bring him home after these guys are gone," Mole Man assured me, then leaned in to say, "You didn't do it, did you?"

"Of course not!"

He nodded. "I knew it. Any lady who cares about a little fluff of fur like Inky couldn't hurt nobody." Then he glanced at Clay and corrected, "At least, not fatally."

"Thanks."

I turned to Detective Jackson. "Hear that? You should have more faith in people. I'm a cat lover. I don't go around murdering people and tossing them into Dumpsters."

"It's not my job to have faith in people." He nodded toward Clay. "That's your lawyer's job. My job is to just nail your butt to the wall."

chapter eleven

I watched Clay Sanderson pace my apartment like a caged animal muttering legalese into his cell phone. Whenever I opened my mouth to speak he held up a finger and shushed me. Sheesh!

So I went over to Mole Man's to retrieve Inky and found Mel down on all fours wriggling a string across the floor for Inky to chase. Inky was looking at him like, *Yeah, right, if I wanted a piece of string I certainly wouldn't have to do tricks for it.*

Mel got abruptly to his feet when he saw me.

"Sorry about letting those guys into your apartment. I really had no choice."

"Yeah, I know. It's not your fault," I reassured him, while I scooped Inky into my arms.

"I actually like cats," he said blinking at me owlishly from behind his thick lenses. "I had a cat named Fluffy when I was growing up."

I smiled. "Well, thanks for taking care of him."

"You know, cats are smarter than dogs. For instance, you'd never find eight cats hooked up to a sled pulling some person around."

I laughed at the image. "You're right about that. Maybe you could cat-sit for me some time, you know, like if I have to go out or something."

His eyes lit up like a kid's at Christmas. "Yeah? That would be great."

What was really great was that Mole Man was not clothed in his Lycra Star Trek pajamas and was acting almost like a normal person.

I returned to my apartment to find Clay without his cell phone growing from his ear and actually in my kitchen attempting to make coffee. Not that I needed any more reason to be edgy, but I helped him out and we were silent while the coffeemaker hissed and dripped.

"Sorry I hit you in the stomach."

He grinned. "That's okay. Under the circumstances, I think you're allowed to lose your cool."

"You probably haven't had breakfast, right? Sorry I can't offer you eggs or anything. Would you like some toast?"

"Sure. That would be great."

I opened my refrigerator. No butter. Checked the bread box on the counter and noticed only one greenish slice of crust shoved to the back.

"Sorry, can't make you toast, either. How about some dry cereal?"

He laughed but it was forced. "Grab your coffee and come and sit with me."

I brought my mug over and sat next to him on the sofa.

We both drank deeply from our cups before he began speaking.

"Tabitha, about this whole murder investigation thing," he began.

"Well they didn't find anything did they? They came in here with their stupid warrant thinking they'd find what? A bloody knife, or something?" I shook my head with disgust. "That's just plain insulting. I mean, even if I was crazy enough to belong to some Satanic cult that was cutting up women as human sacrifices and even if I was sick enough to take a chopped-up woman and toss her in a Dumpster, that would not mean I would be so stupid that I would keep the murder weapon in my apartment, right?"

"Tabitha, you know—"

"And if I really *was* the murderer, why would I keep giving them all these leads? Do I *want* to be caught? If I *wanted* to be caught I'd just stand there and say, *Hey, it was me! I did it!* Even if I was crazy I don't think I'd waste everyone's time with these kinds of games."

"You see—"

"Well, maybe I would do that, if I was crazy, I mean, because if you're crazy then you really don't know what you're doing, do you? I think if you're crazy you're usually the last one to know and—"

"Shut up!" Clay shouted.

"Huh?"

He raked his fingers through his hair and turned to me. He reached and pressed a hand on my knee. "Just be quiet a second, okay? What I'm trying to tell you is that since you appear to be a suspect in a murder investigation, you'll need to take a break from your job at McAuley and Malcolm."

"What?" I jumped up, spilling coffee on the floor. "You have got to be kidding!"

"Now calm down, Tabitha." He got slowly to his feet. "It's only temporary."

"Will I get paid?"

"Eventually. Once your name is cleared and they find out who really did this, you'll get retro pay and your old job back."

"What if they never find out? You're a lawyer, I'm sure you've heard of unsolved crimes before, right?"

He sighed. "You must've known this was coming. You work at a law firm for God's sake, you didn't really expect that the partners would put the firm in a position of having word leak out that their receptionist is a suspect in a homicide investigation."

"I take it back."

"What?"

"I'm not sorry I punched you in the stomach." I wished I'd kicked him in the balls instead. "I want you to go now."

He frowned and walked to my kitchen and put his coffee cup in the sink then headed for the door. He had his hand on the knob to leave then, as an afterthought, he walked back to where I stood, cupped my face in his hands and kissed me softly on the forehead.

While I stood there stunned he silently slipped out of my apartment.

I sank back onto my sofa and covered my face with my hands. I told Inky, "My life's a mess. Can things get any worse?"

In answer to my question the phone rang. It was my mother. She always seemed to sense when I was at my lowest level of nagging resistance. She smelled it like a shark smells blood. Caught worn-out and in a state of complete surrender to my poopy life, I listened to her. Five minutes later, I'd actually agreed to go to both noon mass at Our Lady of Mercy and then afterward to my aunt Ruth's for lunch with her. Mom had even convinced me to wear the parrot earrings my aunt Ruth bought me last Christmas. Obviously, in this state of complete capitulation, I could be convinced to do anything.

Things did not go too badly with my mom. After only a couple of remarks about my skirt being too short for a good Catholic and my hair having no shape, she more or less kept her criticisms in check. I explained to her that I'd been temporarily laid off work and she gave me a check for a hundred dollars. I had a strong feeling that the price for that check would be higher than I'd like to pay, but I took it anyway.

Church turned out to be strangely refreshing. Maybe it was the act of just being forced to sit and do nothing for an hour, or perhaps there was actually something to the saying, what goes around comes around.

Later, as I sat at Aunt Ruth's table stuffing my face with corned beef on rye, I couldn't help but wonder about that. Maybe if I began to attend church more regularly, volunteered to help the elderly and got a job working in a soup kitchen, my crappy life would suddenly make a turnaround.

"Aunt Ruth, do you believe in kismet?"

"Huh? Kismet?" Aunt Ruth wiped mustard from her hairy upper lip. "Is that one of those new fancy coffees they've got at your Starbucks?"

I returned to my apartment with enough corned beef to feed both Inky and me for a week. I tried to coax Inky out from under my sofa with a sliver of the smoky meat but he turned it down. That was my first clue something was not right with my puddy tat. The second clue was the small puddle of bloodstained urine on my kitchen floor.

I hastily wrapped Inky in a blanket and rushed him to a vet. Two hours later Inky and I returned from the clinic. The good news was that the vet concluded that Inky had a very treatable urinary tract infection and only needed to receive a week of medication. The bad news was that the veterinary clinic apparently funded staff trips to Hawaii solely on emergency Sunday visits from panicked pet owners, who felt their pets would die if they had to wait until Monday. I'd squeezed the last of the credit from my replacement Visa to pay the bill.

"You'd better appreciate this," I instructed Inky while reading the label on the pill bottle. "Making you healthy involves me giving up food and might force me to date Doug No-Neck because now for sure I can't pay for the rest of my car repairs."

Inky did not look like he cared that I'd have to sacrifice myself in this way.

The antibiotics said I needed to give Inky one of the little pills two times a day. It seemed simple enough at the time.

First, take cat and pop pill into cat's mouth. Then, retrieve cat from under sofa and pill from across the room. Next, catch cat and ram pill down cat's throat. Retrieve cat from top of kitchen cupboards and pill from under sofa.

Get a new pill and resist urge to simply get a new cat.

Repeat process retrieving cat from bathtub and ceiling and retrieving pill from floor and toilet.

In my final attempt, I ended up leaving Inky suspended from my living room blinds and the pill tangled in my own hair.

This wasn't working. I needed help.

I walked across the hall and pounded on Mole Man's door. He opened and stared at me.

"You look like shit."

"Thanks. Have you ever medicated a cat?"

"Huh?"

"Have you ever had to give a pill to a cat?"

"Well, sure, but why—"

I dragged him across the hall and into my apartment and explained the situation.

"Get a towel," he ordered.

I did as he asked.

"Now get your cat and hold him using the towel."

I got a chair and held Inky at arm's length to keep his claws from my face. I pressed him into the towel while Mel proceeded to wrap the towel snuggly around Inky's small body with only his head protruding.

"Now get me his medicine."

I watched as Mole Man crammed the pill down Inky's throat and managed to keep him from spewing it back across the room. At the end of the procedure I had a new respect for Mel and paid him with the only thing of value I owned, I gave him my aunt Ruth's corned beef.

I called Jenny. When her machine came on I blurted out, "Inky's got a boo-boo on his pee-pee and the vet charged me lots of cash. The cops came to my place with a search warrant. Clay was here, too, but I punched him and then he kissed me on the forehead and I got canned because I'm a murder suspect. Call me."

By now, it was after dinner. I had no food. I had no money and I had no job to make money or to buy food. As days went, it was shaping up to be only second to the day my dad died and I discovered my mom's infidelity.

Maybe it was fate or maybe Lina really did have a clairvoyant link to my head but at that precise moment the phone rang and Lina invited me to meet her for dinner.

"I've got no money to go to dinner," I explained.

"I'll buy."

"Can I order two entrées and take one home with me for tomorrow?"

"I guess…"

"Will you loan me twenty bucks, too?"

"Christ, Tabitha, have you no pride?"

"Desperate times call for desperate measures."

"Fine. I'll loan you twenty bucks. Meet me at Tino's in an hour."

Tino's was a funky Italian place up the road from Pike Place Market. I ordered a Caesar salad, fettuccini alfredo and a lasagna to go. I didn't feel the least bit guilty when Lina only ordered soup.

Until the food arrived I did most of the talking while Lina listened. I rambled and spilled my guts all about my horrid evening and dreadful morning. When the waiter delivered my salad, my mouth was too busy to talk so it was my turn to listen.

"I was wrong to be critical of your dating Lucien and I want to apologize for that," Lina stated.

I paused with my fork halfway to my mouth. "You've always criticized everything I do and you've never apologized before. What's up?"

"I just think criticizing your choice in men goes beyond what my mentorship with you should be about."

I was going to argue that we were no longer in any kind of a mentor–apprentice relationship, but I had a mouthful of salad so I let her comment slide.

"I also wanted to invite you to a party on Friday."

"A party?" I swallowed a mouthful of greens. "What kind of a party?"

"A small dinner party at my place. A few close friends."

"Friday is Halloween."

"Yes."

"Samhain," I said.

She smiled. "Yes. Samhain is a time for honoring and communing with spirits that have passed to the other side. Perhaps you'll hear from your father."

I shrank back with horror and she chuckled lightly.

"I'm not talking about a gruesome exchange. The veil between the worlds is thin now. It is a great time to invite our beloved dead to visit."

"Sounds like fun," I said sarcastically. My throat was suddenly dry and I drank deeply from my water glass. "I think I'll pass."

"Why? Just so you can spend your Friday night boozing it up with your girlfriends like always?"

"What's wrong with that?"

"Nothing, if you do it because it's fun for you. Everything, if you only do it out of habit and lack of anything more fulfilling to do."

I wanted to say no, so I did. "No."

"Why?" She asked with genuine hurt in her voice.

"I'm too depressed to go out partying."

"Nonsense." She waved her hand in the air. "By Friday you'll be bored out of your tree from sitting around in the apartment. You'll be positively dying to get out."

I sighed and caved. "Okay, you've convinced me. I'll come over for dinner but then I'll go out with my friends."

When I returned home I placed the lasagna I'd gotten to go into my empty refrigerator then listened to my phone messages. All three were from Jenny.

The first one was obviously right after she'd heard my blurted message about my morning. "Jeez, I can't leave you alone for a second!"

Her second message said, "Hope you're not arrested, hee hee hee."

She *almost* sounded like she was joking.

The third one just said, "Damn! I'm coming over."

I had just listened to that one when the security buzzer sounded.

I pressed the button to open the door to the building and held my apartment door open. When Jenny arrived she had a six-pack of beer in her hand. She wrapped her big arms around me in a huge hug and whispered in my ear.

"Tabitha, your life is fucked."

I would've laughed if it hadn't been so true.

She ordered pizza even though I told her I'd already eaten. Jenny, being the true friend that she was, ordered two large pizzas from a two-for-one place, paid for it all and only ate a couple of slices before stuffing the boxes into the fridge. She also only consumed one of the beers while I slurped down three.

I whined, moaned, complained and poor, poor me'd for most of the evening. When Jenny left I was so exhausted from crying the blues I fell asleep and slept straight through the night.

Monday arrived without fanfare. I did not need to race around yanking on panty hose and stumbling out the door. It hardly even seemed worth it to shower, so I didn't, but then just after lunch I was bored so I took an extra long shower and made good use of the new shower massager.

It was sunny outside so I took a walk to a bank machine and cashed mom's check. Then I made my way to the corner store and stocked up on necessities like a peach facial mask and low-fat fudge cookies. While my mask hardened I debated the age-old question, just how many low-fat cookies could one consume before caloric intake overrode the low-fat benefits? It became evident that I could eat an entire bag.

When a knock came at my door I was not the least bit surprised. Just like the phone call you're waiting for that always comes when you're in the shower, someone will always show up to visit you when your facial mask is hardening.

I saw through the peephole that it was Clay. He was dressed in his tan-colored suit, the one that I'd always considered my favorite. He looked exceptionally hot. A few days ago I would've rushed to the bathroom to wash off the mask and then applied some makeup. Today, I didn't give a rat's ass what he thought.

"Oh, my God!" Clay exclaimed when I opened the door. "It's a facial mask."

"Why does it have those brown bits on your chin?"

"I believe those are pore minimizers."

"Funny, they kind of look like cookie crumbs."

"What do you want?"

"To come in, for starters."

"How is it that you got in without having to buzz me?"

He shrugged. "Another tenant was coming in when I got here. Are you going to invite me in?"

"No. Say what you came here to say and then leave."

He shifted uncomfortably from one foot to the other.

"Well, um, I talked to Lieutenant McGillvray."

"And…?"

"Are you sure you want me to talk about this in the hall? What will your neighbors think?"

"I'm blackmailing most of my neighbors. That makes me free to do what I want."

"Oh." He cleared his throat. "Okay, well I talked to the lieutenant. They ran the fingerprint from the, er, finger, that you helped them find. The woman was a known prostitute so her prints were in the system."

"Do you have her name?"

"They won't release it until they notify next of kin. She was twenty-one."

"Is that it?"

He nodded and I stepped back and began closing the door but Clay put up a hand to stop it.

"Look, Tabitha, I'm sorry about what happened. I know you're innocent and it's not fair that you can't come to work until you're cleared but that's just the way it is. The quicker this thing is solved, the quicker your life will return to normal, so if there's anything else about this murder that you can remember or—" he swallowed "—see in your mind somehow, you need to let me know so I can help you."

"Anything I give to the police they'll just use against me. They think that the only way I could have any information is to have been involved." I heard a crash and looked over my shoulder to see Inky had swatted a glass off my kitchen counter. "I gotta go and give Inky some medicine. He's sick."

I slammed the door and then leaned up against it as tears pricked the back of my eyes. The woman who died was twenty-one years old. She probably had hopes and dreams for something more in her life than the streets, but she never got the opportunity to reach for those dreams.

Damn. Nothing destroys a facial mask like tears.

chapter twelve

It was time. The last of the light was fading outside my windows. I withdrew the scrying mirror from the drawer I'd squirreled it away in and said a small prayer that using it would not make *me* squirrelly.

Inky attacked my ankles as I crossed the room and placed the mirror on the coffee table. I scowled down at the object, dreading having to use it again, but knowing I wouldn't rest until I did.

The phone rang and interrupted my scowling. I let the call go to the answering machine and Lucien's voice slid out of the speaker and wrapped around me.

"Hello, Tabitha. Tried calling you at work today and your friend Jenny told me what happened." Pause. "I get the feeling you're sitting in your apartment listening to my voice and just don't want to pick up." Another pause. "Are you scared to talk to me?" The mocking tone of his voice was followed by a series of bawk, bawk, bawk clucking-type noises.

I rolled my eyes and walked over to snatch the phone off its cradle.

"You know the entire purpose of owning an answering machine is so that you don't have to take someone's call if you don't want to!"

He chuckled throatily. "Ah, but you *do* want to take my call. Otherwise, you would not have picked up."

"I picked up because I can't concentrate with chicken noises in my apartment."

"What exactly are you trying to concentrate on?"

"If you must know, I was going to give the scrying mirror another chance."

"Now?"

"No, not now, because right now I happen to be talking to you."

"I'm coming over."

"What? No!"

"Promise me you'll wait and not use the mirror until I get there."

"I don't want you to—"

Click.

Damn.

So now I had to get out of my Seahawks jersey and sweatpants and change into clean jeans and a snug black Gap long-sleeved T-shirt. I didn't want Lucien to think I'd let myself go to seed just because I was temporarily out of work. Of course, after changing my clothes I brushed my hair, brushed my teeth, blushed my cheeks and painted my lips then dropped a dot of perfume between my breasts.

Inky sat on the toilet seat watching me. I swear he had a look of disdain beneath his whiskers.

"Don't judge me," I snapped. "I've seen the way you raise your tail in the air every time that slick Siamese comes on that cat food commercial."

The intercom buzzed, and with a wish and a prayer I pressed the button to let Lucien in.

"Let the games begin," I whispered.

I opened my apartment door on his first knock. He held up a paper sack. "I stopped by the store. I'm not exactly sure, but I think I've got everything we'll need."

I couldn't help but think that that was an awfully big bag for a single pack of condoms. He must have bought an entire crate. I was all atingle at the thought but my tingles quickly fell to disappointment when he began unloading the contents of the bag. First, he withdrew an intricately carved wooden wand then four votive candles.

"Oh, so you went to *your* store—" I tried to keep the disillusionment from my voice "—just to pick up a few Wiccan thingamajigs?"

He wagged a finger in my face. "I bet you didn't cast a circle of protection last time you used the mirror, did you?"

I seriously wanted to lean in and suck that finger. Instead, I merely shook my head. "Lina asked me the same question but I'm afraid I don't know much about that sort of thing. I'm not a practitioner of The Craft like she is."

"Lina! Hah!" He snorted. "She's the last one you would want to take advice from on the subject."

He took the candles, looked around, then brought them over to where I'd set up the scrying mirror on the coffee table. I followed him and watched him arrange the candles on the table.

"What do you mean? Who better to advise on these kinds of things than a practicing witch?"

His gaze measured mine. "I'm sure Lina practices many things. I doubt she's a true follower of any. You know what they say, jack of all trades, master of none."

"What are you trying to say? That Lina's not a Wiccan follower?"

He went to the counter and picked up the wand.

"What is it that you said to me when we had coffee together that time? Something about standing in a garage doesn't make you a car, right?"

I frowned. "I still don't know what you mean, Lina is—"

"Look," he interrupted. "Lina is *your* friend. She's not mine. Let's just leave it at that, okay? I don't have to like her to like you, right?"

"Fine." I nodded my head to the wand he was holding. "So you really think all this is necessary?"

He looked momentarily unsure. "Well, it certainly couldn't hurt and frankly the way things are going, Tabitha, you could use some protection."

I blew a strand of hair out of my eyes. "So Jenny told you? About the search warrant and everything?"

He nodded. "It's hard for the police to believe in anything that isn't tangible. Right now I'm sure that the only thing Detective Jackson knows is that you have laid out all his evidence for him. He'd be a fool not to consider you as a suspect when he doesn't have solid evidence leading elsewhere."

"He's a fool anyway."

"Yeah, you're right." He walked over and put his hands on my shoulders. "You have a gift, Tabitha. The fact that you're seeking a way to enhance it to help solve a terrible crime is a very noble thing. I just feel better knowing that if you're going to do this, that you do it as safely as possible and do it right."

I couldn't help but wonder if he would still consider me noble if I followed my desire and unbuckled his belt, unzipped his pants and…

"Are you ready?"

I nodded. "Let's do it." I wished sooo badly I was talking about rolling in between my sheets instead of staring into space.

"I'll cast the circle but I've only seen it done once and I've never actually done it myself. I believe that first—" he looked around and picked up Inky from the sofa, brought him into the bathroom and closed the door "—we need to make sure he's not inside the circle."

"Oh."

He handed me a book of matches and I lit the four candles surrounding the scrying mirror. Lucien turned off all the lights in the apartment plunging us into candlelight. It could have been romantic except for the fact that we were planning on searching for clues to a murder and not doing a lip lock.

Lucien took the wand and pointed it straight out. With intense concentration he walked slowly around my living room in a circle.

He pulled a small card from his pocket and winked at me. "Cheat notes." Then he began to walk the circle again while he murmured aloud, "I cast this circle to protect us from all negative and positive energies and forces on any level that may come to do us harm. I draw into this circle only the energies and forces that are right for us and the most correct for our work."

A third time he walked a circle, this time saying only, "I create sacred space. So mote it be."

I felt a chill skip up my spine as he took my hand and knelt with me in front of the scrying mirror.

"Go for it, babe."

I swallowed my lusty wishes for that comment, took a deep breath and closed my eyes. When I opened them I was gazing into, beyond and through the scrying mirror before me.

I felt an immediate draw, as though a powerful magnet was tugging at my thoughts and pulling them beyond the confines of my control. I was spiraling into a darkness that abruptly twisted to light. Images surrounded and washed over me. The mutilated cat lay inside the upside down pentagram. Hundreds of scarab beetles crawled out of the cat's wound and scurried away. The image washed away to be replaced by the Dumpster. On the edge of the Dumpster stood the naked lithe form of a woman. She was young, hardly out of her teens, with a face that was painted and roughened from life on the streets. Her peroxide blond hair was spiked short. Her fingernails and toenails were painted hot pink. Over her left breast was a tattoo of a red rose and inside the flower there was a single word that was blurred and unreadable. She looked over at me, smiled, then mouthed something I could not hear. I leaned in and heard her singsong voice echo into my ears, "He wants you. He wants you. He wants…"

Standing precariously on the edge of the Dumpster, she rose up onto the balls of her feet and placed her hands together prayerfully then swan-dived into the container.

I came back to reality wrapped inside Lucien's arms.

"He wants me!" I blurted.

Lucien slowly rocked me back and forth and murmured, "Hush now" as if speaking to a frightened child. My face was damp with tears. My clothes drenched in perspiration. I sniffed and hoped I didn't reek of BO.

With a burning need to push the images from my mind, I scrambled to my feet and nearly capsized the coffee table with my knee. Instinctively, I reached to steady the table and noticed with incredulity the votive candles, which had been new when lit, were now mere puddles of hot wax.

"I need a drink."

Lucien unfolded himself from the floor.

"I'll close the circle," he said and retrieved the crib notes from his pocket. He reversed the original process and ended by blowing out what was left of the candles and saying, "The circle is now closed. So mote it be."

He walked toward the kitchen. "I'll get you some water."

I shook my head. "Tequila. Top cupboard on your right."

I went around the apartment and flicked on every light in the place until it looked like high noon instead of midnight. Then I opened the bathroom door and snagged Inky from where he slept on the bath mat. I carried him over to the sofa with me and hugged him close to my chest. I found comfort in the feel of the quick beat of his heart beneath my fingers and the softness of his fur against my neck. Sex would've been better, but a cat cuddle was nothing to sneeze at either.

Lucien brought over the bottle of tequila and two small glasses. He poured us each a shot and we drank without speaking.

Inky, tired of my desperate clutch, wriggled from my grasp and hopped to the floor. With a shaky hand I reached and poured myself another shot of tequila, reveling in the shock of it burning in my throat as I swallowed.

Lucien moved the candles and scrying mirror over to the other edge of the table then sat down on the coffee table facing me, our knees touching.

"We should talk about it."

"I'd rather—" listen to elevator Muzak, run a marathon, pierce a nipple… "—not."

He reached his hands out and held mine. "How about if I talk and you listen?"

"Are you going to whisper sweet nothings in my ear?"

Amusement lightened his features and that was when I realized that I'd just spoken out loud.

"I can't believe I just said that."

Lucien brought my hands to his lips and kissed the inside of my wrists before releasing them. Then he reached into his inside back pocket and pulled out a sheet of paper.

"Here are some of the things you said while you were in your, um, trance."

I stared at him in disbelief. "You took notes?"

"Yeah. Does that bother you?"

I shifted uncomfortably on the sofa. "I don't know. It

just seems weird." Like discovering someone had been spying on you while you were sleeping and then realizing you'd had a dream about making it with a rock star. "How long was I out for?"

He glanced at the slim watch at his wrist. "A few hours."

I scrubbed my face with my fingers. Hours? Sheesh!

"Well, a lot of what you said I couldn't make out but there were a few things." He traced his scribbles with his finger. "You mentioned bugs and beetles a lot." He looked up at me.

I shivered with revulsion and nodded. "And…?"

"You talked about your dad."

My head shot up. "I did? What did I say?"

He touched my knee with his fingertips. "You said you were sorry and that you loved him."

"Oh." I held back the tears. "When Lina was mentoring me she encouraged me to go with my instincts when I had visions but at that time, nothing I saw was clear. Bits of this. Dabs of that. Sometimes my visions made sense and sometimes they didn't. I was with Lina when I had a vision of my dad clutching his hand to his chest and collapsing. Lina convinced me to stay with her so she could help interpret the vision." I snorted my disgust. "Of course, while we were discussing, my dad was dying." I shook the memory away. "What else happened tonight?"

"You kept repeating 'harm ye none' using a very upset tone of voice. You just kept repeating it over and over, like a mantra or chant."

"Harm ye none?" I rolled my eyes and rubbed the back of my neck. "Come on, who talks like that? Do you think I flipped over to the turn of the century?"

"Sounds like the Wiccan Rede to me. What do you re-member from the last couple hours?"

I squeezed my eyes shut. Words left my mouth before I could stop them, "Bide within the Law you must, in per-fect Love and perfect Trust." I had no idea where that came from. It was like I'd heard it before in a dream but not in one of my good dreams that involved me, a couple of buff Hollywood actors and whipped cream. I shuddered and looked up. "I don't even know what I just said."

"It's the first line of the Wiccan Rede."

Huh? "Well…I remember reading the rede in Lina's of-fice. It said something about harming none, but it didn't say anything about law, love or trust."

"The last line of the rede, 'An ye harm none, do what ye will,' is quite often framed or engraved on Craft paraphernalia, but the entire rede is many lines long."

"Well, how would I know it? I don't ever remember hearing those words before. Could I have read it some-where once and just remembered it now?"

He shrugged and I reached for the tequila bottle but Lu-cien took it from my grasp.

"Getting drunk is not the answer."

"I beg to differ. Getting drunk is definitely the answer." The only other way I could think of to clear my head was with earth-shattering multiple orgasms. I glanced up hope-fully but Lucien's face didn't register lust, only concern.

"I wish I knew more about this kind of stuff. I'd like to be able to help you."

"I'm beyond help," I blurted, only half joking.

"I do have contacts who are practitioners of The Craft. Tomorrow I'll make some phone calls and—"

I waved his words away. "That's all right. Don't bother. Lina's always available and, trust me, she'd be more than happy to take me by the hand with this stuff. Lord knows she's tried it before. I'm just not always a willing student."

"She's not the best teacher, either," he replied heatedly.

I opened my mouth to speak and then shut it again.

He reached around his neck and pulled the Pentagram of Solomon from around his neck then pulled it over my head. The amulet nestled between my breasts and the heat of his body radiated from it.

Lucien's finger traced the edge of the long silver chain around my neck pausing at where it dipped between my cleavage. His fathomless dark eyes searched mine.

"You need the protection from the Pentagram of Solomon far more than I do." He leaned in to kiss me and I felt his hesitation. There was no way he was getting out of it this time! I reached to link my fingers behind his neck and drew him close.

His lips met mine and his arms pulled me to him. When his tongue parted my lips, I sighed. When one hand slipped between us to cup my breast, I moaned. When he suddenly jerked away from me, I seriously considered stabbing him through the heart.

"What?" I growled.

He just shook his head slowly from side to side. "Not now. Not right after this." He nodded toward the scrying mirror still on the coffee table. "That would be taking advantage."

"Take advantage. I insist. As a matter of fact—" I stopped short, unable to speak. I felt something nudging my subconscious. Covering my face with my hands I breathed deeply between my fingers and let it come. A vision. A strong one. I gasped and yanked my hands away from my face then placed one over my jackhammering heart.

I whimpered, "Shelby."

"What?"

"The young woman who died. Her name was Shelby. She had a tattoo of a rose over her left breast and she thought she would fly."

"Fly?"

"Her soul." I swallowed thickly. "She wanted to be one with Satan."

chapter thirteen

I decided the best way to handle my current state of unemployment was to fill my days with activities from morning till night. Activities that would get me out of the apartment. Activities that were fun. Activities that were free. I made a pot of coffee and spent two hours that Tuesday morning with pen poised over a sheet of blank paper. I was able to come up with two things. Go to the library. Go to the park.

Then I remembered that I still owed the library twenty dollars for the time I borrowed Italian language tapes and never returned them. I hadn't been able to return the tapes because the Italian guy I was dating had just broken up with me. I'd taken the tapes, dumped them in my trash can and set fire to them, thus making them unreturnable.

Well, Discovery Park was always nice in the fall. A brisk walk through the crunchy autumn leaves could easily kill an hour or two. I heard the *pit-pat-splat* of rain pelting the ground outside my window and scratched off "Go to the park."

I picked up the phone and dialed McAuley and Malcolm.

An angelic voice picked up the phone and sang, "Good morning, McAuley and Malcolm. How may I direct your call?"

I hung up. Stared at the phone for two seconds then redialed.

"Good morning, McAuley and Malcolm. How may I direct your call?"

I hung up again. Who the hell *was* that? I waited a full minute before calling a third time.

"Good morning, McAuley and Malcolm."

"Jenny Arton, please."

"Just one moment," sang the pleasant voice.

"Jenny Arton here."

"Oh, my God, Jen, who the hell is answering *my* phone?"

"Hi, Tab. Her name is Debbie, they got her from a temp agency and, wow, is she great. Never loses a call, gets all the typing done on time. The partners all love her and…of course, not as much as they love you. Everyone's been saying how much they miss you around here."

"Really?"

"Sure."

I sighed. "I'm bored."

"Do your nails."

"Done."

"Do Inky's nails."

"Done. Clipped them, anyway. He wouldn't let me paint them."

"Hmm. What did you do last night?"

"Used the scrying mirror."

"Did it help?"

"No, but Lucien came over and helped."

"Sex?"

"Nope."

"Jeez, that sucks! Well, I'd like to chat more but I've got a stack of work looking at me from my inbox."

"Look, as my best friend in this entire world, you owe it to me to say something to take my mind off my troubles."

"Well, Candy is in Clay's office at this very minute and when she walked in she was crying."

"Really?"

"Yeah. Ah, shit. I gotta go. The Bitch is giving me the evil eye."

I hung up the phone and contemplated what having Candy crying while going into Clay's office could mean. Maybe they broke up! Maybe she was dying! Maybe she broke a nail!

Even though I'd already had my morning shower I decided to have another one and this time I attempted to try out every setting on the deluxe shower massager. I came out of the bathroom half an hour later wrinkled and feeling a need to go to confession. My mother, sensing this need, called and asked if, since I was no longer gainfully employed, I could come over and assist her with scrubbing the grime from behind her toilet.

"Sorry, Mom, I've got a job interview in less than an hour. Gotta go."

Click.

Whew, that was a close one.

I gave up and settled down in front of the TV. Since my sofa was still in the bed position, I was soon fast asleep. I woke up a while later to a sharp knock at my door.

I saw through the peephole that it was Clay. Crap—and me without a stitch of makeup on. Since the last time he was over he'd seen me with a peach facial mask on, I figured he could handle the makeup-free look.

I opened the door.

"Hi."

"Did I wake you?"

"Of course not. It's…" I glanced at my microwave clock. "It's nearly one o'clock in the afternoon."

He smiled. "You've got pillow creases on your cheek."

I narrowed my eyes at him. "Slow day at the office so you drove out of your way to harass ex-employees?"

"Nope. I'm here to take you to lunch."

I opened the door wide. "Come in. Give me five minutes to change my clothes and put on some lipstick."

His eyebrows went up in surprise. "Really? You're not going to give me a hard time about taking you to lunch?"

"Are you kidding? I've got no cash and no prospects for cash. I've got a leftover pizza in my fridge that has to last me all week. If you're buying, I'm going."

I raided my closet and left Clay in my living room while I changed and makeuped in the bathroom. I chose a long denim skirt and a cream cable-knit sweater. I shimmied into stockings, layered on mascara, painted on lipstick and powdered on blush. In under four minutes I was in the living room slipping my feet into low-heeled black pumps and grabbing my blue Gore-Tex jacket from a hook by the door.

While I'd been making myself beautiful, Clay had made himself comfortable sitting on the edge of my bed petting Inky.

"Let's go," I said.

"You're fast. When you said five minutes you weren't kidding."

"I never kid about free food."

He grinned. "I'm used to being kept waiting. Hell, when Candy goes to put on her makeup, I usually settle in to watch a DVD."

I angrily stuffed my arm inside my coat and stated stiffly, "I'm not Candy, or perhaps you haven't noticed."

I yanked up a strand of hair. "No blond here."

I opened up my jacket flasher-style. "No big boobs."

I lifted the hem of my skirt up to my knees. "Ugly legs."

He chuckled and strode toward me. "No. You're not Candy. You're beautiful just the way you are." He grabbed me by the jacket, zipped it up to my chin, put an arm around my shoulders and guided me out of my apartment.

We went to the Emerald Room for lunch. It's a revolving restaurant with a stunning view of Elliott Bay. Naturally, it was pissing rain so the only view was gray and dingy but I sure imagined the gorgeous view. In fact, I'd been imagining dinner with a date like Clay at this very restaurant since I was old enough to like boys. Probably even before that, but in those days I probably imagined eating up here with a pony.

Because it seemed tacky to order two entrées at the Emerald Room and take one home, I ordered just one large lunch, figuring I could always skip dinner. I ordered the swordfish and rice pilaf. Clay had a salad. I ordered a glass of the house white. He had water. His loss.

I sipped my wine and stared across the table at him. He was wearing a navy suit with a crisp white shirt and dark tie. Without a doubt he looked better than he ever had and I wasn't just thinking that because he was buying me an expensive lunch. The thing was, I didn't feel that usual animalistic attraction to him. Sure, he looked sexy and still had that Greek sex god thing going on, though for some reason, I didn't want to undress him with my teeth. Okay, I did want to do that, but not nearly as much as usual.

Then it hit me. Lucien.

Lucien was clouding up my lusty thoughts for Clay. He had my sex drive in such a state of chaotic overdrive I was probably afraid to get worked up over anyone else.

"What's up?" Clay asked, his eyebrows rising in amusement. "You look like you've just made an earth-shattering discovery."

I shook my head slowly from side to side. "You have no idea."

The waiter brought our food and I tried to pace myself, really I did, but the swordfish was heaven, the rice was delectable and the wine was getting to me. It never even occurred to me until we were sipping the best damn coffee in Seattle, sorry Starbucks, that I had not even asked Clay the obvious.

"So, why is it that you decided to come and take me out for such a nice lunch?"

He put his coffee cup down and looked over at me seriously. "I wanted to let you know that I went to bat for you with the other partners. They've agreed to keep you on salary."

My eyes bulged. "You mean I can go back to work?"

"No. You still can't return to your position but you will receive two-thirds of your salary and you'll keep your benefits."

"You're kidding me? I'm going to get paid but I don't have to come in?"

"Well, technically it'll be like you're on a paid vacation. Of course, that can't go on indefinitely. The deal will only be good for a month or so," he explained. "Hell, you won't even need it that long. As soon as they catch the moron who killed that girl or rule you out as a suspect, you'll be back behind your desk disconnecting calls, like usual."

"But what if the cops don't catch him? What if weeks go by but they get no new evidence?"

He leaned in. "I'm in touch with the lieutenant almost daily on this, Tabitha. If something breaks I'm sure I'll hear about it."

I nodded. "Sure. Thanks."

"As a matter of fact, just before I arrived at your place I got a call on my cell from McGillvray and he said they'd found and notified that girl's next of kin. See? They're keeping me in the loop."

"Shelby."

I saw the blood drain from his face. "What?"

"The girl's name. It's Shelby."

"How do you know that? They never released her name."

"I sort of saw it."

"Another one of your vision things? Ah, jeez. I'm afraid to ask but I guess I have to, what else do you know?"

"I saw her in my vision. Slim build, peroxide blonde with spiked hair, a rose tattoo, right—" I pointed just over my own left breast and stopped short. "Are you all right?"

He blew out a breath. "No, I'm not all right and you won't be, either, if you go to the cops with this newest revelation of yours."

I blinked at him. "I wasn't planning on it. They already know who it is."

He whispered roughly, "Don't you get it, Tabitha? You can't tell them that you know her identity and especially her description! What conclusion do you think they'll make with that little tidbit of information, huh? They'll think you know her identity and can describe her tattoo because you were *there* at the scene of her murder, or that *you* were the one who killed her!"

His hand was in a white-knuckle fist on the table. I reached over and covered his hard fist gently with my fingers.

"I'm touched you're so worried about me, but don't be. I haven't done anything wrong."

He yanked his hand back and rolled his eyes. "Do you know how many times I've seen innocent people go to jail?"

"No. How many times?"

"I don't know and that's not the point."

The waiter headed in our direction then quickly turned to go the opposite way at the sound of our angry tone.

"Oh. I thought that *was* the point."

"No. The point is that it does happen. Innocent people go to jail. The system's not perfect."

"Thanks for trying to make me feel better," I said dryly. "I know the system isn't perfect, but nothing's perfect."

"What does that mean?"

"Just that. Absolutely nothing in this world is free of flaw."

I pursed my lips together because I really wanted to tell him that A) it's so wrong to ply a woman with swordfish and then remind her that she could go to jail, B) he was not exactly going to win lawyer-of-the-year if this was how he usually talked to his clients and C) he really did look damn hot in that suit.

Instead I blurted out, "You know, Clay, I used to think *you* were perfect."

"Me?" He sank back into his chair, his anger switched to stunned surprise.

"Yes, you. I thought you were the most attractive man that I'd ever laid eyes on. I drooled over you for almost two years."

He grinned. "You did? What happened?"

"I guess I got over it."

His smile faltered. "Got over it? Just like that?"

"Well, no, not just like that."

He nodded knowingly. "There's another guy."

I didn't answer.

"It's that guy who sent you that mirror thing, right?"

"Lucien? Maybe."

"No maybes about it."

We were quiet for a moment and then Clay reached his hand across the table and linked his fingers with mine.

"I had a thing for you, too, Tabitha," he whispered hoarsely.

"You did? Guess it's a good thing you got over it, what with Candy and all."

"I never said I was over it." He released my hand and signaled the waiter for the check.

When he pulled his Miata up to the front of my building I turned to thank Clay for lunch and for the good news about my paycheck, but the words got lodged in my throat.

"What's wrong? Do you have something in your eye?"

I touched my forehead and closed my eyes tight. After counting to ten, I slowly opened them again.

"Oh, my God, she's pregnant."

Clay shifted uncomfortably in his seat. "Who? What are you talking about?"

"Candy. She's pregnant. That's why she was crying this morning in your office. She just found out." I swallowed the lump in my throat. "And you're going to marry her."

"Wait a second, I never told you—"

"You didn't have to."

"So this was one of your visions, huh?" He shook his head slowly from side to side. "I have to admit, it's very strange seeing it happen up close, even if it's not completely accurate. I never told Candy I'd marry her. That doesn't mean I'll shirk my responsibilities, either." He shrugged. "In this day and age pregnancy isn't enough of a reason for marriage and a man can be a father without the license."

Some men might be able to support a woman and child without the license but Clay couldn't. I didn't even need to have the vision to know that. I looked at Clay and felt sorry for him. I'd seen it all. The wedding. The baby. The angry divorce two years later.

I leaned in and kissed him gently on the mouth, then patted his cheek softly.

"Thanks for the lunch."

I was glad to get that lifelong dream of having a meal at the Emerald Room off of my To Do list, but it had left me with a bad taste in my mouth.

chapter fourteen

Now that I knew I was getting paid two-thirds of my salary just to sit on my ass, sitting on my ass had actually become an appealing thought. With my feet up on the coffee table, Inky and I shared some dry cereal and watched *The Price is Right* while cheering on the trailer trash. Our plans for later in the day involved moving my sofa bed and vacuuming beneath it. After that I could either A) tackle removal of the mildew in my shower, B) exercise to improve my poor muscle tone or C) ignore both problems and watch soap operas. The possibilities were endless.

Martha called when *The Price Is Right* was almost over. I was relieved to hear her voice.

"It's good to hear from you," I said and meant it. "Were your mother-in-law and sister-in-law angry about your skipping out of the shower?"

"No. I think they were relieved."

"It all worked out, then."

"I'm actually calling about what you said about the baby. You said I should go to my OB-GYN and get him to do another ultrasound." Her voice had grown softer. "That was because you saw something that was wrong with the baby's heart, right?"

I debated lying, then decided against it. "Yeah, but maybe I'm wrong. Maybe the baby's fine."

"You weren't wrong. I had another ultrasound. The baby has hypoplastic left heart syndrome."

"Oh, God, I'm sorry, Martha!" I hoped it wasn't as bad as it sounded.

"Don't be sorry. If it wasn't for you they probably wouldn't have noticed until after he was born. The damn technician should've seen it on my earlier ultrasounds, not that there was anything we could've done even then."

"You called the baby *he?* Did you find out the sex then?"

She chuckled. "No, but you called the baby 'a little guy.' Since you were right about the heart thing, I'm betting you're right about it being a boy."

I didn't deny it.

"How serious is this heart thing?"

"Serious. Maybe surgery. Maybe a transplant. I just wanted you to know that you were right and that I'm glad I found out now. It's better than having to deal with the news later on."

Getting news like that at any time couldn't have been good.

"I also told Sonya that you should be the one to get my job when I go on maternity leave and with the baby's health being what it is, I won't be coming back to work, either. The job's going to be yours permanently."

"Thanks, Martha, but the way my situation is right now, who knows if I'll be coming back to McAuley and Malcolm."

"Well, personally, I think it sucks that they aren't letting you come to work."

I brushed cereal crumbs from my Seahawks jersey and shrugged. "It's not so bad."

"Well, as Clay's secretary, I do know a little of what's happening with you." She lowered her voice. "I know you didn't do it, Tabitha, and I told Clay that if you need a character witness or someone to testify about your psychic ability, man, I am so there for you."

"Um, well, thanks. You know, there is one thing I was hoping to find out."

"Anything."

"The girl who died, Shelby, she was a prostitute, right?"

"Yeah, that's what the cops said."

"Is there any way that you could find out what area of the city she worked?"

"Why?"

"To tell you the truth I'm not sure. It just feels kind of important."

"I'll see what I can do."

I went for a walk through the October drizzle to the store to stock up on cleaning supplies then trudged back to my apartment. When I returned I saw that Martha had already left a message on my machine with the information I'd requested. I sprayed cleanser on my shower tiles while contemplating what to do.

I came up with a plan. It wasn't necessarily the best plan but I could always blame it on inhaling the dimethyl ethylbenzyl ammonium chloride that I'd sprayed in the bathroom.

I called up my friends and asked them to come over, and one by one the three musketeers made themselves comfortable in my apartment. Jenny arrived with a gift. She had bought me a canary-yellow nightgown with a black cat on the front. She also sported new canary-yellow hair, Ashen Allure, courtesy of a sale at Neuman's Drugs.

"Um, thanks for the nightie," I said, holding it up questioningly. It was probably the ugliest nightgown I'd ever seen.

"Well, you're officially a cat person. You'll have to expect gifts like that now. Pretty soon people will be giving you all kinds of cat knickknacks."

"Really?"

Jenny nodded sagely.

"So, when are you going to tell us what we're all doing here?" Jenny asked.

"Yeah, I traded two shifts to get the night off," Lara piped up.

"And I had to leave Jeff pouting in the apartment because he thought I was holding out on him about what I was doing," added Cathy.

"Well, girls, you'll be thrilled to find out that we are trolling for hookers tonight," I announced.

My three friends shared identical looks that said *You have got to be kidding.*

"Look, we know you're bored, Tabitha," Jenny began,

"but it's Tuesday so the Skin Spot has drink specials with their male exotic dancers tonight. I make a motion we reconvene this meeting at that location."

"I second that," said Lara.

"Third," added Cathy.

"Whoa." I held up my hand to stop them parading toward my door. "We are on the lookout for hookers, specifically hookers who may have known Shelby Kent—the prostitute killed and tossed into that Dumpster."

"How exciting!" Jenny rubbed her hands together. "This is like some kind of undercover thing, right?"

"What kind of undercover thing?" Lara glanced down at her blue jeans and sweatshirt. "I'm not dressed up to pretend to be a hooker."

Cathy frowned down at her own attire, which consisted of jeans and a red cotton shirt. "If you give me a second to put on more makeup and tie this shirt under my boobs, I might be able to pull it off."

I sighed and explained slowly, "We are not going to act like hookers. We're going to go and talk to hookers."

"Oh," they chimed together.

"Don't you think that kind of takes all the fun out of it? I mean, it's your field trip, Tabitha, so you're the boss but, personally, I think we could spice it up a bit," Jenny suggested.

We stopped at a McDonald's drive-through and picked up burgers and shakes for our adventure. My Escort reeked of a combination of fried food and perfume while I took the drive down to Klinsky Road.

"It's a good thing it stopped raining," Cathy commented. "I don't think hookers work the streets in the rain."

"Of course they work in the rain," Lara insisted. "If they didn't work in the rain in Seattle they'd never work."

"That's right," Jenny agreed. "Hell, they probably make more money in the rain 'cause then they have that whole wet T-shirt thing happening."

I was beginning to rethink bringing my friends along on my little escapade.

"Oh, there's one! There's one!" Lara squealed and pointed at a woman in a black Lycra cat suit and stilettos.

"Don't be pointing and shouting," I hissed. "Besides we're not going to be talking to just any hooker. I'm looking for Shelby's corner. I want to talk to the ones who worked near her."

I drove up and down Klinsky road so many times I finally had to stop and get gas. While I was getting gas, my friends went into the convenience store to stock up on reinforcements, namely jalapeño chips and diet soda.

Once we'd all loaded back inside the car I headed down the street. With a deep breath and a silent prayer I steered to the curb at the corner of Klinsky and First.

"Is that the one?" Lara asked, wide-eyed behind her black-rimmed glasses.

"She looks kind of scary," Cathy said anxiously.

"Yeah, why can't we talk to that one across the road with the cool white boots?"

I let out an exasperated breath. "I'm going to do the talking. You guys are just here for moral support, okay?" I climbed out of my car, and walked around the front, up the curb and toward the woman in the flaming-orange wig and the hot-pink vinyl miniskirt who walked four steps to the left, turned, walked four steps to the right.

"Um, excuse me, miss?" My voice wavered a little around the edges.

Miss Orange Wig turned and eyed me skeptically but didn't stop her pacing. "Yeah?"

"I was wondering if I could have a word with you?"

"Honey, I don't get paid to talk." Four steps to the right. "And I ain't running no circus show, either." Turning, four steps to the left. "If you and your friends are going to park there, you're gonna scare off all the legitimate customers."

"I just want to talk to you a second." I fell into step beside her, turning, walking four steps to the right. "I could give you ten bucks if you answer a few questions." Turning, four steps to the left.

"Make it twenty." Turning, four steps to the right.

"Okay, twenty."

Abruptly, she stopped walking and stuck out her hand.

"I'll go get it." I headed toward the Escort and motioned for Jenny to roll down the passenger-side window. When she did, I whispered, "Pass me my purse."

I dug out a twenty then turned to find Miss Orange Wig right behind me.

"Do I smell fries?"

I gave her the twenty but she leaned in toward the car. "One of you gals got fries in there."

"Sorry, we ate all our fries," Jenny said.

"Man, I'm starving. What's in that bag over there?" She asked, pointing a long, orange-painted nail toward the McDonald's bag on the floor by my seat.

"My Big Mac, I didn't get a chance to eat it yet," I replied.

"Tell you what, I'll answer your questions for the twenty and the Big Mac."

I rolled my eyes and asked Jenny to pass me the bag. I thrust it into Miss Orange Wig's waiting hands. While she unwrapped the burger and bit into it I talked.

"I wanted to speak to you about Shelby Kent."

Miss Orange Wig stared with disgust down at her burger then over at me. "I can't be eating and talking about my friend getting cut up for rat food at the same time." She belched. "I'll get indigestion."

"Hey, you said you'd talk if I gave you the burger and the twenty, so talk!" I shouted.

"Don't you be yelling at me, or I'll take your burger and the twenty and see you in hell."

I blew out a breath. "Fine. I'm sorry. Now about Shelby, do you remember anything about the night she went missing?"

"I already told all this to the cops," she whined, stuffing the last of my burger into her mouth.

"Please?"

"Well, like I've told everyone who's asked, Shelby was a good shit, you know? But she wasn't very particular about the kind of folks she took off with. She'd go with anybody and do anything for the right price. She had the goods, too—young, skinny, so she always got the price."

"So did you see who she went with that night?"

Miss Orange Wig tossed the empty burger wrapper and bag back through my passenger window and Jenny ducked to avoid getting hit in the head with them.

"She wasn't out here long. She said she was meeting a regular and going to some big party."

"Did she say where the party was, or who was going to be there?"

"Nope. And I can tell you I tried to get her to take me."
She looked skyward and made the sign of the cross. "Lord,
I'm glad she didn't let me go with her. She said they only
wanted her and that was all."

"So were you here when she got picked up?"

"I wasn't here in this exact location. I was over in the
alley." She nodded the orange wig in the direction of a
dark lane between a crumbling brick hotel and a parking
garage. "I was kind of indisposed at the time."

Yuk.

"Okay, so you didn't see who picked her up."

"I never said I didn't see. I just said I was indisposed."

I closed my eyes and willed myself not to grab her by
the shoulders and shake her fillings loose.

"So did you see who came to get her, or did you not?"

"As I told the cops, there was a man in a dark car."

"A man? White? Black? Hispanic?"

"White."

"That's it?"

"Well, he was wearing a baseball cap, and I'm pretty sure
the guy was a regular. Shelby sometimes went to some kind
of religious meetings with a guy. It may have been him.
He'd pay her to go, so she didn't mind. Actually, she said
she was kind of into it."

"Do you know where these meetings were?"

She shook her head and the orange wig bobbed with
the motion. I asked her a few more questions and then
Jenny had a couple inquiries of her own. We left Miss Orange Wig to work her corner and I drove my friends home.

That night, in the comfort of my own bed while dressed
in canary-yellow flannel, I dreamed of a shapeless form in

a hooded cloak that deliberated and plotted to kill again. It was a celebration, although it definitely wasn't a Tupperware party.

On Wednesday, Inky and I spent a boring day as couch potatoes. The phone didn't ring once and even the shower massager had lost much of its appeal. I was tempted to drink the rest of my medicinal tequila for excitement, but I convinced myself that drinking hard liquor while watching soap operas was too depressing. Even for me.

Getting paid to sit on my ass was quickly losing some appeal, too. After twelve consecutive hours of television watching, I was convinced that my whites could be whiter and I'd never obtain that elusive just-showered freshness. In short, I was losing my mind.

Thankfully, the phone rang Thursday morning only seconds after Inky and I had settled into our TV-watching position, snacks in hand.

"Hello?"

"Are you still bored?" Jenny asked.

"Let me check." I glanced around. "Yep. I'm still bored. Nothing remotely exciting has happened to me since Tuesday night when you tried to buy sexual secrets from the orange-wigged prostitute. Why are you asking?"

"Because I thought that if you were really and truly bored with nothing else to do today that you wouldn't mind giving your best friend a lift after she got off work."

"Where are you going?"

"I'm meeting Brad at Pike Place Market."

"Who is Brad?"

"My parents' gardener's son."

"Sorry I asked and I'm sure I'll be equally sorry that I asked why you're meeting him at Pike Place."

"He works there at a fish market. He wants me to meet him before he gets off at six and pick out a piece of fish, then we're going back to his place and he's going to cook it for me."

"That's almost romantic, in a stinky-fish kind of way."

"Yeah, I thought so, too, except that it is absolutely pouring outside and it's supposed to continue to pour for the rest of the day. If it's still raining at five o'clock I'll never get a cab and make it down to Pike's by six."

"So you want me to be your five o'clock cab ride."

"Pleeeeease?"

I popped some cereal into my mouth then fed a nugget to Inky. I relented. "Okay. It'll take my mind off what I've been thinking about."

"Oh, and what have you been thinking about?"

"I've been thinking about how I want to find Lucien and drag him into bed with me."

"Are you serious?"

"Yes. No. Maybe."

"Wow, bored *and* horny. That must be awful."

"It is."

It took a while for me to come up with a plan regarding Lucien. I was still working out the details when he threw all my planning out the window and called me.

"I thought I'd invite you to lunch."

"Lunch? You want to take me to lunch?"

"Yes."

"There's a lot of that going around."

"What?"

"Nothing. When?"

"Today, if you're not busy."

"I am so not busy."

"Great. Come by the store around noonish."

Click.

I wondered if it was possible to seduce someone over a lunch hour. Maybe, if only I convinced him to make me lunch at his place, or at a motel. I ran my fingers through my hair and decided that I would not continue to act like a slut no matter how proud Jenny would be of this behavior.

Lina called while I was eyeing my wardrobe critically.

"I just wanted to remind you to be at my place for six tomorrow."

"Six o'clock. Got it. You remember that I'm meeting Jenny and the girls later, right? I'm not planning on staying all night."

"You say that now, but who knows?" Lina said tightly. "Maybe you'll be having so much fun you won't want to leave." I heard her talking to someone else nearby. "Sorry, Tabitha, I've got to go. The library is having an author signing today and it's just nuts around here."

"Anyone I know?"

"Narda Kaminsky."

"The romance writer?"

"Yeah. Don't tell me you read that stuff?" She spoke with derision.

"On occasion." Every time one of Narda Kaminsky's books came out I ran and bought one. They're the perfect blend of escapism and erotica. Given the way my life was going, I clearly needed both.

I could almost hear Lina tsk-tsking before she disconnected.

I went back to my clothes and tried to decide which of my outfits would convince Lucien Roskell to have a nooner with me.

An hour later, I'd showered, blown dry and burned the top of my scalp with the curling iron. I tucked myself into my WonderBra and poured myself into a clingy seafoam knit dress with a short skirt and a plunging neckline that, according to The Bitch, was inappropriate office attire. I scrutinized my reflection in the mirror and concluded that I was well balanced between sexy and loose. Perfect.

I was done the makeup thing a few minutes later, glanced at my watch and wondered what I would do with myself for the next two hours before meeting Lucien. I couldn't sit, hell I couldn't even lean against a wall in my apartment without wearing Inky's hair as a fur coat. It was in that moment when it occurred to me that the library wasn't too far from the Scrying Room.

I arrived at the Emerald City Library with intentions of meeting one of my all-time favorite authors. It never occurred to me that there would be hundreds of other women with exactly the same idea. I looked at the long lineup snaking across the main room and decided it really wasn't a priority to have my copy of *Passion in Paradise* signed. Instead, I elbowed my way through the crowd across the autobiography section until I found Lina's office. I knocked but there was no response. I tried the door and peered inside and saw she wasn't there. Oh, well, I'll just leave her a note to say hello. I walked around her desk, sat in her chair and reached across her daybook to snag a pen and a scrap of paper: "Came by to say hi. Sorry I missed you, Tabitha."

I dropped the note onto her daybook and my gaze landed on her margin scribbles. I frowned at an address written in Lina's lazy scrawl in the upper right corner, 811-156th Avenue. The address of the vacant building. My fingers rose of their own volition to trace the address and when my flesh came into contact with the paper my head began to swarm with a thousand images: grotesquely maimed animals, their bodies impaled inside inverted pentagrams, their faces contorted with the agony of their deaths. I yanked my finger away from Lina's daybook and rose unsteadily to my feet.

I left the library grateful to have my lunch with Lucien to distract me from the images in my head. On my way to the Scrying Room I drove to a Dairy Queen drive-through and picked up a thick chocolate shake. Nothing says soothing, placating comfort for strung-out nerves than fat and calories. At least this way I wouldn't eat so much on my lunch with Lucien. I would appear less than my usual piggy self and I'd also free up my hands and mouth for more sexually-oriented activities.

I applied more lipstick, then got out of the car and smoothed my dress. When I entered the Scrying Room, the sight of a tall, stunning redhead working the counter accosted me. I felt the confidence in my sexy-slut appearance fly out the window. I slowly approached her feeling like a bulldog at a poodle show. I hated her.

The redhead looked up. "Hi, can I help you?"

"My name is Tabitha. I'm here to see Lucien."

She smiled broadly. "Hello, Tabitha. I'm Heather."

Heather. As in the woman Lucien had chatted with on the phone when I'd been at his place. They worked together and were probably sleeping together. I despised her. I wanted to reach across the counter and pluck her eyes out.

"Nice to meet you," she said and stuck out her hand for me to shake it. Her silver bangles jangled at her delicate wrist making me loathe her even more. "I was just telling my husband the other day that I wished Lucien would meet some nice girl. Then Lucien told me he was expecting a gorgeous brunette to show up for a lunch date today. I almost didn't believe him, but here you are, and you're absolutely stunning."

I shook her hand warmly and tossed her a face-splitting smile. I loved her. I wanted to reach across the counter and kiss her perfect face and then I wanted to adopt her as a sister.

"Lucien is in a meeting with a client and is running a little behind schedule. He's hoping you could meet him."

She glanced up when a young couple in gothic makeup stepped into the shop.

Heather quickly scrawled a number on a notepad and handed it to me. "You can use Lucien's office in the back to call him on his cell."

I walked through the rear entrance where utility shelves were crammed floor to ceiling with boxes. To my right was a door and I took a guess and stepped inside. The large room had a heavy oak desk, burgundy chairs, filing cabinets and in a corner there was a fridge, microwave and coffeemaker. It looked like Lucien's office doubled as the staff lounge. I arranged myself in a burgundy leather chair behind the huge desk and reached for the phone. I pressed a button for an outgoing line and dialed the number that Heather had given me.

"Hello?"

"Hi."

"Sorry I couldn't be there to meet you. Is it a problem for you to meet me for our lunch?"

"No problem. I've got no other plans." Besides maybe making out in your Saab after we eat.

"Great. Can you meet me at the Seattle Art Museum?"

"The art museum?" I picked up a pen and began doodling on a notepad that was filled with other scribblings.

"Yeah, I'm in a meeting here but I should be finished by the time you arrive. I'll meet you in the café."

"We're having lunch at the museum café?"

"Yeah, best salad nicoise in the city."

"Okay. Sure." I felt my hopes for a romantic lunch followed by a passionate groping in his back seat fading fast.

I hung up the phone and sighed. I glanced down, appalled at the doodles I'd drawn on Lucien's notepad. I'd added a variety of phallic symbols next to his tame doodles that were mostly cubes and cobwebs. Okay, I was definitely sexually frustrated. I tore the page from the pad. I didn't want to toss it into his trash where he might see it, so I folded it and tucked it into my purse. When it was a small pressed square, a message that he'd written in the corner of the pad stared up at me: "Pacific Refuse Inc." and a phone number.

I felt a tickling in the back of my mind. It was not unlike when you've forgotten something important. I was

sure that tickling could easily be confused with the skit-
tishness that accompanied a sexual dry spell so I ignored
it and tried to drum up real enthusiasm for a visit to the
museum.

I paid for my Escort to be slotted in a parking garage
at First Avenue and Union Street. The sky was clearing
and the autumn day warm so I left my jacket in the car
and hoofed it the block down to the art museum. My
confidence was buoyed when a construction crew on
University Street whistled and hooted as I walked by.
That same confidence plummeted when I realized the
noise was directed to the buxom teenager in short-shorts
behind me.

I was seated at a small circular table in the café with
a menu. I noticed the special of the day was Willamette
Orchard Salad with pears and toasted hazelnuts. What
I really wanted to satisfy my appetite was not listed on
the menu but walked smartly into the restaurant a
minute later.

He paused at the table, his gaze traveling keenly over my
body. "Wow. 'She walks in beauty like the night, of cloud-
less climes and starry skies,'" Lucien whispered. He bent
and planted a smoldering kiss on my cheek.

After that, it was hard to keep my mind on lunch, but
Lucien appeared content with food and conversation.
Damn. I had the smoked salmon chowder and Lucien
feasted on the nicoise salad with rosemary potatoes. I
listened while Lucien talked excitedly about art. After
we ate, he insisted on escorting me on a tour of the
museum.

"Do you realize the Seattle Art Museum has thousands of objects and close to fifty-eight hundred artworks?"

"You're not planning on showing me all of them are you?" I asked dryly.

He threw back his head and laughed. "You're bored."

"No, I'm not." Yes, I was. "I just didn't select shoes to stroll through a museum."

He glanced down at my Burberry knockoff ankle-strap sandals with the three-inch heels.

He leaned in and murmured into my ear, "I promise you a foot rub later." Then, in his regular tone he announced, "We don't need to go any farther." He waved his hand to the exhibition we'd arrived at. "This is what I wanted to show you."

I looked around the alcove, which displayed a variety of carved masks.

"Hmm. Interesting." *Not!*

He placed a hand on the small of my back and led me to a corner where a grotesquely carved wooden goat head, with flaming eyes, sat staring back at me.

"I found this among my brother's private collection and knew the museum would love it for this exhibit."

I swallowed uneasily. "What is it?"

"An etching on the back refers to it as the Horned God." He shifted his weight from one foot to the other. "I've done a little reading on the subject and it seems horned gods were worshipped in most of the world for centuries. They've always been part of a polytheistic belief system that accepts many gods. Amazing, isn't it?"

My eyes would've glazed over if I hadn't felt the pull of the vulgar mask before me.

I shifted uncomfortably. "Um, you know, I find it hard to find anything linked to the devil amazing." I flicked an irritated gaze at him. "Actually, I think it's repulsive."

"You just have to keep an open mind."

"Someone once told me that if you're too open-minded, your brains will fall out."

"Clearly there's no danger in that happening to you," he said curtly. "Sorry for thinking that you'd find a piece of art interesting."

I whirled and planted my hands on my hips. "You invited me to lunch, remember? Not an art lecture. Thanks for the meal. See ya around."

I walked away as quickly as was possible given the ankle-strap sandals and the marble floor, but wasn't exactly speedy. He caught up with me a few inches later.

"Sorry, Tabitha. You're right."

I was? Wow. There's a first for everything, I guess.

"I know this is last minute but I thought we could go out tomorrow night. With it being Samhain the store's open late but I thought, in the spirit of the evening, that we could catch a scary movie at the Megaplex."

I felt my anger dissolve but then remembered I had already double-booked my evening.

"I'm invited to a dinner party at Lina's and meeting my friends at Jimbo's afterward. Besides, I'm banned from the Megaplex."

He laughed.

"You know, you're welcome to come by Jimbo's after you close up."

He hesitated then nodded. "Maybe I will. If not, can I

get a rain check on the movie? A different theater than the Megaplex, of course."

Gratefully, we were able to end our lunch date on a positive note, if not a sexually-satisfied one.

I arrived back at my apartment with sore feet that really could've used a foot rub, and a sexual itch that really could've used a good scratch. Sigh. Back to the shower massager.

When I emerged from the bathroom I noticed that Inky had knocked my purse from the counter to the floor and used the contents for batting practice across the linoleum. I scooped the stuff back into the bag pausing at the folded square of paper from Lucien's office. The words *Pacific Refuse Inc.* left an anxious feeling in the pit of my stomach. I closed my eyes and could see the name of the garbage company emblazoned on the side of a Dumpster with a pentagram spray-painted over top.

I pulled Detective Jackson's card from my junk drawer and dialed his number.

"Yeah, of course we checked out the refuse company." A touch of annoyance colored his voice. "Pacific Refuse collects for half of the city of Seattle. It was a dead end."

"But the building has been vacant for a while, hasn't it?"

"Listen, I talked to the owner of the building personally. He took off down to Florida a couple of months ago when his son ran him and his store broke. He wants to sell the property for land value but figures now 'cause of the murder he'll have to tear the building down first. He can't do that until we're finished our investigation. The old guy also figures that with all the loose ends he was tying up before the move, his son must've forgotten to call and cancel the garbage company."

"Then the son's been paying Pacific Refuse to pick up at a vacant building? That doesn't make sense and if he stopped paying, the refuse company wouldn't just leave one of their huge Dumpsters there. They would've retrieved it."

Detective Jackson let out a world-weary sigh. "Listen, Nancy Drew, the guy said he was on an automatic payment plan with the garbage company, so Pacific Refuse would probably continue to pick up there as long as he had money in his account."

I hung up the phone and my fingers went instinctively to play with the amulet against my chest. Something didn't feel right about this whole Dumpster thing and something didn't feel right about my life, period.

I pulled out the phone book and looked up the number for Pacific Refuse. After punching my way through a dozen choices on the voice mail message tree I was finally connected with Lucy in accounts. Figuring the best way to get information was to pass myself off as another detective, I adopted my best business voice.

"Well," Lucy began with hesitation, "I wasn't the one who talked to your partner when he called. That was probably Derek, but he's away on vacation."

"I just need you to confirm a few things for me. I take it the owner of the property has already called to cancel service with you?"

I could hear her pecking on a keyboard before she answered. "Yes, now I remember, I took the call from Mr. Jaskowiak myself. He called last week and asked us to cancel service and stop withdrawals from the bank account that he shared with his son. The funny thing was, we weren't taking withdrawals from that account anymore."

"Really? How were you being paid, then?"

I heard her tap away a few more times. "Well, payment was made through automatic debit of their bank account up until the beginning of August, but then it was stopped."

"So he called to stop service when he moved a few months ago?"

"Yeah, but I guess he didn't remember doing so. You know how old people are. He also didn't remember sending in another check."

"Another check?"

"Yeah. First, service was canceled, but then we received a check that paid us in advance for a few months."

"So that's why you never removed the Dumpster?"

"Uh-huh."

"Maybe it was the owner's son who sent the check?"

"Could be. Mr. Jaskowiak did say his son took care of most of the bills, so that's probably what happened. Anyway, service is canceled now and I already mailed him a check for the credit on his account, that's all he cared about."

"Is there any way that you can figure out where that paying-in-advance check came from?"

"I doubt it, but I can try."

I gave her my phone number then disconnected, feeling exhausted by my stint as a fake detective. I settled onto my sofa and for the rest of my day I channel-surfed and snacked with Inky stoically by my side, although he was prepared to leap to my assistance at a moment's notice to nibble a dropped potato chip or pretzel.

I called Jenny hoping for a detour from dullsville.

"Hey, I was just going to call you. My date's been canceled for tonight so I don't need you to drive me. Oh, and Jeff called Cathy and Cathy called Lara and Lara left me a note while I was out...."

"And...?"

"And Jeff was saying that in honor of Halloween he's buying drinks tomorrow night at Jimbo's. He's got some big announcement."

"What kind of announcement?"

"Dunno. Cathy told Lara it was a surprise."

"Maybe he won the lottery."

"If he won the lottery I'm not sticking to Halloween drinks, I want champagne."

I was afraid to ask but did anyway, "What kind of Halloween drinks did Cathy come up with?"

"A couple sound good... Hemorrhaging Brain and Woo Woo."

"Oh. Sounds—" ulcer inducing, vomit promoting, hangover encouraging... "—interesting. I'm still going to Lina's for dinner first, but I'll meet you guys later."

"That's fine. Jeff said he won't be able to show up until after nine anyway."

"I guess he's working the late shift at the Scrying Room. That reminds me, I asked Lucien to join us tomorrow night."

"Oooh, now that's interesting. Think he'll show?"

"I have no idea." But I felt my nipples tingle in anticipation.

Lina was right. I'd been so bored all day Friday that I could not wait to get to her house.

What does one wear to a Samhain party? This was the

question I asked myself while staring into the dismal abyss of my closet. I needed to do laundry. Badly. Oh, well, after a few trial-and-error sessions I settled on fake designer black crepe pants with an unknown white sticky stain that I'd tried to blot out. I also chose a basic black turtleneck and had spent an hour picking off the cat hair. Moreover, just to irritate Lina, I completed my outfit with a jack-o'-lantern pin that had eyes that flashed when it was turned on.

A call came in while I was slipping my feet into low-heeled shoes and it turned out to be Lucy from Pacific Refuse.

"I just wanted to let you know, Detective, that I found a copy of the check."

"What check?"

"The check that was sent in to pay for Mr. Jaskowiak's refuse removal. I remembered that we do keep copies of checks when they're written by a third party."

"Who was the third party who wrote the check?"

"It was a company check and it was used to pay for pickup at two separate locations. Mr. Jaskowiak's property was one of them."

Goose bumps rose on my arms, hair stood up on the back of my neck and a chill zipped up my spine. I figured this would not be good.

"What was the other?"

"A place with a cute little name. The Scrying Room."

I pulled up in front of Lina's two-story turn-of-the-century home in North Queen Anne shortly after six o'clock. From the street, the house wasn't exactly alight with warm welcome, but from the half-dozen cars parked out front I figured I wasn't the first guest to arrive.

Up and down the street trick-or-treaters ran haphazardly, their eyes aglow with the need to fill their bellies with candy. I understood that need. I'd stopped at a grocer and personally stocked up on a bag of mini-chocolate bars, and at this moment was trying to cram as many as possible into my purse. I needed to medicate with chocolate and, hopefully, Lina had liquor. Lots of liquor. I also needed to make a phone call to Lieutenant McGillvray. A call that I knew would have to be made and would result in locking up a murderer whom I'd considered sleeping with.

chapter fifteen

I postponed the call. No matter what evidence I had, I still could not believe that Lucien was a killer. Had a killer body, yes. Could possibly suck the life out of me with one mind-blowing orgasm, oh yeah. But murder someone in cold blood? I shook my head and my fingers reached to clutch the Pentagram of Solomon. I still had not been able to make myself take it off. I tucked the amulet inside my sweater while I debated, contemplated and became frustrated over what to do.

Obviously, I needed to pass on the information to the police but I was sure that it could wait until later. Not that I was confident enough in Lucien's innocence that I was going to meet up with him.

Alone.

At night.

On Halloween.

Just to give him the opportunity to explain himself. I could be in lust but, contrary to anyone else's opinion, I was not stupid.

I was hoping Lina would be able to use her talents to get a clearer vision of Lucien Roskell than I could. Considering how much she hated him, I doubted she'd be willing. If she wasn't, maybe Shelby Kent would be.

Then again, maybe pigs would fly and it would rain men.

I took the bag of little chocolate bars that I'd bought and jammed a few into my overflowing purse. I wanted to be prepared in case Lina's idea of dinner was eye of toad, hair of newt or something vegan.

While I tried to shove just one more miniature Kit Kat into my small purse my little finger snagged a purple cord. I tugged and yanked free the small protection satchet that Lina had given to me to carry around. Well, protection is all fine and good, but when faced with the choice, I'd have to choose chocolate.

With the satchet removed from my purse, I was able to cram in three more miniature chocolate bars. I tossed the satchet in the direction of the passenger seat but missed and it landed, spilling dried herbs all over the car floor. Damn. I leaned sideways and scraped up what I could and stuffed the bits back into the small white cloth sack. My fingers felt something cool and smooth mixed in with the herbs and I held it up to the interior light of the car. It was a small brass scarab.

My head began to whirl. A vision of a smudged blue tattoo of the beetle engraved not between the thumb and forefinger, which Lina had described, but on what appeared to be someone's shoulder. I dropped the brass insect with revulsion and leaped from my car. I walked around to the curb and breathed crisp fall air into my lungs. Only sheer willpower and the disgusted look of a mom and her little ballerina trick-or-treater gave me the willpower not to vomit.

"Don't look at that bad lady," the mother chastised her daughter. "She's a drunk like Uncle Lou."

"Hey," I shouted at the lady. "I'm not even drunk yet! I'm just having a bad day. So there." For emphasis, I stuck my tongue out at the kid, which caused them both to run off in horror from the psycho female leaning against the Ford Escort.

This is what my life was coming to. I frightened small children on Halloween without even the benefit of a costume. To make myself feel better I stuck my hand inside my jacket and turned on the blinking jack-o'-lantern pin on my sweater. I walked up to Lina's front porch where I was immediately plunged into darkness. Guess Lina wasn't giving out treats. I rang the bell. Lina opened the door seconds later.

I shouted, "Trick or treat!" And stuck my hands out.

She offered me a crooked smile. "Come on in."

"Before I come in I want to know why you put a little brass beetle in what was supposed to be my protection satchet?"

She looked me up and down. "Merely part of the charm I concocted specifically to ward off the Scarab Sentry. Come inside."

"I was serious about the trick-or-treating. I've had a bad day and I need you to give me candy or I'm not coming in."

"By the looks of the chocolate in the corner of your mouth I'd say you've already treated yourself."

I licked away a smudge of Kit Kat and folded my arms across my chest. "That is not the point. When someone rings your bell and says 'trick or treat' you're supposed to provide a treat."

She sighed. "Sorry, I don't have candy. How about a glass of red wine?"

"That'll do." I stepped across the threshold, removed my jacket and handed it to Lina who had also chosen the black look. Only in contrast to my pants and sweater, she wore a straight-cut black wool dress that reached her ankles. Her long black hair was pinned back with a large gold clip.

"How quaint." Lina smirked at my jack-o'-lantern pin. "Give me your purse, too, you won't need it in there."

I handed her my pocketbook and she turned and hung it by the handle on the same hanger as my jacket.

"Lina, I think I've figured out who killed Shelby Kent."

Her posture stiffened, then relaxed, as she turned back to face me.

"You used the scrying mirror to get your answer?"

I shook my head. "No, just deductive reasoning."

"Well, well, well…aren't you a little Nancy Drew?"

"Yeah, so I've heard."

"Did you call the police with this newfound knowledge?"

"No, not yet. I wanted to talk to you about it first, get your take on it."

Her eyebrows rose in amusement. "As if my opinion has ever meant diddly-squat to you."

"Diddly-squat?"

"Come now, the rest of the group are gathered in the dining room." She nodded for me to follow but I was still trying to decipher what the hell diddly-squat meant. When she turned to walk away I placed a viselike grip on her arm.

"Wait a second," I said, staring at her in disbelief. "Don't you even want to know who did it?"

She shook her head. "Tabitha, my dear, if you imparted this information to me now, at this moment, would it change Shelby Kent's outcome in the slightest?"

"Well, no, but the refuse company was paid with a Scrying Room check. Don't you see? It was Lucien!"

Her face flickered with disbelief then anger, before she recovered.

"I'm not surprised."

"But maybe it's not him! Maybe I'm missing something. I don't want to go to the police if I'm not right."

"We can discuss that later. Come. We shouldn't keep the others waiting. It would be rude. We'll chat more after the ritual."

"Ritual? What ritual? I'm here for dinner!"

I followed in her wake, flinging words at her back.

She glanced over her shoulder. "I also indicated that Samhain is a time for communing with spirits and that a séance might help you contact your father."

I dug my heels in. "Séance? The word *séance* never left your lips. I would've remembered."

Lina turned and with exasperation explained that a séance was merely a meeting to receive spiritualistic messages.

"Almost like your predictions or your dreams but in a more contained environment."

"Is this a Wiccan thing? I don't remember ever discussing séances with you."

I saw conflict in her face as if she were debating what to tell me. When she decided she said, "Tabitha, I know I've always led you to believe that I've followed strictly Wiccan ways but I'm actually a follower of many paths, Wiccan, Druidry, Christianity—and many pagan and non-pagan beliefs."

"Jack of all trades, master of none." I mumbled Lucien's quote about Lina.

She narrowed her eyes. "I enjoy leaving myself open to many different spiritual arenas. There's no need to limit ourselves to one area when we can learn something from all. So are you staying, or going?"

"Do you think I could contact Shelby Kent through this thing?"

Lina pursed her lips thoughtfully. "I can't tell you which spirits will contact you, Tabitha."

My stomach began to beg for more than just chocolate. "Okay, but we still get to eat, right?"

"Yes. Afterward."

I followed Lina down a darkly paneled hallway that opened into a large living room where walls were painted a rich burgundy and held elaborate oil paintings. I felt a twinge of fond remembrance for the times Lina and I had sat in this very room together. Her, in the role of teacher, and I, in the role of smart-ass student.

A fire crackled in the stone fireplace. A pan flute played a soulful tune from the stereo in the corner and Lina's stiff, formal furniture had been pushed against the walls as if to allow for dancing. Only the half-dozen people gathered in the room did not look like partners I'd want to dance with.

"Why is everyone wearing masks?" I whispered into Lina's ear.

"They are an outer symbol of our aspirations. By wearing them we align ourselves with positive forces and sympathetic magic."

I really didn't want to wear a mask but I was all for anything that would bring something positive into my life.

Lina reached a side table and produced two eye masks with sparkling sequins, one was purple, the other gold. She took the gold one and held it out to me.

"I want the purple one."

"Fine."

She handed me the purple one and I stretched the elastic over my head and covered half my face with the mask. Lina did the same with hers only on her it actually looked good, as if she were a Mardi Gras goddess or something. There was no doubt in my mind that on me the mask just looked stupid.

Lina clapped her hands and the people at the opposite end of the room became silent and walked to form a circle in the center of the room.

Lina took me by the hand and we joined the circle. Everyone present wore masks. Two other women wore half masks with sequins like mine, a man in blue jeans had an ogre mask, two men in dark suits wore long rubber goat masks that covered their faces and someone had a Richard Nixon mask on.

"Welcome all and thank you for coming," Lina began, her voice firm and authoritative. "There was a time when men and women only had the earth, sun, moon and stars to entertain them. The changing seasons were celebrated as were the cycles of change and renewal in life."

Lina broke away from the circle to dim the lights and turn down the music. As she did this she spoke. "All Hallow's Eve or Samhain is a holiday where the veil between the seen and unseen worlds are thin. Spirits, both good and bad, can pass through the veil and, therefore, we take precautions."

She strode to a corner table adorned as an altar with fall leaves and dried flowers. She lit some incense sticks then returned to the group.

"On this evening we are reminded that death is merely a new doorway that our spirit enters."

I mumbled under my breath, "Personally, I'm hoping to keep away from that door for a while."

Lina's lips formed a tight smile. "Please refrain from talking during the ritual."

Sheesh!

"Now we will cast a circle. While the circle is cast I ask that you chant along with me, *Our Circle is filled with spirit and sight, and all the things that are holy and right.*"

The group walked clockwise around the area three times reciting the little diddy.

I giggled to a woman on my right, "It's kind of like a Wiccan ring around the rosy."

"Shhh!"

Okay!

One of the goat-masked guys left the room just as we came to a stop.

Lina stated, "Our circle is cast. Hail guardians of the

watchtower of the East, powers of air. Blow stale energies away and fill our lungs with fresh life. Let our words create a new safe place. Blessed be."

Everyone repeated, "Blessed be."

"Hey, I thought we weren't allowed to talk," I said.

Lina elbowed me in the ribs. After that I figured it would be best if I just kept quiet. I couldn't wait for the thing to be over with. My stomach was making begging noises for food and the cooking smells emerging from the kitchen only made it worse. I was hoping the goat-masked guy who'd left was coming back with a big tray of food.

I tried to tune everything out. It was kind of like attending church as a child only you didn't get to sit.

Lina did lots of talking about conquering our fears and at one point an apple was cut to symbolize one thing and some people pulled Tarot cards, but I declined to participate in the card thing. Lina softly commented that we should allow a chance for energies to resonate through us.

I found myself wondering whether I could lock my kneecaps so that I could sleep standing up like a horse. Even though Lina had suggested we close our eyes, I figured I'd better keep mine open. I didn't want to fall over.

My gaze landed on the fire. I watched it spark then stretch and sway. Among the flames, shapes formed, their terrifying pictures writhed hypnotically. I saw Shelby Kent's slaughtered body lying in a crimson pool where blood flowed freely over the rose tattoo above her breast, and now a single word pulsed and glowed inside the flower. Purity.

Someone's hand clamped onto one of mine. Whether it was happening in reality or was a hallucination, it was hard to tell. Air felt squeezed from my lungs. I was drowning. My arms flailed for a life preserver and found none. I fell to the floor on my knees, and felt my cheap knockoff pants tear in the left knee. Damn.

Lina ordered someone to get me a glass of water then tugged me to my feet.

"I have to go." I took off out of the living room as fast as my bleary eyes would let me.

I heard Lina's quick footsteps. I reached for my jacket and purse as she put a hand on my shoulder.

"You just had some kind of overwhelming vision. You should explore it further. I'll help you."

"No."

"Please stay. There are things I should tell you." She glanced furtively over her shoulder and suddenly looked all of her fifty years.

"I'd rather—" dive naked into a pool of piranha, listen to a country music marathon, cheer on the 49ers instead of the Seahawks… "—not."

I stumbled out the door, aware only that Lina had slammed it behind me and that it had begun to rain. At the end of the sidewalk I lifted my face to the dark, starless night and let the icy shower wash away the vision and shock me back to the present.

"Damn, that feels good," I breathed.

A father motioned away his little boy in a Pokémon costume and shouted, "Stay away from the weirdo, son."

"Get lost!" I yelled after them. Apparently hallucinating removed my ability to formulate a good comeback.

I fished in my purse for a Kit Kat, unwrapped it feverishly and shoved it in my mouth. Enjoying the gooey sweetness of it, I rummaged around for my keys.

I needed to call Lieutenant McGillvray and Clay Sanderson but there was no way I wanted to go back inside Lina's house to use the phone. I'd just find a pay phone. Fast.

I opened the door to my Escort, buckled my seat belt, turned the key in the ignition and felt cold sharp steel pressed against my throat.

"Pull away from the curb and start driving. You know where to go."

I met Jeff Jaskowiak's dull, vacant eyes in the rearview mirror.

chapter sixteen

"I've already called the police, Jeff." Fear iced through my veins.

"Nice try. Get going."

I directed the car slowly along the street.

"I did call the cops. I told them all about you. How your real last name is Jaskowiak. How your father owns the property where Shelby was murdered and that you've been practicing satanic ritual killings. Your father found out so he hightailed it to Florida. It was the satanic stuff that your father disapproved of, not the fact that you're gay."

"Well, aren't you a regular Sherlock Holmes."

"Nancy Drew, actually."

"Ha!" he spat, and I felt the spray hit me in the back of the neck. "Good to know you can joke, Tabitha, it shows you've got a good spirit."

I tightly clutched the steering wheel. "Good. But not

pure. That's why you chose Shelby, right? Because of her tattoo?"

"It was more than the tattoo. She came to some of our meetings and instructed us on animal sacrifices. She had a pure thirst for evil, felt her soul would fly and merge with Satan's if we performed the ritual just right."

"She was willing to die?" I asked stunned.

"Some people are willing to make personal sacrifices in the name of pure depravity." He pressed the blade of the anthame into my larynx and I felt it bite into my flesh. "If you had any sense you'd be afraid."

I was afraid all right, so afraid that I'd probably already wet myself, but I wasn't about to let him know that. Tangled with the fear, though, was a nail-splitting fury. It was the anger that spurned me on as a small rivulet of blood dribbled down my neck from where he'd cut me.

"What was the big announcement you were going to make at Jimbo's tonight?"

"Oh, I'm still going to make it. There's plenty of time for that. Unfortunately, you won't be around to hear it." He chuckled softly. "I'll be telling everyone about the great job my dad got me in Florida and that I'm leaving in the morning. Then I'll excuse myself for the evening and catch my flight to Mexico, which leaves at midnight."

I wheeled my car down roads that were usually crowded with vehicles, but this evening traffic was light. The wipers kept an impossibly normal rhythm to the insanity inside my car.

"So, how many are in your satanic group?" I asked, trying to keep him talking, while I hoped it would stop him from lobbing my head off.

"There's only me."

I frowned and my eyes met his again in the mirror. I wanted to nod toward the goat mask I'd seen tossed onto the floor, but I was afraid nodding would end up being the same as slitting my own throat. The ritual knife he held was shockingly sharp.

"I know what you're thinking," he said, his voice surprisingly even. "You're thinking one of the drones from Lina's group is with me on this."

"Not one of the drones. Lina herself."

"No. Although I did try to convince her and she was game in the beginning. However, once things went beyond cats and rabbits she couldn't handle it."

"So she knew all along it was you?" The betrayal felt like a heated blow, like hot sauce in your contact lens solution.

"Actually, she believes it's the Scarab Sentry since they approached our group last year. They were the ones who instructed us on ritualistic killings, but they were amateurs. I knew we needed to go to a higher plane. They didn't agree. Neither did Lina. So Shelby and I separated from the rest of the group."

I couldn't help but wonder why Lina didn't report Jeff. Had she not suspected him? Before I could ask, he answered, "When Lina heard Shelby was dead she immediately blamed the Scarab Sentry. Any suspicions she had about me were quashed when I told her I'd spoken to the Sentry and they'd confessed to killing Shelby but threatened to kill me if I reported it."

"But the Sentry was never involved in Shelby's murder?"

With his free hand he yanked the collar of his shirt to the side to reveal the bluish tattoo of a scarab beetle on his right shoulder. "I tried to bring them along but," he conceded, "I was never much of a team player. Shelby and I started our own group, just the two of us. Now, of course, it's just me."

We were nearing the corner of 156th Avenue and Eighth Street. I could feel a trickle of sweat between my breasts, a dripping circle of perspiration under my armpits and beaded droplets had formed on my forehead. I was a putrid puddle of panic.

The only thing I could think of was to keep him talking.

"So you put the bug on my windshield and the virus on my office computer."

"Just trying to scare you off. When Lina began having visions of you solving this thing, I got worried."

At Jeff's indication, I steered my car around back.

"Kill the engine."

"Could you please not say the word *kill?*"

"Just get out. Slowly. If you try to run, I'll make it worse for you."

"You're going to kill me. What could be worse?"

"There are myriad ways to kill someone with a knife, Tabitha, we could count the ways while I slowly dissected you."

I announced, "Getting out now. Slowly."

I tugged the amulet out of my sweater and clutched it desperately while reciting the Lord's Prayer inside my head. I figured with the prayer and pentagram I was covering as many Christian and pagan bases as I could.

Jeff bent to retrieve a small black sport bag from the floor of the back seat. While he was bent at the waist it occurred to me I could leap onto his back and swiftly disarm him. Then I remembered I wasn't a superhero. I was only a receptionist and a semiunemployed one at that.

When he turned to face me, his eyes were no longer vacant. They were alive with madness. They were sparkling with lunacy. They were glistening with insanity. If he'd been a wolf his tail would've been wagging with the excitement of the kill.

Me, I wasn't feeling excitement. I was feeling the complete opposite of excitement.

"You'll see, Tabitha," he cooed as he placed the knife in the small of my back to encourage me to walk. "I'm going to make you fly."

When we walked into the dark building, the same building where Shelby had breathed her last breath, he added, "But first I'm going to make you beg."

Once in the main room, Jeff ordered me to sit. He pulled from the sport bag a large, black pillar candle and matches. He lit the candle, chanting softly under his breath, then pulled a silver skull ring out of his pocket and slipped it onto the third finger of his left hand.

"Look, Jeff, you don't have to do this," I whimpered. "You can leave me here and take off. By the time anyone finds me you could be long gone."

He knelt in front of me. Smiling wistfully, he touched the tip of his knife to my cheek. "You talk too much."

Reaching inside his bag, he retrieved a roll of duct tape and sliced off a long strip that he used to bind my hands behind my back. He cut another strip of tape from the roll and plastered it roughly across my mouth.

Then everything happened at once. A shot rang out. There were lots of scuffling noises. I was knocked to the ground where I tore a hole in the other knee of my crepe pants. Damn. Then the room was flooded with light from half a dozen flashlights. Cop flashlights.

Jeff was cuffed and bleeding from the shoulder where he'd been shot near his Scarab Sentry tattoo. I assumed it would have to get redone, but then again, he probably wouldn't need it where he was going.

Jail.

Hell.

Wherever.

Detective Jackson tore the tape from my mouth and released my hands. He muscled a thick hand on my elbow and dragged me outside where Clay Sanderson bounded over to wrap me in an enthusiastic and protective embrace.

Clay stuck around at the police station while I finished repeating my story to Lieutenant McGillvray and Detective Jackson umpteen times. Then finally I signed it in triplicate. As we walked from the station, Clay said, "Whenever you feel up to returning to work, I hope you'll consider accepting the position of my assistant. I think you've more than earned it."

"Thanks. I'll think about it." I smiled tentatively.

Then Clay took off to meet up with his pregnant fiancée, so he released me into the loving arms of Jenny Arton.

After her hug, she stood with thick fingers planted on her wide hips and shook her head. "Damn. Look at that. You ruined your best pants."

"I know." I blinked back tears.

"And you missed Halloween drink night at Jimbo's."

"I know." I felt exhaustion give way to anger. "Damn.

I really wanted to try a Hemorrhaging Brain and a Woo Woo."

She draped an arm across my shoulders and I could feel the tremble in her body as she led me into the drizzly night.

"I guess this isn't the best time to say Doug called to demand the rest of the payment for your car repairs."

"I'll call him tomorrow," I offered. Suddenly, working a second job or going on a date with No Neck didn't seem so bad. Practically anything was better than dead.

"Sheesh, I sure could use a drink, or a smoke. Can I bum a cigarette off you?" I asked.

"Sorry, buddy, I quit tonight. I thought if Tabitha can quit, then so can I."

Figures.

"I knew you wouldn't be happy about missing Jimbo's so while I was waiting for the cops to let you go, I called Lara and Cathy and told them to go to the booze store and buy all the fixings. We're making drinks at your house and then we're having a pajama party."

"But I only have one bed."

She shrugged. "It'll be cozy, and anyways, we'll be too drunk to care."

"I love you, man." I sobbed.

"Hey, don't start with that!" Jenny protested, her own voice wavered with emotion. "Wait until you at least have a few drinks."

The drive back to my apartment was quiet. I was relieved Jen didn't feel the need to fill the air with questions or chatter. Lara and Cathy were already waiting out front when we arrived and, in addition to booze fixings, they'd pocketed stale pretzels from Jimbo's to add to the ambiance.

Half an hour later I'd become an expert on mixing together strawberry schnapps, Baileys and grenadine to make a Hemorrhaging Brain. I'd become even more of an expert at drinking them.

"I can't believe my roomy was a murderer," Cathy slurred. "How'd you figure out it was him, Tab? Was it a premonition?"

"Kind of a psychic moment combined with a Nancy Drew moment." I licked strawberry schnapps from my fingers. "You were the one who told me he didn't like you seeing him without a shirt on and Lina thought the Scarab Sentry had tattoos on their hands. Then I had a vision of a tattoo like that on someone's shoulder."

"That's what showed you he was the killer?" Jenny quizzed.

"Well, no. It was the fact that I found out from Lucy at Pacific Refuse that the owner's son always paid the bills and that Jeff told me his dad had been so ashamed of him he'd moved to Florida."

"Only his dad wasn't ashamed of the fact that Jeff was gay," Lara guessed. "He was ashamed of him being into satanic stuff."

"Yeah, but the kicker was when I started thinking Lina was involved in something bad, too, but she was the one who had called the police as soon as I was gone and discovered Jeff had skipped out in the middle of the ritual. She began to suspect something when I said the Scrying Room paid for the dumping of the body but she still felt the Scarab Sentry were to blame for the murder."

"So she really could've been the one to put this all together earlier," Jenny said, with mouth agape. "She *is* a loser."

"We all knew Jeff and none of us suspected him," I pointed out.

My intercom buzzed and Lara pressed the Talk button since she was closest. It was Lucien. She looked to me and I nodded for her to let him in. My friends immediately started packing up their stuff.

"What are you doing?" I sputtered.

"You *are* going to take advantage of the fact that he'll be all emotional so that you can get the guy in the sack, aren't you?" Jenny asked.

"A pity fuck?" I asked in an appalled tone.

My friends turned their eyes questioningly toward mine.

"Of course," I replied.

Jenny sniffed. "I've never been prouder of you than I am at this moment."

She opened the door and they all filed out as Lucien rushed in. He lifted me off my feet in a rib-cracking hug and then tenderly he touched his lips to the bandage at my throat.

"Do you want to talk about it?" he breathed hotly against my neck.

"No. I'd rather—" My mind went blank. "I'd rather just have you kiss me."

He did.

Don't miss the book that *People* magazine called "Spring's Best Chick Lit 2004."

Fat Chance

Deborah Blumenthal

Plus-size Maggie O'Leary is America's Anti-Diet Sweetheart. Her informed column about the pitfalls of dieting is the one sane voice crying out against the dietocracy. She is perfectly happy with who she is and the life she leads. That is, until she gets the chance to spend quality time with Hollywood's hottest star and she vows to be the *skinniest* fat advocate ever. But is it possible for Maggie to have her cake and eat it, too?

Available wherever trade paperbacks are sold.

If you liked **Dating can be Deadly,** you'll love…

The Pact

by Jennifer Sturman

A mystery for anyone who has ever
hated a friend's boyfriend

Rachel Benjamin and her friends aren't looking forward to Emma's wedding. The groom is a rat, and
nobody can understand what Emma sees in him.
So when he turns up dead on the morning of the
ceremony, no one in the wedding party is all that
upset. Is it possible that one of the five best friends
took a pact they made in university too far?